PRAISE

"Turn on the lights and check your locks before settling down with Jess Lourey's latest thriller. *The Laughing Dead* is a tense, twisty read that will grab you by the throat and won't let go until you race to the very last, spectacularly creepy page."

—Melinda Leigh, #1 *Wall Street Journal* bestselling author

"Jess Lourey slays in this spellbinding, spine-tingling mystery and thriller about Evangeline Reed, a complex and intriguing protagonist whose personal history and desire for justice make her perfect to take on the case of the Laughing Dead. The story explores Van's dark and tragic past, her struggles with guilt and forgiveness, and her fight for redemption and deliverance from evil. Writing from multiple perspectives, Lourey weaves an intricate tale of despair and hope, leading to an explosive and gripping climax that had my jaw dropping to the floor."

—Yasmin Angoe, author of the Nena Knight trilogy and *Not What She Seems*

PRAISE FOR *THE TAKEN ONES*

Short-listed for the 2024 Edgar Award for Best Paperback Original

"Setting the standard for top-notch thrillers, *The Taken Ones* is smart, compelling, and filled with utterly real characters. Lourey brings her formidable storytelling talent to the game and, on top of that, wows us with a deft stylistic touch. This is a one-sitting read!"

—Jeffery Deaver, author of *The Bone Collector* and *The Watchmaker's Hand*

"*The Taken Ones* has Jess Lourey's trademark of suspense all the way. A damaged and brave heroine, an equally damaged evildoer, and missing girls from long ago all combine to keep the reader rushing through to the explosive ending."

—Charlaine Harris, *New York Times* bestselling author

"Lourey is at the top of her game with *The Taken Ones*. A master of building tension while maintaining a riveting pace, Lourey is a hell of a writer on all fronts, but her greatest talent may be her characters."

—Danielle Girard, *USA Today* and Amazon #1 bestselling author of
Up Close

PRAISE FOR *THE REAPING*

"Mystery and horror mix in a creepy novel whose suspenseful ending hints at a very special sequel."

—*Kirkus Reviews*

"*The Reaping* is so much more than a mere thriller. There are complex characters, unpredictable settings, and a mix of supernatural and mystery elements that drive this tale to a unique finale."

—Bookreporter

"There are just some books—or series—that grab you and don't let go, and this is one of those."

—*Madison Daily Leader*

PRAISE FOR *THE QUARRY GIRLS*

Winner of the 2023 Anthony Award for Best Paperback Original

Winner of the 2023 Minnesota Book Award for Genre Fiction

"Few authors can blend the genuine fear generated by a sordid tale of true crime with evocative, three-dimensional characters and mesmerizing prose like Jess Lourey. Her fictional stories feel rooted in a world we all know but also fear. *The Quarry Girls* is a story of secrets gone to seed, and Lourey gives readers her best novel yet—which is quite the accomplishment. Calling it: *The Quarry Girls* will be one of the best books of the year."

—Alex Segura, acclaimed author of *Secret Identity*, *Star Wars Poe Dameron: Free Fall*, and *Miami Midnight*

"Jess Lourey once more taps deep into her Midwest roots and childhood fears with *The Quarry Girls*, an absorbing, true crime–informed thriller narrated in the compelling voice of young drummer Heather Cash as she and her bandmates navigate the treacherous and confusing ground between girlhood and womanhood one simmering and deadly summer. Lourey conveys the edgy, hungry restlessness of teen girls with a touch of Megan Abbott while steadily intensifying the claustrophobic atmosphere of a small 1977 Minnesota town where darkness snakes below the surface."

—Loreth Anne White, *Washington Post* and Amazon Charts bestselling author of *The Patient's Secret*

"Jess Lourey is a master of the coming-of-age thriller, and *The Quarry Girls* may be her best yet—as dark, twisty, and full of secrets as the tunnels that lurk beneath Pantown's deceptively idyllic streets."

—Chris Holm, Anthony Award–winning author of *The Killing Kind*

PRAISE FOR *BLOODLINE*

Winner of the 2022 Anthony Award for Best Paperback Original

Winner of the 2022 ITW Thriller Award for Best Paperback Original

Short-listed for the 2021 Goodreads Choice Awards

"Fans of *Rosemary's Baby* will relish this."

—*Publishers Weekly*

"Based on a true story, this is a sinister, suspenseful thriller full of creeping horror."

—*Kirkus Reviews*

"Lourey ratchets up the fear in a novel that verges on horror."

—*Library Journal*

"In *Bloodline*, Jess Lourey blends elements of mystery, suspense, and horror to stunning effect."

—*BOLO Books*

"Inspired by a true story, it's a creepy page-turner that has me eager to read more of Ms. Lourey's works, especially if they're all as incisive as this thought-provoking novel."

—Criminal Element

"*Bloodline* by Jess Lourey is a psychological thriller that grabbed me from the beginning and didn't let go."

—*Mystery & Suspense Magazine*

"*Bloodline* blends page-turning storytelling with clever homages to such horror classics as *Rosemary's Baby, The Stepford Wives,* and *Harvest Home.*"

—*Toronto Star*

"*Bloodline* is a terrific, creepy thriller, and Jess Lourey clearly knows how to get under your skin."

—Bookreporter

"[A] tightly coiled domestic thriller that slowly but persuasively builds the suspense."

—*South Florida Sun Sentinel*

"I should know better than to pick up a new Jess Lourey book thinking I'll just peek at the first few pages and then get back to the book I was reading. Six hours later, it's three in the morning and I'm racing through the last few chapters, unable to sleep until I know how it all ends. Set in an idyllic small town rooted in family history and horrific secrets, *Bloodline* is *Pleasantville* meets *Rosemary's Baby*. A deeply unsettling, darkly unnerving, and utterly compelling novel, this book chilled me to the core, and I loved every bit of it."

—Jennifer Hillier, author of *Little Secrets* and the award-winning *Jar of Hearts*

"Jess Lourey writes small-town Minnesota like Stephen King writes small-town Maine. *Bloodline* is a tremendous book with a heart and a hacksaw . . . and I loved every second of it."

—Rachel Howzell Hall, author of the critically acclaimed novels
And Now She's Gone and *They All Fall Down*

Praise For *Unspeakable Things*

Winner of the 2021 Anthony Award for Best Paperback Original

Short-listed for the 2021 Edgar Awards and 2020 Goodreads Choice Awards

"The suspense never wavers in this page-turner."

—*Publishers Weekly*

"The atmospheric suspense novel is haunting because it's narrated from the point of view of a thirteen-year-old, an age that should be more innocent but often isn't. Even more chilling, it's based on real-life incidents. Lourey may be known for comic capers (*March of Crimes*), but this tense novel combines the best of a coming-of-age story with suspense and an unforgettable young narrator."

—*Library Journal* (starred review)

"Part suspense, part coming-of-age, Jess Lourey's *Unspeakable Things* is a story of creeping dread, about childhood when you know the monster under your bed is real. A novel that clings to you long after the last page."

—Lori Rader-Day, Edgar Award–nominated author of
Under a Dark Sky

"A noose of a novel that tightens by inches. The squirming tension comes from every direction—including the ones that are supposed to be safe. I felt complicit as I read, as if at any moment I stopped I would be abandoning Cassie, alone, in the dark, straining to listen and fearing to hear."

—Marcus Sakey, bestselling author of *Brilliance*

"*Unspeakable Things* is an absolutely riveting novel about the poisonous secrets buried deep in towns and families. Jess Lourey has created a story that will chill you to the bone and a main character who will break your heart wide open."

—Lou Berney, Edgar Award–winning author of *November Road*

"Inspired by a true story, *Unspeakable Things* crackles with authenticity, humanity, and humor. The novel reminded me of *To Kill a Mockingbird* and *The Marsh King's Daughter*. Highly recommended."

—Mark Sullivan, bestselling author of *Beneath a Scarlet Sky*

"Jess Lourey does a masterful job building tension and dread, but her greatest asset in *Unspeakable Things* is Cassie—an arresting narrator you identify with, root for, and desperately want to protect. This is a book that will stick with you long after you've torn through it."

—Rob Hart, author of *The Warehouse*

"With *Unspeakable Things*, Jess Lourey has managed the near-impossible, crafting a mystery as harrowing as it is tender, as gut-wrenching as it is lyrical. There is real darkness here, a creeping, inescapable dread that more than once had me looking over my own shoulder. But at its heart beats the irrepressible—and irresistible—spirit of its . . . heroine, a young woman so bright and vital and brave she kept even the fiercest monsters at bay. This is a book that will stay with me for a long time."

—Elizabeth Little, *Los Angeles Times* bestselling author of *Dear Daughter* and *Pretty as a Picture*

Praise for *Salem's Cipher*

"A fast-paced, sometimes brutal thriller reminiscent of Dan Brown's *The Da Vinci Code*."

—*Booklist* (starred review)

"A hair-raising thrill ride."

—*Library Journal* (starred review)

"The fascinating historical information combined with a storyline ripped from the headlines will hook conspiracy theorists and action addicts alike."

—*Kirkus Reviews*

"Fans of *The Da Vinci Code* are going to love this book . . . One of my favorite reads of 2016."

—*Crimespree Magazine*

"This suspenseful tale has something for absolutely everyone to enjoy."

—*Suspense Magazine*

Praise for *Mercy's Chase*

"An immersive voice, an intriguing story, a wonderful character—highly recommended!"

—Lee Child, #1 *New York Times* bestselling author

"Both a sweeping adventure and race-against-time thriller, *Mercy's Chase* is fascinating, fierce, and brimming with heart—just like its heroine, Salem Wiley."

—Meg Gardiner, author of *Into the Black Nowhere*

"Action-packed, great writing taut with suspense, an appealing main character to root for—who could ask for anything more?"

—Buried Under Books

Praise for *May Day*

"Jess Lourey writes about a small-town assistant librarian, but this is no genteel traditional mystery. Mira James . . . flees a dead-end job and a dead-end boyfriend in Minneapolis and ends up in Battle Lake, a little town with plenty of dirty secrets. The first-person narrative in *May Day* is fresh, the characters quirky. Minnesota has many fine crime writers, and Jess Lourey has just entered their ranks!"

—Ellen Hart, award-winning author of the Jane Lawless and Sophie Greenway series

"This trade paperback packed a punch . . . I loved it from the get-go!"

—*Tulsa World*

"What a romp this is! I found myself laughing out loud."

—*Crimespree Magazine*

"Mira digs up a closetful of dirty secrets, including sex parties, cross-dressing, and blackmail, on her way to exposing the killer. Lourey's debut has a likable heroine and surfeit of sass."

—*Kirkus Reviews*

PRAISE FOR *REWRITE YOUR LIFE: DISCOVER YOUR TRUTH THROUGH THE HEALING POWER OF FICTION*

"Interweaving practical advice with stories and insights garnered in her own writing journey, Jessica Lourey offers a step-by-step guide for writers struggling to create fiction from their life experiences. But this book isn't just about writing. It's also about the power of stories to transform those who write them. I know of no other guide that delivers on its promise with such honesty, simplicity, and beauty."

—William Kent Krueger, *New York Times* bestselling author of the Cork O'Connor series and *Ordinary Grace*

THE
LAUGHING
DEAD

THRILLERS

Unspeakable Things

Bloodline

Litani

The Quarry Girls

SALEM'S CIPHER THRILLERS

Salem's Cipher

Mercy's Chase

CHILDREN'S BOOKS

Leave My Book Alone! Starring Claudette, a Dragon with Control Issues

YOUNG ADULT

A Whisper of Poison

NONFICTION

Rewrite Your Life: Discover Your Truth Through the Healing Power of Fiction

Better Than Gin: A Coloring Book for Writers

THE LAUGHING DEAD

A STEINBECK AND REED THRILLER

JESS LOUREY

THOMAS & MERCER

Text copyright © 2025 by Jess Lourey
All rights reserved.

Published by Thomas & Mercer, Seattle
www.apub.com

Amazon, the Amazon logo, and Thomas & Mercer are trademarks of Amazon.com, Inc., or its affiliates.

EU product safety contact:
Amazon Media EU S. à r.l.
38, avenue John F. Kennedy, L-1855 Luxembourg
amazonpublishing-gpsr@amazon.com

ISBN-13: 9781662514166 (paperback)
ISBN-13: 9781662514159 (digital)

Cover design by Caroline Teagle Johnson
Cover image: © Silveri / Plainpicture

Printed in the United States of America

THE
LAUGHING
DEAD

CHAPTER 1

Just Judy

August 24, 1986

Judy Morsa had to face facts: She'd been stood up.

On her sixteenth birthday, no less.

The prickling heat in her cheeks was part anger, part humiliation. After all, she was the dum-dum who'd let a Dairy Freez customer convince her to run away. He'd been such a sweet talker. He didn't see her as Just Judy (what her Sauk Centre High School classmates called her when they noticed her at all). No, to him, she was as cute as a soap opera star.

He had sworn it up and down the moment he'd laid eyes on her.

The sunshine-blowing might not have worked with another girl, but Judy's mom—a teenager at the time—had died in childbirth, and Judy's dad had ditched her right before making tracks, never to be heard from again. Gramma Anne raised her, swore that she was a good girl and nothing like her no-account, blow-with-the-wind father. But what, Judy thought, if she was *exactly* like him? What if she was *destined* to explore the great wide world? It was easy to imagine when talking to Troy no-last-name, his elbows on the ice cream counter, his hair slicked back like Emilio Estevez's in *The Outsiders*.

He wanted Judy so bad, and after all, didn't we all need love?

So she'd thrown off her apron, hopped in his firethorn-red Camaro, and taken off west down I-94, Phil Collins's "Against All Odds" thumping out the speakers. In that moment, it felt like God himself was on her team, and she found herself grinning so wide her face nearly cracked.

The first night was fun. The second less so.

And the third? Well, you were looking at it.

They were supposed to have seen the Oak Ridge Boys play at the Minnesota State Fair, but on their way to the grandstand, Troy'd gone off, said he had to use the can. She'd waited for him until the concert was half-over, her hair scraped into a greasy ponytail, her stomach tight from sugary fair food.

He never showed.

She'd been crashing at his place, didn't have a ride of her own, didn't even own a quarter to call home. She might have stood, paralyzed, in front of the grandstand forever if someone hadn't shoved a Dairy Delight postcard in her hand, prestamped. She took it as a sign to let her gramma know she was okay. She fished around in her purse for a pen and scribbled a note. It made her feel a little better, dropping it in a mailbox. Then she hoofed it back to Troy's house, though it took the better part of an hour. Thankfully, she'd been born with a good sense of direction. Gramma Anne said Judy was a homing pigeon, a bird who'd always fly back to her, and sure enough, Judy realized on the walk that she missed Gram dearly. She'd learned her lesson. She preferred stability, liked knowing the rules so she could follow them, and she'd given all that up for the first guy who showed her some attention? Jeez Louise.

She was feeling good and sorry for herself by the time she rounded the block to Troy's little house. The neighborhood was quiet except for the eerie creak of that widow-maker branch that sounded like it was gonna drop from his backyard oak any second. She'd warned him he better take care of it before it killed someone. Freddie Nistler back in

Sauk Centre had been paralyzed from the chest down when he'd camped below a widow-maker—everyone in town knew about his accident.

Troy had laughed when she'd told him about Freddie, said maybe he *liked* playing Russian roulette with God, and then he hauled her over his doorstep like they were in a movie. Her cheeks flared up all over again as she remembered that she'd honest-to-Pete *swooned* when he'd carried her like that. She shook her head and crossed his backyard, giving the tree a wide berth. Her heart skipped when she spotted a light in his kitchen—maybe it'd just been a misunderstanding!—but then she remembered she was the one who'd left it on. *Sigh.*

At least the key was still under the flowerpot. She let herself in, looked around, and for the first time saw the house for what it was: not a magical lovers' hideaway but a single guy's grody pad, all secondhand furniture and blacklight posters and poop streaks in the toilet bowl. She wrapped her arms around herself, wondering how dumb she actually was, like was she medically stupid?

The thing was, he'd probably found someone even thicker, and that's where he was right now. Well, good luck to them both. Judy intended to get a good night's rest and call her gramma first thing in the morning to come get her. They'd have a laugh about what a fool Judy was, and then she'd swear she'd never leave Sauk Centre again, and she'd mean it.

Turned out the great wide world was kinda crappy.

She didn't feel like sleeping in the same bed she'd shared with Troy, so she tried the couch. When that didn't work, she figured she might as well tidy up his place. That way, he'd remember her fondly, or at least not track her down and demand she return the girl's clothes she'd found stuffed in a bag in the back of his closet.

She cleaned the crusty kitchen and was halfway through the bathroom when a wild idea landed: She would cut her butt-length hair right now, hack it all off! She'd never let her gramma so much as trim it, but if not now, then when? It'd mark her growth, prove she was going back home a different person. Changed. Wiser.

It wouldn't be a waste if she'd learned something, right?

She discovered surprisingly sharp scissors in his junk drawer and got to work. She hummed as she sliced, the *slick* of the blades so satisfying. The hair fell in silky sheets.

She waited to peek in the mirror until she was all done. Then, her head feeling unbelievably light, she studied her reflection. She liked how she looked, hair nice and short like Winona Ryder's in *Lucas*, but the color was off. Hers was blond, and Winona's was black. Judy'd always been good at chemistry—it was her favorite class, and not just because Mr. Wand told her she had a gift—and what was hair dye but simple science? So she boiled some water, poured it over coffee grounds, let it steep, and then tossed in some ice cubes to quick cool it. Once her homemade dye was the right temperature, she mixed it with Troy's Pert and slopped it on her head.

Forty-five minutes later, she rinsed it out.

It looked great. For real.

She was smiling at her reflection—the short-haired brunette staring back was someone who took charge, who didn't let men push her around—when she heard a noise at the rear door. Her breath fluttered. Troy! Boy, was he going to regret ditching her when he saw how awesome she looked now. She raced to the door and tore it open.

Her stomach fell. "Oh, it's you."

The man's voice was deep, his face furrowed. "What did you do to your hair?"

Did he sound mad? She suddenly found it difficult to swallow. "How'd you find me here?"

He closed his eyes for a moment. When he opened them, his face was smooth, his smile radiant. She relaxed instantly. "Your boyfriend ever show up?" he asked.

She crossed her arms and cocked a hip. "No. You like my hair?"

"Love it." His smile, impossibly, widened. "So, you gonna wait around for that putz, or are you ready for a real man?"

Judy thought of her gramma. She was for sure already worried sick. One more night wouldn't change anything. "Can you buy me a meal?" Judy asked, reaching for her purse. "Cuz I'm hungry. And I have to be home tomorrow."

"You got it," he said.

Something about his tone, landing in the crack between a threat and a promise, made her feel like she had to pee. She didn't want to think about that too much, so she hurried to follow, locking the door behind her. He was still a few feet away when she opened her mouth to tell him it'd just been her sixteenth birthday. Except, instead of words, she heard a scream like a fox caught in a trap.

Her skin rippled with goose bumps as she tried to figure out what had made the noise. By the time she realized it was the widow-maker hurtling toward them, it was too late. The limb—as thick around as a grown man and surely as heavy as a cement truck—had flattened him on his back, quick as a blink.

Horror punched her in the chest. No *way* had he survived that. A three-inch branch could kill you if it fell from high enough, and this one had to be a hundred times bigger. She froze in panic, every bit of first aid she'd ever learned tumbling out of her head. The dude lay on the ground beneath the limb, pale, mouth slack. He reminded her of the Wicked Witch trapped below the house. She was sure she'd see blood pouring outta him any second.

Oh no oh no oh no I should have never left Sauk Centre.

Then, suddenly, unexpectedly, his eyes popped open.

He's alive! Her legs gave out, grateful tears running down her face. "I'll call an ambulance."

"Stop." His voice was commanding. He coughed, the sound wet and throaty, then, unbelievably, wriggled out from beneath the massive branch like he was scooting from beneath a car whose oil he'd just changed.

Her mouth gaped open. *It can't be.*

He rose to his feet. Brushed himself off. He wasn't bleeding, didn't hold himself like he'd just been pancaked. When he offered her his hand, he appeared . . . annoyed?

"Hurry," he said. That was it.

Judy glanced over at the huge branch. Nothing had slowed its fall, nothing except his body.

She took his hand and let him lead her into the blue-ink night.

CHAPTER 2

Van

Mother Mary looms over my bed, hands crossed at her waist. She's clothed in the commune's female uniform of an undyed skirt and long-sleeved blouse, her hair bound in a tight knot behind a swoop of bangs. Her smile is gentle, her deformed cheek pulling at her face. Mothers don't normally enter the girls' dormitory. It's our job to keep it neat and peaceful. Every now and again, one will come in to check our hygiene, or to usher out a girl who's sick. Even rarer, Father will hide under a bed to make sure we're not gossiping.

But mostly, it's just us Sisters.

Mother Mary leans over and whispers, "The Lord gives sight to the blind." Her breath's hot in my ear, and this close, she smells like fresh-baked bread. "He lifts up those who are bowed down. Use your vision to see the righteous path."

I should be worried that she's here, but Mother Mary's my favorite. It's not really in what she does, or even what she says—she's nearly mute, this burst of speech a rarity. It's in the soft smile she always wears, like she has gotten a peek at the end of the story and it all turns out fine. I feel my mouth curve in response. It's after lights out, so I'm forbidden to speak. A smile is all I have to offer.

But then, a stomach thump of worry: If it's lights out, I shouldn't be able to see her so clearly. And why can't I move?

My lungs squeeze. I realize I'm pinned to my bed, entirely immobile, able to see only Mother Mary's face, her smile so benign, but widening, stretching, her eyes beginning to bleed and her teeth sharpening to fangs. I'm terrified to look away, but a sudden movement behind her pulls my gaze, the only part of me I can move.

Father?

He's dragging a Sister out of the dormitory.

Saliva thickens in my mouth like cold honey, making it difficult to swallow. The girl makes no noise. I can't see which Sister it is, only her hands clawing at the air, trying to escape.

The grin sawing at Mother Mary's face blurs through my tears.

I slam my eyes shut.

When I open them again, I'm in a new place, no longer lying on my back. In fact, I'm hovering just above an open window suffocated by snaking green vines. A shadow crawls through the gap and slips across the floor, the vines rustling to follow. I'm pulled along overhead like a balloon on a string. The intruder enters a tiny bedroom, where a woman lies on a bare mattress, her arm thrown over her face. Is she drugged? She doesn't twitch as the vines encircle her wrists and ankles. Once she's restrained, the shadow jumps on her stomach, unhinges her jaw, and pours something down her throat.

The rotting mouse scent of it burns my nose. *Poison.* Is it airborne? I try holding my breath, but a kick to my gut pushes out all my air, followed by something warm and wet and rough caressing my face.

The sensation is enough to break the paralysis. I am able to cry out.

The nightmares began to slip away, leaving a trail both sticky and sharp.

I'd returned to my body, my bed, my apartment. To *now*.

A dog lay on my chest, licking my face, her breath bologna scented.

"Enough, Owl." I turned so her tongue didn't breach my mouth. "Can you get off?"

Her butt began wiggling furiously, and she gave an excited little growl-yip. Well, as little as anything that came out of a seventy-five-pound boxer could be.

Her weight made breathing difficult. I tried again. "I'd like to sit up now."

She took my words as an invitation to raise her rear in a classic downward-facing dog pose, a string of slobber leaking past her underbite. I finally rolled over to unseat her, rubbing at the claw indents she'd left on my belly. My sleep terrors unsettled her. This was the third time she'd thrown herself across my body, trying to shield me from the darkness, and I hadn't been fostering her a week.

I glanced at the digital clock. 12:45 a.m.

I rubbed at my face, wisps of both awful nightmares clinging to the contours of my brain. Had there been a Mother in the first one? I stretched until my spine popped. Until recently, I'd rarely dreamed about my cultlike upbringing at Frank's Farm. It was one of the few mercies I'd experienced since escaping it. The second horrible dream had contained vines, that much I could remember. A shadow. Poison?

I shook my head, the details of the second nightmare also slipping away.

Good riddance. I hadn't slept well since my Bureau of Criminal Apprehension colleague Harry Steinbeck and I'd returned from Duluth a few weeks earlier, where we'd been working a case, him in the role of scientist and me as a cold case agent. I brought my wrist to my face, my smartwatch app telling me that I was averaging four hours a night. The lack of sleep was blurring my edges. I stood, wading through my comfort junk. The thrumming in my body told me that more rest would be hard to come by this evening.

"Wanna go for a walk, Owl?"

She woof-barked. I put a gentle hand on her nose. "Shhhh, girl, you don't want to wake the neighbors. They might call the cops on us."

I slipped out of my pajamas and into black jeans and a black sweatshirt. It was late April, which in Minnesota could bring anything from a blizzard to a heat wave. It'd been a mild week, so I was hoping the predawn dipped more toward the latter. I grabbed my quilted jacket and tugged a knit cap over my white-blond hair before looping Owl's Gentle Leader around her face.

Like most boxers, she bounced more than walked.

I considered for a moment bringing my gun and badge, but I didn't want them to become a crutch I used to soothe myself when I was off duty.

I am safe. I am grown. I am free.

My therapist had offered the mantra to use when the childhood memories closed in: Frank's magnetic abuse, the never-ending cleaning-cooking-laundry-sewing-prayer in the name of our Father, one dorm for the Sisters, where we weren't allowed light at night, one for the Brothers, and a separate house for all the Mothers except the one Frank chose to share his bed.

I am safe. I am grown. I am free.

I stepped into the cigarette-scented hallway, down the stairs, out of my building, and into the slumbering city. My apartment might be small, but you couldn't beat the location, right on Loring Park, a thirty-four-acre oasis plopped between downtown and uptown Minneapolis. Beneath the jarring yellow of streetlights, winter crashed into summer everywhere I looked: ghostly shards of ice still gripping the pavement, air drunk with the scents of silver and green, tender buds quivering on the trees, gambling that the morning would bring sunshine rather than deadly frost.

The conflict of spring.

Owl's claws clicked on the sidewalk as we strolled. I enjoyed the nip in the air and the quiet, eyeballing the cameras everyone seemed to have hooked up on their porch. They imparted a false sense of security as far as I was concerned, but what was the alternative? Dwelling on the murders that went unsolved—over half—or the daily crosses that we carried, from annoyance to evil, that were out of our control?

Naw, I wasn't going to judge a person for buying a little peace.

Owl sniffed everything she could, rushing from one invisible smell pocket to the next. She was an enormous fawn-colored dog with a gremlin face and paint-stripping farts. She'd come in through the domestic violence Safe Housing program at the animal shelter where I volunteered, needing a temporary home while her owner got her life back on track.

She was my first foster.

Until last week, my contributions to Animal Haven had consisted of scraping poop out of cages and exercising the animals. I was in a raw spot from the Duluth case when she came in, though, and something about her big, apologetic eyes—she looked proactively sorry for everything—had tugged at my heart. I peeked at her chart and found she had two broken ribs courtesy of her owner's boyfriend. That made me see red, but it wasn't until she let out a mournful yowl somewhere between a moo and a bark when I walked away from her cage that I realized I had no choice but to take her home.

My place wasn't the best setup for her. My hours at the Bureau of Criminal Apprehension were erratic, and my apartment was a studio. But it was better than the shelter. They did God's work, but the smells and sounds hyper-stressed an animal's nervous system. Most creatures preferred a quiet home. Even one as small as mine was better than a cage, especially if the foster got regular exercise, which I made sure Owl did.

She paused in front of an import store. The front window display had changed since we'd walked past yesterday. Where before it'd featured peacock-bright batik skirts and stacked rain sticks, now it was crammed with hand-carved wooden masks, some frowning but most of them grinning widely, all of them gape-eyed.

Their soulless gazes iced my gut.

Owl growled low in her throat.

"You too, girl?"

But she was glaring at the alley a few feet away. Before I could ask what was wrong, a rumpled-looking guy in a scarlet scarf jumped out, fists in the air, the gesture menacing. I snapped into an offensive posture as Owl lunged at him. It took all my strength to hold her back.

"Stand down," I told him roughly. "You're scaring my dog."

He was a good foot taller than me, wearing layers of clothes, all of it shabby except for the bright knit scarf. His head was bare, his smile nearly toothless. He abruptly dropped his hands and began to walk in the opposite direction.

"Father knows best," he called over his shoulder, cackling.

My skin lifted from my bones, the details of tonight's first nightmare suddenly flooding back.

Except that it hadn't been a nightmare.

It'd been a memory dipped in the paint of time and run through my subconscious. Father Frank *had* dragged Sister Veronica away, like in the nightmare, except he'd hauled her out of the church, not our dorm. Mother Mary and all the rest of us had watched in shock as he slammed her head into the side of a metal trough on his way to violently baptizing her, blooms of blood staining her light hair before she disappeared beneath the water.

Veronica's crime? She'd told outsiders what went on at the Farm.

I gritted my teeth at the memory.

I'd allowed it to happen, we all had, Mothers and Sisters alike, not interfering because you didn't dare question Father Frank Roth. Sister Veronica was irreversibly brain damaged afterward. His abuse stole her mind and left her body a shell. It shattered me.

There'd been no consequences for what he'd done.

That was who Frank Roth was, the sick fear he commanded, and I knew exactly why he—and my life on the commune—had started visiting my nightmares for the first time since I'd left: I was searching for him. Thanks to what I'd learned up in Duluth, after more than fifteen years of hiding from my childhood, I was now running toward Frank.

And it was for the most horrifying reason of all.

I believed that in 1998, he'd abducted my partner Harry's little sister.

CHAPTER 3

Van

Harry Steinbeck was a meticulous BCA forensic scientist who dressed like a 1950s Wall Street executive. He was also, frankly, a panty-dropping hottie. It amused me to no end how uncomfortable the attention paid to his Michael Fassbenderesque good looks made him.

Me, I was about ten years his junior, worked cold cases, and had more interesting things to do than pick up after myself. We never would've been partnered—uptight scientist, rule-bending investigator—if not for COVID thinning the BCA's ranks, but the matchup had worked. We'd consulted on several cases since and actively worked three: what the media called the Sweet Tea Killer, followed by the Taken Ones abduction, and finally a third that'd required us to head north to Duluth, Harry's old stomping grounds.

Up there, we'd looked into a deadly practice that the locals in a nearby town referred to as a reaping. That case had only recently resolved, and I'd been avoiding Harry since discovering that his sister's kidnapper shared a rare trait with my father: heterochromatic eyes. Frank had been doing a lot of traveling back then, gone for long stretches of time, and Harry's sister had been seen entering a car that matched the description of the one Frank drove.

I'd last crossed paths with Frank right before my eighteenth birthday. The feds had been hauling him away—handcuffs and all—for tax evasion, effectively breaking up the commune. When I realized in that moment that I felt *bad* for Frank, that my impulse was to *protect* that monster rather than celebrate he'd finally encountered some form of justice, I'd walked away from it all—the only family and home I'd known—and never looked back.

But now I had to. For Harry.

Frank Roth might be dead, for all I knew—fifteen years was a long time—but I needed more intel before I flattened Harry's life with the possibility that my father had abducted his sister. I couldn't do that to him without an excellent reason, something more than what he'd uncovered in Duluth. I'd been doing some borderline unethical research to track Frank down ever since, putting out feelers about my father and his current whereabouts. I was poking ghosts, hence the crap sleep I'd been having plus the nightmares, including the memory of Sister Veronica's near-drowning and mutilation.

Father knows best.

My stomach twisted as I recalled the vagrant's words. I had no father, not that I claimed. Hell, Owl was the closest thing I had to family, and she'd return to her real home in a week or two. I shook my head, returning fully to the present. The man in the red scarf was long gone.

Lucky him, because I wanted to punch something.

I glanced back at the import store's wall of grinning faces as my phone rang. I jammed it to my ear. "Yeah?"

"Evangeline." Harry's rich voice was strained. "You're needed. It's urgent."

CHAPTER 4

Gina the Jester

August 26, 1986

Gina Penchant fit the lemon wedge into her mouth, a perfect puzzle piece slotting into place. She shuddered, her eyes slamming closed. "Ohmygawd," she yelped. "It's so sour!"

Lindy and Pru laughed uneasily.

The girls sat in the center of Gina's room, a faded blue rug protecting them from the splintery floor. They were close enough to feel one another's body heat, to smell the zing of nerves. Gina's twin bed was shoved against the wall. Its headboard abutted the board-and-cinder-block shelves her father had helped her set up, the ones holding her Nancy Drew collection—she'd been garage-sale hunting the books since she was eight—plus her primo cootie catchers, favorite childhood toys, glittering stones, shells, everything she'd accumulated in her sixteen years, all of it arranged neatly and dusted weekly.

The collection paled beneath Gina's pride and joy, though: her movie posters.

Her brother, Sam, worked at the Waite Park theater and brought them home for her when the movie run ended. She'd scored *Clue, The*

Jewel of the Nile, Ferris Bueller's Day Off, and her favorite, the Wall of Cruise: *Risky Business, Legend, Top Gun.*

Gina'd never say it out loud, but she thought she and Tom would get along just fine, especially if her rabbit-brown hair were magically blond.

Hence tonight's forbidden activity.

Their parents *definitely* wouldn't approve. That's why they'd agreed to meet at Gina's. With her mom and pop out for the evening, they could skip asking for permission and go straight to begging forgiveness tomorrow. It was luck her parents had wanted to catch a flick at the Starlite Drive-In tonight *and* had allowed Gina to have a sleepover in the middle of the week. She took it as a sign that God wanted her to be blond.

"Ready?" Gina asked.

The other two nodded. They resembled solemn aliens—or asylum patients—with the plastic grocery bags tied below their chins and sprigs of hair sticking out of the dozens of holes they'd poked into them, the tufts drawn through with a crochet hook. The professional hair-dye kits sold at Ben Franklin came with salon-quality masks, but they couldn't afford those, and anyways, the bags'd work just fine.

That's what Gina swore, and she was pretty sure.

She'd also convinced Pru and Lindy that the thirty minutes their hair was soaking would be A-plus time to try out the Ouija board she'd smuggled home from school. The game was being passed around Rockville Senior High like a take-home hamster, hitting the house of every fifteen-to-eighteen-year-old who didn't have super-religious parents (or who wasn't too chicken to defy them).

"Tomorrow," Gina said, lifting the checkered quilt and sliding out the game from beneath her bed, "we'll be blond *and* cool."

Pru giggled. Lindy stayed silent, her eyes trained on the Ouija game.

"You sure we should do this?" she finally asked, picking at a cuticle. "I heard Mike Webber called forth a demon that took over his little brother."

Gina huffed. "*Called forth?* Danny Webber was a glue-eating devil *long* before Mike played with a Ouija board."

The laughter was real now, cutting through their nerves.

Gina'd always been good at that, a natural clown who set people at ease, and that was her role in the threesome. *Gina the Jester*, her dad called her. He'd be upset about her hair—he thought bottle blondes looked cheap—but he'd never been able to stay mad at her longer than a day. Gina tried not to take advantage, but there were times when a girl had to do what a girl had to do.

She gave the signal, and they all reached for their assigned lighteners. Gina dipped her protruding strands in the bowl of lemon juice as best she could. Pru did the same with her hydrogen peroxide. Lindy—who'd five-finger-discounted the Sun-In—sprayed it across the top of her head. Gina sniffed. Did the Sun-In smell like cinnamon? Hard to tell over the lemon juice's bite. Hair fully dunked, she twisted the strands to release the excess liquid and sat up.

Pru followed suit, pushing her glasses back into place. Lindy gave her crown a final spritz.

They beamed at each other, their exposed hair dripping onto the towels they'd thrown over their shoulders. They were supposed to heat the strands while they dried, but none of them owned a hair dryer.

"Ready?" Gina asked.

Pru and Lindy nodded. Gina held out her hands for them to grasp. Once they were a connected triangle, the Ouija board its center, Gina uttered the words that all Rockville tenth graders knew to say.

"Ouija, please tell *me*, who will I mar-*ee*?"

The next step was to put their hands on the planchette, but Gina had frozen.

Lindy was the first to tug free. "What's wrong, dork?"

The color had drained from Gina's cheeks. "Nothing."

"Gene?" Pru asked, reclaiming her own hand.

Gina swallowed, poking at the teardrop-shaped game piece. "It's nothing, really." Her eyes flashed to Tom Cruise peering at her over his Ray-Bans. "It's just that . . . what if it tells us we're gonna marry someone gross?"

She'd used four nails to put up the *Risky Business* poster—no cheap putty—to ensure it lay flat over her veiny plaster wall. She *knew* she was destined for better things than a dull life in Minnesota, marrying some regular guy, never leaving her mark on the world. How could she fall asleep every night beneath Tom Cruise's studly gaze and not believe that?

Lindy punched Gina in the arm, her earlier jitters ousted by Gina's cold feet. "The board just tells you about your *first* husband. You can have two." She said this last part with certainty. Gina and Pru were Catholic, but Lindy was Lutheran. In her church, there were actual divorced folks. Well, two, and they'd divorced each other, but wasn't that proof it was possible?

Gina rubbed the spot where Lindy'd hit her. It'd been a hard punch, but she supposed that between their hair and the board, they were all on edge. Time to lighten the mood. "Okay," she said, "but what if it's *Kevin?*"

Pru and Lindy squealed. Besides playing varsity baseball *and* football, Kevin Quick was a doctor's son and the first Rockville kid to own a pair of Girbaud jeans. The thought of marrying him infused their blood with Pop Rocks.

They were so tweaked that when a loud knock came at the front door, they all jumped.

"It's him!" Pru shrieked. She sucked in air, her voice dropping to a whisper as she stared at the Ouija board. "And we didn't even touch it."

"How's that possible?" Lindy's eyes were comically wide. Between her expression and the hair sprouting from the plastic bag, she was a dead ringer for a hapless housewife in a 1950s sitcom.

Gina stood, brushing off her rump and wearing a wicked smile. "If it is Kevin, he's about to see me with a Cash Wise Foods bag tied to my head."

Pru clapped her hands over her mouth. "You wouldn't!"

"Watch me." Gina stepped out, closing the bedroom door behind her.

Pru and Lindy clutched each other in thrilled disbelief, enjoying the electricity arcing between them.

"Should we listen?" Lindy asked.

Pru nodded so emphatically that her glasses slid halfway down her nose.

They gallop-crawled over to the door and slammed their ears against it. Their mouths became perfect circles when they caught the rumble of conversation. Gina was talking to a man!

They immediately fell away from the door, howling with laughter. *No. Way.* It didn't sound like Kevin, but it was definitely a guy, and Gina *for sure* looked like a knob with her alien hair in a grocery store bag. They shook their heads, delighted tears rolling down their cheeks. Only Gina. They'd be bragging to everyone at school about it tomorrow, about how funny their friend was, how brave. And wait, was that a girl's voice along with a guy's? She sounded young, about their age. She must be bugging out, seeing Gina with her hair like that!

When Gina returned a minute later, they were still grinning.

"Was it Kevin?" Lindy sang. "Is he gonna marrrryyyy—" Her mouth snapped shut at Gina's expression. She looked like she'd seen her own ghost.

Pru flew to her feet in concern. "What happened?" she asked Gina. "Was it the police?" It was a silly question. She had no idea where it had come from.

"Yeah, no." Gina was trying to untie the bag beneath her chin, but her hands were shaking too much. "It was just somebody selling stuff."

"What kinda stuff?" Lindy asked. Gina was clearly lying, and it made Lindy's mouth dry.

Unable to work the knot, Gina finally ripped off the bag, the already-blonding strands twisting and grabbing at her hands like snakes. "I dunno," she said moodily, dropping onto her bed. "Encyclopedias." She drew her chin into her neck, her expression dark. "Hey, I think you two should go. I don't feel too good."

Pru and Lindy exchanged a look. Lindy was the only one with her license. She'd driven Pru. Both their parents believed they were staying overnight, had in fact demanded a tithe in chores for the privilege of a weeknight sleepover.

"You sure you want to be alone?" Pru asked. "Should we track down your mom?"

"No!" Gina said, too quickly. She tempered her voice. "Sorry. I just want to rest. I'll feel better soon." She flopped onto her back, the lemon juice still in her hair.

"Let's at least wash this stuff off," Lindy said, standing. She was surprised how wobbly her legs felt.

"Please," Gina begged, draping an arm over her face. "I have a headache."

Lindy gave Pru a *What the hell?* eye bulge. Pru turned her hands palm up.

"Fine," Lindy said, suddenly annoyed. How like Gina to be a drama queen. Sure she was fun, but only because it made her the center of attention. Like when Lindy landed the role of Audrey in the school production of *Little Shop of Horrors*, and Gina got the part of the killer plant, and she upstaged everyone. Playing a *plant*. Probably Gina'd decided it wasn't fair Lindy had the *actual* Sun-In and so she was kicking them out.

Hopefully their hair didn't fall out before they got home.

Lindy stormed out of Gina's bedroom, Pru on her heels.

Pru grabbed Lindy's arm before they reached the car. "What do you think that was about?"

Lindy shook her off. "I think it was Gina being Gina. You know she'd rather die than give up the spotlight."

They didn't say another word the whole ride. Lindy dropped off Pru, then drove the four minutes home. Her parents were watching *Simon & Simon* and didn't even glance up as she passed. She was able to sneak into the shower and head to bed straight after.

Gina's hair was clean and dry, her new caramel highlights glossy in the moonlight, when her parents finally arrived home from the double feature. They wouldn't normally have checked on their daughter, not so late, not when she was having a sleepover, but Lindy's car wasn't in the driveway. It was Gina's father who entered her room after she didn't answer his knock.

"Gina? Jester Girl?"

Still no answer. He flicked on the light. Blinked, his eyes not connecting to his brain.

Gina lay on her bed, the Ouija board clutched to her chest, her dry eyes forever open, an unbending jack-o'-lantern grin spread across her cold, dead face. He tried to reach for her but fell to his knees instead. He opened his mouth to yell, but no sound came out.

He was frozen.

His daughter. His baby girl.

His wife rushed in moments later. Her scream mobilized him. He wasn't sure what he told the 911 operator, but he thought it was something about that awful smile and the skinny yellow snakes in her hair, like she was Medusa.

When word of Gina's death reached school the next day, Lindy felt like she'd been sheeted with ice. *You know she'd rather die than give up the spotlight.* That's what she'd said, her very last words about her best friend, before driving away and leaving her alone with the haunted Ouija board.

All their classmates whispered that Gina'd killed herself, but Lindy didn't believe it. Refused to. And she'd chew on those awful final words about Gina every year on the anniversary of her death.

They never got any easier to swallow.

CHAPTER 5

Van

How like Harry to word it that way. *Evangeline. You're needed. It's urgent.* Crisp. No nonsense.

It hadn't been hard to avoid him while I waited for a hit on Frank's whereabouts. Harry'd texted twice. I ignored both. Our departments were in different wings of the BCA headquarters, and when we were not sharing an active investigation, there was no reason for our paths to cross.

Until his phone call just now telling me I was needed, that was.

He'd given me an address and little else. I was familiar with the location. It was across Loring Park from my apartment, maybe a twenty-minute walk.

It was also the women's shelter where Emily, Owl's owner, was staying.

That was information I shouldn't have. When someone took in a foster under the Safe Housing program, they were informed that they'd be caring for the animal for an indeterminate period of time. That was it. Any further information was kept private to protect the person temporarily surrendering their pet. But Owl had seemed so heartbreakingly sad, even when I got her out of the shelter, that I pulled a few strings to track down Emily Barris's name, phone number, and current address. A little visitation wouldn't hurt anyone, right? She and I agreed to meet at a bench in Loring Park, halfway between our places. Owl was so excited to see her that she nearly turned herself inside out, and I'd had to look away from the naked tears Emily shed as she squeezed Owl's face and told her how much she missed her.

The end always justified the means.

We'd scheduled two more meetups since. At the most recent, Emily had said she hoped to be out of the shelter and in a place of her own by the end of the month. I'd promised I'd keep up the visits until then. She was so grateful that she'd hugged me.

I didn't like the cold rock that'd dropped into my gut when Harry gave me the address. I hoped whatever was happening there had nothing to do with Emily. I hurried Owl back to the apartment, made sure she had fresh water and her favorite stuffie, and drove to the address. I wanted my vehicle close. Two Minneapolis PD cars and an unmarked were parked in the street when I pulled up. I'd done a ten-year stint in MPD homicide and could pick out a detective's car with one eye tied behind my back.

I studied the shelter, a sprawling Victorian, white with emerald-green accents. Based on its size, I estimated it housed eight bedrooms. I'd probably driven past it a bunch of times, not guessing who was inside. People all over the world lived next to safe houses and didn't even know. Using actual homes gave the clients, mostly women and children, a chance to feel something like normal as they figured out their next steps.

Having the police swarming this one wouldn't do them any favors on that front.

Harry stepped off the Victorian's wraparound porch, his sculpted face tense, his hands tucked in the pockets of his navy peacoat, a gray cashmere scarf wrapped around his neck. His wool fedora matched his coat perfectly.

Of course Harry was dapper in the middle of the freaking night.

I waved as I crossed the street. His jaw clenched in response. Was he upset about something? But no, as I drew closer, I saw that he wasn't mad.

He was *worried*.

CHAPTER 6

Van

"Sorry to call you out at this hour." He offered me shoe covers and gloves.

His scent—a faint cedar with a metallic note—normally put me at ease. Not now. Not with him holding himself rigid, refusing to make eye contact.

"What's up?" My own shoulders had tightened in response to his body language, but I tried to keep my voice light. Something was off, a premonition just below my radar. Was it the house? The neighborhood?

"A suspected homicide," he said, circling but not actually answering my question. He held open the front door, staring straight ahead, still not looking at me.

My neck hairs stood at attention as I glided past. Harry had never been loquacious, was allergic to speculation, but this was circumspect even for him. The night clerk glanced up as we entered, nodding at Harry. The foyer we stood in likely used to be grand, but it'd since been walled off, a desk placed right inside the front door. A camera was mounted on the far wall, matching the one I'd spotted on the porch.

"Cause of death?" I asked as I slipped on the booties and gloves.

The night clerk buzzed us through. Harry held this second door, too, his words tight. "Possibly poison."

My apprehension tripled. What'd gotten under his skin? He wasn't mad I hadn't returned his texts, not Harry. The man didn't have a petty bone in his body, which was a damn waste from where I sat. Something about this murder had unsettled him, and he'd had a front row to more gruesome crime scenes than anyone I knew.

"Connected to a cold case?" I asked. There'd be no other reason to call me in.

He shook his head once, curtly. "No idea."

That did it. My stomach circled and landed on its back. Harry was one of the best forensic scientists in the state, if not the country. It wasn't out of pocket for him to be called to a crime scene on short notice. But I worked strictly cold case. With MPD already here and no cold case in sight, why had I been brought in?

It wasn't an academic question.

A BCA agent showing up uninvited risked alienating the responding police department, particularly if that BCA agent was me and the responding department was the Minneapolis PD. Created in the 1920s in response to Chicago mobsters using the Minnesota landscape from Saint Paul to Two Harbors like a playground, the BCA had no jurisdiction of its own. It started small, basically a mobile backup team. In the '30s, it grew to include a statistics division, and in 1947, it built the first forensic science laboratory in the region. It'd since become one of the finest labs in the nation, renowned for its crime scene processing and evidence analysis, thanks in no small part to Agent Harry Steinbeck. The BCA had continued to add agents and field offices on top of founding one of the first dedicated cold case departments in the country.

My department.

The one I stuck to unless another agency requested help.

Well, mostly stuck to. I wasn't afraid to massage a rule. Harry refused to, though, and the fact that he'd called me in on an active murder investigation with no connection to my department unsettled the hell out of me. I concentrated on keeping my expression smooth as I struggled to find a reason I was here—or better yet, a reason Harry *refused to tell me* why I was here—but there was no time. We'd stepped into a paneled hallway containing four doors, all of them constructed of identical cheap hollow core, any charm the old house might have held stripped away to make efficient use of the space.

An MPD officer guarded the second door in.

I didn't recognize him. There was some small grace in that. I'd done my best to avoid homicide since they'd as good as driven me out after my partner died two-plus years earlier. I hoped to continue that trend.

Harry tossed me an apologetic glance before stepping past the officer and into the room, this time not doing me the courtesy of letting me go first. I didn't care, but he sure as hell would. My gut plummeted another level. This was wrong, all wrong, a sharp-toothed warning humming for my attention, telling me to turn and run.

Obviously, I did the opposite. I hadn't gotten this far in my career or my life by showing fear. I strode past the officer, eyes clear and shoulders back, keeping my movements slow and smooth as I scanned everywhere for threats.

I found myself inside a cramped living area. It was overheated and smelled like soup. From the tall ceiling and elegant wainscoting, it appeared to have been a large dining area now divided into smaller spaces. It contained a couch, TV, and tiny fridge with an electric teakettle balanced on top. The floor was crowded with stacks of boxes, sparkling-water cans, and garbage bags stuffed with what looked like clothes.

I assumed the door on the opposite wall led to the bedroom, and judging by the commotion coming from inside, that's where the victim was.

The only other opening was a single window straight ahead.

A window surrounded by painted green vines.

Exactly like the one I'd seen in this evening's second nightmare.

I sucked in a breath—Had I been here? Had I witnessed someone else here?—before sliding sideways into myself.

It was happening again.

My visions were back.

CHAPTER 7

Robin the Red

August 29, 1986

"These seats suck," Robin Seer yelled, her arms crossed in irritation.

"They're better than standing," Chuck hollered back. "And Angus Young is God."

It was the same thing he'd been saying since he scored the concert tickets two days earlier outside the Minnesota State Fair. They'd gone to the fair on a lark—Robin was craving Sweet Martha's cookies—and spotted some guy scalping the passes out front. AC/DC and the Met Center were in a different universe from the fairgrounds, but the guy swore the tickets were good, that he couldn't make it to the concert and figured he'd unload them somewhere with a lot of foot traffic.

Chuck had immediately started haggling with the man.

Robin told Chuck she'd meet him by the cookies.

Thirty minutes later, he found her in the snaking line outside Sweet Martha's Cookie Jar. He'd dropped thirty dollars for two general admission tickets and spent the rest of the day crowing about how Angus Young was rock-and-roll royalty, a god, *metal as hell*. Now that they were in the audience, Robin had to admit that the guitar player was fun to watch, kick-marching across the stage in his schoolboy uniform.

"I'll grab us beers at intermission, 'kay, Red?" Chuck said as the chords of the next song rang out. "I don't want to miss a second of this."

She leaned back and blew a breath up her face, determined to make the best of it. There were worse places to spend a Friday, after all. The people-watching alone was epic. Old dudes in their worn Zeppelin and Iron Maiden T-shirts, their stringy armpit hair hanging outta the holes where the sleeves used to be. The rock ladies were even more interesting, with their big hair teased to the sky, choice eye shadow, and frosty lipstick. Robin'd aimed for that look herself, though her hair was a bummer. Her parents wouldn't allow her to perm it, and it was too thick to get the rise she wanted otherwise. But she'd layered blue-purple eye shadow like a galaxy on each lid, just like she'd seen Grace Jones wear it, and three swipes of blue mascara gave it the perfect pop.

Plus, no one's lips were frostier than hers.

Combine that with the Blondie T-shirt she'd nabbed at Goodwill, her shredded jean shorts, and her favorite white cowboy boots and she was "pure Betty," according to Chuck. She glanced fondly at him. His feathered hair made him look like a prince from the side. They'd been dating since eighth grade, after he'd asked her if he could carry her books from chemistry to English. It took all of a week before she'd scrawled his name in a heart next to hers across all her textbooks' paper-bag covers.

They'd been inseparable ever since.

They planned to attend the same college come fall. Alexandria VoTech, him for welding, her for interior decorating. They weren't going to share an apartment—her parents wanted them to wait to move in together until they were married, and she'd agreed—but they'd be living on the same block. Her heart blossomed thinking about it. She pushed a lock of dark hair behind his ear and returned his smile when he flashed it at her.

"It's 'Shot Down in Flames'!" he yelled.

She nodded indulgently and kissed his cheek. Chuck was a doofus, but he was *her* doofus. Her head was on his shoulder when she spotted the man over by the beer stand. Her eyes narrowed. Small world.

"Babe!" she yelled, getting to her feet. "I see someone I know."

She didn't stand a chance against Brian Johnson's shriek. "Be right back!" she hollered anyhow. Chuck patted her hip but didn't glance her way.

The band was playing "Fly on the Wall" when she returned several minutes later.

"You missed the raddest rendition of 'Back in Black,'" Chuck yelled when she dropped into the seat next to him. His gaze remained locked on the stage. When she didn't respond, he reluctantly dragged his eyes to her.

What he saw turned his hands into fists. Robin's pretty eye makeup was running down her face, making it look like a clown'd barfed on her. Not to mention her arm had a visible handprint on it.

Chuck jumped to his feet, scanning the crowd. "Who did that to you?"

Robin tried to dab at her face with the hem of her shirt, but it was a losing battle. She tugged Chuck back into his seat. "Don't worry about it."

"I *am* worried about it." He ran his hands gently across her hair, her arms, her legs, searching for more injuries. "What happened?"

She tried to shrug him off. "Someone thought he knew me, and he didn't, that's all. Can we watch the show?"

The sudden break between songs left a vacuum where Chuck's voice was too loud. "He hurt you?"

"Not as bad as I hurt him," Robin said, a grim little smile on her face. "I kneed him in the balls when he wouldn't let go. The girl he was with looked nearly as shocked as him."

Chuck's face scrunched up, and then he started laughing as the notes of the next tune rang through the stadium.

Robin scowled. "What's so funny?"

"This song, Red." He pointed toward the stage. "It's 'She's Got Balls.'"

He hooted and pumped his fist into the air. Anything he said after that was drowned out by the music. He grew happier as the night wore on, and she felt herself shrink smaller and smaller. They watched the rest of the show, including both encores. Robin asked to be taken straight home after.

Chuck yammered the whole drive. He was too high from seeing his favorite band live to even offer to walk her to the door, which he'd done every other single time he'd brought her home. He *did* watch her, though, to make sure she made it inside.

He'd think about that a lot.

About how he'd ignored her to focus on the band, how he'd let her walk up her sidewalk alone, how he hadn't even kissed her good night. It wouldn't have changed anything—at least, he hoped it wouldn't have.

Robin the Red still would have died that night, approximately four hours after he dropped her off.

When Robin's mom discovered her smiling in bed the next morning, at first it didn't even occur to her that her daughter was gone, that's how wide Robin's grin was.

CHAPTER 8

Van

Before I could react to the awful realization that my visions had started up again, a fish-belly-white man in his early sixties with thin, perennially wet-looking hair and Richard Nixon jowls strode from the bedroom, somehow managing to make this shit situation even worse.

"Welcome to my scene, Reed," Detective Dave Comstock said cheerily, holding an evidence bag in one paw. "Always nice to see your little face."

I fought for my bearings.

Comstock was the reason I'd left the MPD. He and I'd worked homicide together, and I'd never seen him not wearing a cheap suit and cheaper shoes. He'd been friends with my former partner, Bart Lively. Like Bart, Comstock was a skilled investigator, but that's where the resemblance ended. Comstock had played pals with me when Bart was alive, but the second Bart keeled over from a heart attack while eating a chicken-and-peas TV dinner and watching *Dateline*, Comstock let his real face show. Turned out he'd always been jealous of our clearance rate.

He had no idea that it came courtesy of my visions. No one did.

When my "sight" hit, revealing a crime in progress or one just completed, I'd share it with Bart. Naturally I'd tell him it was a hunch, and he and I would do the boots-on-the-ground work to catch the criminal. But once Bart died, there was no one in the Old Guard to provide me cover, and the rumors about me being a witch spread quick as spilled gasoline, with Comstock lighting the match.

But I wasn't a witch. I was a woman who'd been regularly terrorized as a kid and so had sharpened to a razor's edge the instinct that every human possessed. Who hasn't connected two seemingly unrelated facts to come up with an unexpected truth, or felt a tingle telling them they were being lied to, or had a dream about someone they hadn't seen in years the night before running into them on the street? I had a theory that folks with large doses of these instinctual gifts gravitated toward law enforcement, but my point was, it wasn't magic. It was a human capacity that I'd been given a heftier dose of than most, and it came in the shape of me seeing real-life crimes taking place as I slept.

I'd never confessed my visions to Bart, the best man I'd known before Harry. When Comstock told people I was some sort of witch, he wasn't going on anything but bad faith.

It didn't matter. It took no time at all for the group at the MPD to make my life hell. From stupid stuff like slipping salt into my coffee, hiding all the toilet paper in the women's restroom, and letting the air out of the tires on my personal vehicle all the way to big stuff like freezing me out of cases.

When I couldn't take it anymore, I left, landing at the BCA.

For a blessed while, the visions stopped. I hoped I might be free.

But I'd had flare-ups since, most recently in Duluth. I'd been praying for a longer reprieve before the next bout, hoping that the green-vined poisoning I'd witnessed only hours ago had been a regular old nightmare.

It wasn't looking good on that front.

I tried to pull up details of the vision—the vines, someone climbing through the window—but my brain was circling too hard. Why was Comstock here? *His* scene, he'd said. More pressing, I still didn't know why Harry had called me.

"So glad you're happy to see me," I told Comstock, my voice droll. I had no choice but to play it cool because Investigator 101 dictated that if it felt like a trap, you were already in one. The only way out was through. "Wish I could say the same for your saggy face."

This earned me an appreciative grunt from the officer guarding the hallway door. I should have stopped there, should have reined myself in, but it wasn't in my nature. "You keeping busy since the Taken Ones?" I asked.

Next to me, Harry sucked in his breath, a small noise scolding me for baiting Comstock, but the man had made my life hell on earth during that case. It'd almost cost us two lives. Believe me, I'd been in no hurry to work with him again after getting screwed out of the MPD, but I'd figured we could at least remain professional. I'd been wrong. I hadn't turned him in for his misconduct, but neither had I pretended he hadn't done what he'd done. Other detectives let Comstock feel right when he was wrong—he had seniority, plus an arrogance that made it easier for most people to just go along with him. Not me. I wasn't gonna soft-shoe for anyone.

Comstock's eyes glittered. He knew what was passing between us, me bringing up the Taken Ones. I was warning him that he'd better be on guard, that I wasn't going to forget that he'd shown his ass. "Yeah, I've been busy," he growled, "but not too busy to request your presence."

It was only a lifetime of practice that kept the shock off my face. *Comstock* had wanted me here, not Harry? Why hadn't Harry warned me? I could feel his dopey eyes on me, but I was too pissed to look his way.

"Speaking of the Taken Ones," Comstock continued, "I'm doing you a professional courtesy now, same as you did for me then. After this, we're all good."

And just like that, he'd volleyed my warning right back to me. I strained for equilibrium.

"Yeah, nothing I love more than being woken up in the middle of the night," I said, my voice heavy with sarcasm. He didn't need to know I'd been out walking Owl. "That for sure clears away all your past calcified crap."

He laughed. It sounded hollow.

"Sorry about the hour," he said, his tone matching mine. "Killers can be so inconsiderate. But I think you'll be thanking me for the invite." He held up the evidence bag he'd been gripping while we played shit ping-pong. "Seems you have a personal connection to this particular scene."

I took a step forward, my mouth suddenly so dry I could taste my teeth.

I squinted.

The bag held my Minneapolis Police Department ID, the one I hadn't seen since I'd shoved it into a box that I'd crammed into the back of my closet more than two years ago.

CHAPTER 9

Van

I tried swallowing and just barely kept myself from coughing. "Where'd you find that?"

I'd never been inside this room, or even this shelter. My only connection to the place was Emily Barris, and I certainly hadn't fished out my old ID to bring along the three times we'd met in Loring Park. *Dammit.* I hoped I didn't run into her tonight. I didn't think she could pretend we were strangers.

Comstock's expression grew hard—what did he see playing across my face?—but his voice stayed easy. "Why don't you come see for yourself."

I now understood why Harry couldn't tell me who'd requested me, or why. I'd never have come inside if I'd known the setup that awaited, and not seeing this through would have been the worst of the terrible paths available. My chest tightened as an appalling suspicion bubbled to the surface. I shoved it down. I needed to stay on my toes.

My legs carried me forward through sheer willpower into a bedroom that was as cramped as the living room. It held a dresser, a portable closet stuffed with clothes, a lamp, and a double mattress. A body lay on the mattress, a sheet covering it.

The acid smell of vomit seared the air.

The squeeze in my rib cage tightened at the sight of the two uniformed officers standing next to the bed, watching me with wary eyes. Comstock joined them, looking like the cat that'd swallowed the canary.

"Your ID was found over there," he said, pointing to the floor near the bed. "Right in the path the killer would have had to take. I bet you have a real good story for how it got there."

I opened my mouth, hoping my voice sounded more solid than I felt. "A lot of people in and out of a shelter, plus this is my neighborhood, more or less." I aimed my chin at the bagged ID. I should have stopped talking—guilty people talked—but I couldn't seem to keep my trap shut. "Besides, I haven't seen that for years."

There was no overhead light, only the lamp near the bed. It made the shadows severe, cutting Comstock's face in half. "You been here before?" His voice was needling. "You know the victim?"

"She has no idea who the victim is," Harry said curtly, appearing at my elbow. "I didn't tell her, as you requested. And you know she's never been here before, or she would have said something by now."

Honest Harry, too good for this world. I was going to split his heart wide open.

Because I didn't just have visions.

I was also a murderer.

CHAPTER 10

Lovely Lulu

August 30, 1986

"Order up, Lovely Lulu!"

Lulu Geldman smiled. "Thanks, Caesar."

He gave nicknames to all the waitresses. Lulu told herself it could be worse—just ask Krusty Kathy. She grabbed the nearest hot pad and used it to slide the double-plated entrées onto her table-size tray. When she'd first started working at Chi-Chi's, she'd been overwhelmed by the food selection, mostly because it all looked the same: an island of molten cheese. But after three months, she could tell the enchiladas apart from the chimichangas from the flautas. It was little things—a hint of green sauce here, the height of the cheese mound there.

Of course it all tasted the same, but that was above her pay grade.

She adjusted her strapless bra (*Wearing it'll be like smuggling two grapefruits in a rubber band,* Kathy had cautioned during training, and she wasn't wrong) beneath the off-the-shoulder embroidered flounce blouse all the girls at the downtown Minneapolis Chi-Chi's were required to wear. Then she bent at the knees and slid the tray onto her shoulder. One wrong move and she'd have eighty pounds of edible lava burying either her or an innocent customer, but you didn't land the prime lunch shift by being a coward.

Lulu sailed through the packed floor, her hips swishing, her black hair tied into a high ponytail, a red-lipsticked smile painted on her face.

She felt every inch the Lovely Lulu.

She slung those plates like she'd been born to it and nodded agreeably when her table asked for water refills. They'd need all the help they could get washing down that slop.

"Lulu!" Tawny, a waitress who should have been working the floor above, appeared looking panicked. "You gotta help me. I have a birthday on the second floor. You free? Pleeeeezzee."

Lulu glanced around her section. She had a dozen tables, three that'd just been seated. The hostess was supposed to stagger them, but she was new. Lulu tugged up her bra with a snap. "Sure, but it's gotta be quick."

Tawny looked ready to weep with relief. "You're a doll."

Lulu tucked her tray in a corner, and they took the stairs two at a time. As far as Lulu knew, the City Center Chi-Chi's was the only one that occupied more than one floor, not to mention a third of a city block. Each level had its own kitchen, with a dumbwaiter connecting them. Usually, waitstaff stuck to their floor, but no one wanted to sing the birthday tune alone. They'd learned it in training, sung to the tune of Queen's "We Will Rock You": "Buddy it's your birthday, big day, happy day, you got cake on your face, such a disgrace . . ."

Surely they were breaking a million copyright laws.

"How old's the kid?" Lulu asked when they reached the next level.

Tawny grimaced but didn't respond.

Lulu groaned. "It's a *man*, isn't it. A college dude with his goons."

"Worse," Tawny said as they rounded the corner. The second floor was impossibly busier than the main level, but even so, it was easy to pick out the table of too-loud guys in suits. Businessmen in town for a convention, judging by the boat-size margaritas in front of them.

Tawny ducked into the kitchen for the fried ice cream, lighting its sparkler as she walked. Lulu followed, and they both belted out the song, laughing the whole time. If they couldn't enjoy the job's ridiculousness, what was the point? Lulu raced back downstairs afterward, her entire shift passing by in the same hectic blur.

By the end she was exhausted, and—judging by the bulge in her apron—at least eighty dollars richer. She joined the rest of the waitstaff near the main-floor Corn Chip Island, two huge warming drawers kept constantly stocked during rush. At the end of the lunch and dinner shifts, the staff got to take home whatever the customers hadn't eaten.

"Thanks, Caesar," Lulu said, accepting the empty paper bag he offered her. She was sick of everything corn, saw ears and chips and kernels dancing through her dreams, but she didn't want to hurt his feelings.

"Welcome," he said. He glanced shyly at his feet. "You work Monday?"

"Naw, it's my day off."

He leaned against the counter. "Lucky."

Monday was September 1, and on the first of every month, the restaurant was slammed with people who'd just gotten their welfare check. Those folks always asked for extra chips and salsa and rarely tipped. Some of the staff minded, but not Lulu. She filed it under easy charity work.

"Not lucky," she said, shaking her head. The smell of the chips finally got to her, and she began filling her bag. "I have a dentist appointment."

"Your teeth are beautiful," Caesar said.

Lulu had only a moment to wonder if he was trying to get in her pants—fending off line cooks was her least favorite part of the job—when Chris, another kitchen worker, popped his head in from the staff-only door. It led to an alleyway where they took their smoke breaks.

"Guy out there wants to talk to you," Chris told her, jabbing his thumb behind him.

Caesar's brow furrowed, but he gave her a pat on the arm before returning to his cleanup duties. Maybe he'd only been being nice.

"Who is it?" Lulu asked.

"I dunno," Chris said. "Am I your secretary now?"

"Dude," one of the waiters said before Lulu could ask a follow-up question, "come here and check out these three chips stuck together. They look like a throwing star!"

Chris rushed over, letting the door close behind him. He stank of cigarettes and alleyway garbage when he passed, carrying the temporary heat of the outdoors on his clothes. Lulu glanced at her watch. Her mom worried whenever she came home later than expected, but it would only take a minute to see who was out there, if it was anyone at all. The cooks liked to play dumb pranks. She had a moment of concern that it was one of the men she'd sung "Happy Birthday" to, but they'd seemed harmless enough, so outside she went.

She returned minutes later.

Only Caesar noticed how upset she looked, but she was gone before he could ask.

Lulu's mom peeked in her daughter's bedroom the next morning when Lulu's alarm wouldn't stop going off. "Honey, you shouldn't set it if you want to sleep in. I've told you once, I've told you a million times, that—Lulu?"

Her beautiful girl lay in bed, her back to the door.

Martha Geldman would tell police that Lulu looked asleep, but all of a sudden, she sensed something was terribly wrong. She didn't know if it was her mother's instinct or the result of two decades of nursing, but when she darted forward to flip Lulu around, her heart was already hammering at her throat.

Her only child flopped onto her back.

She had no pulse and wore a clown's lurid grin.

CHAPTER 11

Van

When my visions first began on Frank's Farm, I'd assumed they were a circus of horrors created by my sick brain. Then, one day after Frank was arrested and I'd fled the commune, I was buying a pack of cigarettes when a familiar face caught my eye on the overhead television.

It was a man I'd been having nightmares about for weeks.

He was being arrested for sex trafficking.

That was the moment I realized the ghastly crimes I'd witnessed in my dreams were *real*. I broke down crying in the middle of the gas station, great gasping sobs of relief as I watched the monster being led away in handcuffs. *I hadn't been hallucinating.* My dreams were windows into actual crimes, which meant that the predators could be stopped.

I could use my talent for good.

I earned my GED in record time and went directly into the University of Minnesota criminology program. Once I graduated, I joined the Minneapolis PD. Worked my way up to homicide, had the great good fortune to land Bart as a partner. For ten blissful years, I was able to channel my visions into justice. The relief of catching the murderers, the rapists, the child molesters—whose crimes looped in my brain as I slept—was unmatched.

But after Bart died and I left the MPD, a trio of pedophiles began haunting my sleep. Without steady Bart by my side, the visions of their abuse drove me outside myself. I couldn't see straight, couldn't figure out how to stop the horror that awaited me every night. The few minutes of sleep I carved out were filled with children being tortured.

When I couldn't take it anymore, I forced each of the three pedophiles to drink poison.

The press caught wind of it, somehow learned that the poison had been mixed into the last thing they'd each drunk, and speculated that there was a serial killer at work. They dubbed "him" the Sweet Tea Killer.

That killer had never been caught.

Of course she hadn't. Except for one slipup, I'd covered my tracks. If a life in law enforcement didn't teach you how to successfully get away with murder, I didn't know what did. Not that I took it lightly. The murders tormented me almost as much as the men's crimes had. I'd snipped a lock of hair off the victims so I could remind myself that I was no better than them. After those three, I swore I'd never let my visions drive me to violence again, and I'd been true to my word. With Harry by my side, I'd even been able to again start using information gathered from the visions in my investigations. I hadn't confessed the source of the details to him, not yet, but for the first time since Bart was alive, I had it once again under control.

So no *way* was my appalling suspicion true, no *way* had I sleep-walked into this place and poisoned some woman I'd never met. There had to be some other explanation for why my old ID was here.

But as I stared at the sheet-covered body, my worry grew.

"Who called it in?" I was stalling, pushing back the inevitable, feeling the walls close in. My cheek twitched, and I couldn't hide it.

"Her ex," Comstock said. He watched my every move, a predator sniffing for weakness. "He swears he was just dropping by to give her some of her stuff." He raised his hand, palm out, a *before you ask* gesture. "And yes, he's already been taken in."

Relief hit me like a truck, and I almost laughed out loud. An ex? Then we had our suspect, and a good one. Statistically, an abusive partner was the reason most women ended up in a shelter, and it was not unheard of for them to track down their girlfriends and wives to finish what they started.

I clung to this life raft. *It wasn't me. I hadn't killed the person beneath the sheet.*

"So you ready to see her face?" Comstock taunted, his gloved hand over the body. Had he covered the victim for theatrics? "You're not too delicate?"

"Screw you and your bullshit, Comstock." I was angry now. He and I'd been on gnarly crime scenes together in the past. He knew I was no delicate flower. He was jerking me around, and now that I knew the ex was on the hook, I could think clearly again. My new best guess was that Comstock had planted the ID here as some sort of sick joke. "Let's see it."

"As the lady commands."

He lifted the sheet.

Emily Barris, Owl's owner, lay beneath, a ghastly joker's grin stretching her dead cheeks.

CHAPTER 12

Just Judy

September 3, 1986

It was a coincidence that a firefighter being treated at the hospital where Martha Geldman worked overheard the nurses talking about Lulu's terrible death, a coincidence that the same firefighter also knew about Robin Seer's passing. When he called up Amos Anderson, a friend and *St. Cloud Times* reporter, to tell him about the two bizarre cases, Amos had already heard word of Gina Penchant's grinning corpse—the whole county was talking about it.

Since the three curious deaths had all happened within days of each other, Amos was sure he had something. He threw together a rushed article that hit the front page below the fold, even requesting and viewing the county coroner's photos (though they'd never make it into the paper). He couldn't sleep without his lights on for weeks after seeing those snaps—three forever frozen fairy-tale princesses, grinning like ghouls, stiff as stone.

He called them the Laughing Dead, figured he'd make a name for himself by being the first to connect what he felt certain were three murders, become known as the guy who helped nab a serial killer.

Folks read the article, talked about it for a hot minute, but it didn't gain any traction. Part of the problem was that the deaths had happened in three different counties. The other issue was most people decided it was just three tragically unfortunate, unconnected teen suicides. Not a serial killer and certainly not news, not compared to Bert Blyleven coming to town to sign baseballs or the rumors that the yearlong Hormel strike was ending.

And so the hubbub, small as it was, quickly passed.

Judy Morsa would never see the *St. Cloud Times* article. If it'd landed on her lap, she might have read it for its salaciousness, but it would never have occurred to her that it applied to her. She was just a sixteen-year-old girl trying to make sure life didn't pass her by. Still, it took her all of ten minutes to realize she'd gone too far by leaving Troy's place with the guy. What was that saying her gramma always used? *Don't bother stepping out of the frying pan if you're going straight into the fire.*

And here she was, crackling in the flames.

A tear raced down Judy's cheek. Gramma Anne was probably sleepless with worry. Judy had been gone for more than a week. She should demand he take her home. She should and she *would*, as soon as he returned. After the widow-maker fell on him, they'd just driven around for days, a lot of it consisting of him telling her to wait in the car while he ran in somewhere, a farmhouse outside of Rockville here, a Maple Grove house there. He really loved that she was good at chemistry, though, and had her tell him what she could do. He also took her to a concert, a real one at an arena, not a state fair show. Then, after a few days of that life, he'd driven through the night to Judy-didn't-know-where. She'd fallen asleep with the Minneapolis skyline still visible in the rearview mirror. She hadn't woken until the car stopped. The sun had been rising, turning the sky the color of Tang.

She'd rubbed her eyes. "Where are we?"

He smiled that nice smile, grinned so big that his big goofy ears moved. She still couldn't believe that tree hadn't crushed him like a bug. The guy had to have nine lives.

"Your new home," he said.

She blinked, staring at the ghost-gray two-story house in the woods, half its windows smashed out and squirrels peering out of holes in the siding. She was positive he was pulling her leg. Too bad he was as serious as a heart attack. He showed her around, helping her see his vision for the place, gave her lots of attention the first day there, like Troy had, and then he'd disappeared.

Also like Troy had.

The only difference was *this* guy had locked her up.

He'd trapped her in a second-story bedroom with a jug of water and some granola, plus a white enamel pot that he said she could use like a toilet. She curled her nose and told him that was gross.

He laughed and said she was cute.

Then he left.

She held out for twelve hours before she peed in the pot. Twenty-four before poop, and her cheeks burned the whole time. The room smelled like an outhouse now, and there wasn't even a window to crack. Well, there was, but it was papered over and nailed shut.

Judy was thinking she wouldn't mind hauling off and throwing that pee-pot through the glass and breaking out of there if he didn't come back soon, when she heard footsteps outside the door. She sat up in bed, which was the only furniture in the room besides the white enamel can and an empty dresser. No books, not even for coloring in.

"You better let me out of here!" she cried. Had it been two days already?

A click-tumble told her he'd slid a key into the lock. She didn't know why her heart was beating so hard. He was just a man. She saw them all day long at the Dairy Freez, had male teachers. What could one guy do to her?

But it wasn't him who walked through the door.

It was a woman, her eyes sunken, her skin the sick yellow of old squash. She balanced a baby on her hip. Her face lit up when she spotted Judy. "I *knew* you'd be young!" she said.

It was a weird thing to say.

Judy guessed the lady was in her early twenties, dark hair cascading down her back, her nose tossed with freckles. Her baby was so cute. Judy felt a stab of jealousy. Babies and Barbies, she loved them both.

Judy rubbed her arms. The house didn't have heat. "Where am I?"

The woman stepped closer, her face screwing up. Judy thought it might be the pee-pot stink. "Why, you're home," the woman said, her face relaxing.

Had she been confused by Judy's question and not grossed out after all?

Judy felt her ice melt a little, but she still needed to get back to Sauk Centre. "I actually live with my gramma. If it's no sweat, I'd like to go see her now." She'd carefully avoided saying *I'd like to* go home *now*. She didn't want to offend the woman, not when she was being so hospitable, and besides, she seemed like someone who'd be easily spooked.

The woman pooched out her bottom lip, her chin wrinkling in obvious disappointment. "Sure, if you want," she said slowly. Then her eyes widened like she'd just had a rad idea. "But you wanna stay a little longer? Baby Charles is getting bored with only me to play with."

She held out the pudgy child. He made a cooing sound.

Judy knew she shouldn't take the infant. She should go home. But Baby *Charles*? He was reaching out to her now, too, his arms so chubby that it looked like someone had snapped rubber bands where his wrists should be.

She thought of the man who'd brought her here. He was handsome, with that square jaw and that beautiful smile. He'd been a gentleman, too, lying next to her the first night without so much as kissing her.

"Fine," Judy said, accepting the baby.

He immediately clutched her shirt and nuzzled his face into it. Judy laughed, then blew a raspberry on his neck. He squealed so loud that she almost didn't hear the woman say how pretty Judy would look when she grew out her hair.

Almost.

CHAPTER 13

Van

I stood in that bedroom staring at Emily's death mask of a face for all of five seconds, her horror-movie smile gutting me, before turning heel. Her death, my ID on the scene? I needed to see what was on the other side of that vine-painted window.

Let Comstock think what he wanted about why I fled.

Harry followed me out, the moon staring down with her milky eye. "I apologize for not giving you a heads-up," he said.

He sounded troubled. Good. I kept walking, not stopping until I reached the exterior of Emily's window. "You want forgiveness, go to church."

The window was only a few feet off the ground, easy to crawl through, not even a decorative bush to slow an intruder. I shined my phone flashlight on the ground. No visible footprints in the frozen brown grass below. I scanned the light back up, slowly. The window was open a half inch. The hot, soup-scented air leaked out, offending the crisp spring night.

"They think someone broke in?" I asked, pointing at the opening.

Harry shook his head. "Hard to be sure with only an eye check, but Comstock thinks no, she liked a hot room and a cool breeze."

I glanced back at the window frame. It likely held layers of fingerprints. None of them would be mine. *None.*

"The victim's ex-boyfriend is the likely suspect," Harry continued, "and Comstock knows it. But once he found your ID, he had every right to call you in."

I snapped the light onto his face, my tone icy. "How kind of you to help him ride me."

Harry shielded his eyes. I should've been taking my anger out on Comstock, but Harry was here. Still, I hated the hurt look on his face. I softened my stance. "You promised him you wouldn't tell me why you called me?"

A muscle jumped in his cheek. "It was important there be no appearance of impropriety in processing the scene. We can't give a jury any reason to throw out the case."

Golden-hearted, rule-following Harry. If I could have punched him in the throat right then without him knowing it was me, I'd have done it in a blink. "Got it," I said.

He stepped closer. "Evangeline," he began.

"Look, I don't need a babysitter." I wanted him off my back while I figured out what my next steps were. "I'm fine. If I'm acting off, it's because that whole scene was horseshit."

Harry nodded, his posture relaxing.

I drew in a deep breath. I was in no way connected to this crime, and the sooner it was confirmed that the ex was responsible, the better. I turned off my flashlight and slid my phone into my pocket.

"Explain the smile," I demanded.

Harry pushed his hat up so I could better see his eyes. "*Risus sardonicus.* It's caused by a sustained spasm of the facial muscles. Certain poisons can cause it, as can *Clostridium tetani.*"

"*Clostridium tetani?*" I really wanted to thump him now.

He nodded, as if it should be obvious. "The bacterium that causes tetanus."

"How's it transmitted?" A shadow passed on the other side of the window. Had Harry's techs arrived?

"It's usually passively introduced through a break in the skin," he said, his eyes also flicking to the window, "with puncture wounds, burns, and crush injuries being the most common entry points."

I considered this. "So not person to person."

He shook his head.

I squeezed my eyes closed, picturing Emily's body. Her joker's grin had been the most obvious feature, but there'd been other clues. "But you're leaning more toward active than passive poisoning because of the bruises at the victim's neck and wrists suggesting she'd been held down." I opened my eyes. "Assuming those weren't shadows?"

Harry's expression was grim, but respect swam to the surface. "They were not. If she was poisoned, the evidence suggests she didn't take it willingly."

I leaned forward, my outward calm finally snapping. "I need in on this case, Harry."

His face was so perfect, so eerily symmetrical, that he reminded me of an angel. "Why was your ID in there?"

I looked away. Looked back. Decided to tell him the truth. "I have no freaking idea."

He slid his hands into his pockets, revealing his belt. Of course it matched his shoes. "You know I don't control assignments. If you want this, you need to connect it with a cold case."

I grimaced. He wasn't telling me anything I didn't know. I'd scour the BCA files, see what I could stretch to say it was related. There had to be some way in. With access, I could figure out what had happened to Emily, close her case, *bye-bye finito* to all the weirdness swirling in the air.

Harry was quiet for a few beats, letting me think. "You didn't respond to my texts the other day," he finally said.

I drew down my eyebrows. "*That's* what you want to talk about right now?"

He smiled softly. "Did you read them?"

"Nope." He held on to his patient expression, which irritated me to no end. I blew air out of the side of my mouth, making a loose lock of hair dance. "Fine. What'd they say?"

"Just that I wanted to speak with you."

I rolled my eyes so hard I saw yesterday. "You're speaking with me right now."

He nodded. "It can wait." He glanced back at Emily's window. His expression was clear: *You have bigger things to worry about.*

Well, that did it. No way was I going to have him feel sorry for me. "Either you tell me what you texted about or I'll crawl down your throat and pull it out."

"That won't be necessary." His look of discomfiture was immediately replaced by an intense gaze, followed by a few uncomfortable beats of silence. "I was wondering what happened in Duluth that has you avoiding me ever since we returned."

CHAPTER 14

Van

Fat chance I was about to tell him that I was worried my cult leader of a father had abducted his innocent baby sister. "Me avoiding you? You're imagining it."

I was betting that a gentleman like Harry would never argue with me about my perspective on a personal matter, and I was right. After some vague words followed by a few beats of silence, he and I agreed it was best for me to leave the scene.

On the drive back to my apartment, I had an unhinged moment where I considered Patty Devries might have planted my ID on that scene to frame me. She was the one person who could nail me for the Sweet Tea killings. My only slipup had been accidental, Patty coming home early to see her pedophile husband thrashing on the floor, me standing over him as the poison I'd forced him to drink at gunpoint coursed through his body.

I shook my head to release the paranoid thought. If she'd wanted to cause me trouble, that would have been the time. Instead, she'd packed up her daughter and fled the country. Besides, no way would she have killed Emily to get back at me. Patty had nothing to do with my ID being on that scene.

If it had actually been mine. I was still betting Comstock had planted it.

Once I got home, I headed straight to my closet, throwing aside the clothes piled in front of it. My nervous energy agitated Owl. I took a moment to soothe her before returning to dig for my old ID. I knew it was weird that I'd kept something that reminded me of a job that had ended on such a sour note, but any piece of evidence that I was free, that I could decide when to eat or what to wear or *who I was*, I clung to like a ledge on a cliff. That meant not only hanging on to what others considered garbage for far too long but also storing every expired driver's license, student ID, and badge in a plastic bin that I kept in the back of my closet.

The bin that I'd just pulled out.

If I found my MPD ID inside, then all this was exactly what it looked like: Comstock placing a copy near the victim to mess with me just like he'd done back when I was in homicide. And the more I thought about it, the more confident I was that Comstock had decided to bring a fake along to the next crime scene he was called to. Planting it would hassle me to no end, not to mention give him the opportunity to declare we were even after the Taken Ones case.

It was catastrophically bad luck that I'd ended up knowing the victim on the case he'd chosen. If I'd had an ounce of sense, I'd have fessed up on the spot that she and I'd crossed paths. If it came to light now, I'd look guilty. But I didn't think anyone except Emily Barris knew we'd met. Once I confirmed my ID was in the bin, this would all be over. Comstock could play his sick little game, minus me caring.

"Prepare for one problem to disappear," I told Owl.

Her rump wiggled supportively.

I lifted the lid, certain I'd see my ID on the top. It would've been the last item I'd stored in there.

Except . . . the identification card was nowhere to be found.

My heartbeat thudded. I started throwing cards and photos aside searching for it, and then finally emptied the bin out onto the floor. Still no sign of it, so I started putting everything back in piece by piece, even though my legs were cramped from kneeling for so long.

It was no use.

My Minneapolis Police Department ID was gone.

Or rather, it'd found its way to Emily Barris's death scene. I sat back on my heels, overcome by a terrible, lonely calm.

CHAPTER 15

Van

I closed the bin, returned it to the rear of my closet, and then stood, electricity shooting from my nerves. A heavy blanket of shame covered me. *I am a murderer.* I glanced at the bathroom door. I knew it wasn't healthy, but I couldn't resist the pull. I was zombie-legging it toward the drawer where I stashed the hair I'd snipped from my three victims, certain I'd spy a lock of Emily's hair joining the rest, when Owl nudged my hand, whining. I glanced down into her chocolate-brown eyes. They held more feeling than I experienced in a week.

I sighed, her presence allowing me to reclaim just enough of myself. "Fine," I told her, rubbing her velvet ears. "I don't have to look right now."

She went to grab her tug-of-war rope, suddenly overcome with joy. A reluctant smile pushed at my mouth. After a few minutes of playing with her, the worst of the shame had passed, enough that I could get to work. No way had I killed Emily, and the quickest way to prove that would be to figure out who had. I slid pizza boxes off my small glass dining table and opened my laptop, intending to see what I could uncover. Emily's Facebook page was private, as was her Instagram. Her LinkedIn profile told me nothing other than her past two jobs, both in human resources. My head was starting to grow heavy when my email dinged.

Few people had my address. I didn't need it to be *easier* to get a hold of me. But when I saw the incoming was from Jobber, the guy I'd asked to help me track down Frank Roth, my heart did a leprechaun kick.

He was a classmate from my MPD training days who now worked the private sector.

I'd reached out to him because he owed me one. I'd been his beard at our graduation, plus a few other events. He wasn't gay, just really unpleasant. I told him it would've been cheaper to grow a personality than to keep buying me dinner, but he hadn't heeded my advice. Once we left school, he'd gone the cop route for a few years before becoming a borderline shady private investigator.

Exactly what I needed.

My plan for what to do if I found Frank Roth remained vague. In the pixelated black-and-white photo of Caroline Steinbeck that the cops had distributed after her abduction, she was cute, young, generic, but not familiar. No way had she been in the girls' dorms with me. I saw the Mothers far less often than the Sisters, but Caroline would have been too young to be one of them. In other words, it was impossible Caroline had been on the Farm.

Frank had disappeared for weeks at a time, however.

He might have built other enclaves. If so, Caroline could still be living at one of them.

If Frank had abducted her. *If* she was still alive.

Both of which were incredibly long shots. So I'd reached out to Jobber, figuring I'd first locate Frank and decide next steps from there.

But my balloon of hope deflated when I read Jobber's subject line: No Luck.

Well, at least I didn't have to waste my time reading the email.

I leaned back in my chair, stretching until my spine popped. The sky outside was growing rosy. I rubbed my eyelids with the heels of my hands. I could do more research on Emily Barris, hoping to uncover the name of her ex or some other helpful information explaining why she might have had my ID in her room, or I could scrape out an hour of sleep and pray it was enough to get me through the day.

Owl nuzzled my hip.

I glanced down, having a hard time remembering how I used to live without her. Poor thing didn't even know she'd lost her person. I'd find a way to break it to her, just not yet.

"You're such a nag," I told her lovingly. "You're lucky you're cute."

I set the alarm on my watch, made sure the REM tracking app was cued up, and crawled under the blankets. As I stumbled over the threshold into sleep, my last troubling thought was that I better hurry up and find out what happened to Harry's sister before Comstock hamstringed me for Emily's murder.

The nightmare finds me almost immediately.

I'm walking toward the deepwater creek from my childhood, but something is terribly wrong. The once-clear stream is black, its wet oiliness lewd against the blue sky. Its banks are lined by figures I almost recognize, but their faces have twisted into grotesque masks made of bark, their arms twisted branches, their hollow eyes following my every step. The scent of rotting wood is overwhelming.

That's when I spot Frank Roth kneeling at the river's edge, his back turned to me. His shoulders convulse rhythmically, as if he's scrubbing something in the black water.

My horror sharpens when I realize what he's actually doing.

He's not washing clothes, of course he isn't.

He's baptizing Veronica until she drowns. My heart stutters as his arms plunge into the water, holding her beneath the surface. I stumble forward, fighting the thick sludge that clings to my feet.

It's not until I reach his shoulder that I see it's not Sister Veronica he holds underwater.

It's me.

Frank Roth grips my shoulders, shoving me down into the cold, suffocating depths. The water closes over my head like an icy shroud. I thrash, my lungs burning. I'm tangled in the muck, the cold seeping into every pore, my father's face looming above me, a cold, distorted mask. His grip is unyielding. On the banks, the grotesque trees sway, their whispers a mocking laughter. The cold numbs my senses, and I feel my consciousness fraying at the edges.

I'm about to slip away when Owl's whining pulls me from the depths.

I woke shivering, tangled in my blankets.

CHAPTER 16

Van

"What're you in the mood for today?" Alexis asked. She was a brown-eyed brunette in her early thirties who volunteered at the same shelter as me. She also taught yoga when she wasn't slinging drinks at Magnolia's coffee shop, the closest restaurant to the BCA.

I'd parked in the Bureau lot and hoofed it over. My alarm had gone off for so long before I woke that Owl started harmonizing with it. I'd sat up, more tired than I'd been when I'd first dropped off to sleep. My watch confirmed I'd been out for an hour, and my heart rate had stayed steady. That meant I hadn't had a vision or a nightmare, that I'd actually gotten brief rest, even though it felt like I'd run a marathon.

After a quick shower and a walk for Owl, I'd taken off thinking of only one thing: coffee.

"Two large mochas." Chocolate could only improve the experience.

"You got it." Alexis showed her dimples before she walked over to the machine. Magnolia's was morning-rush busy, but she always gave me personal service. She wanted us to be friends and—I suspected—more. "How's Owl?"

She'd been at Animal Haven when I'd taken the doggo home. Since she'd offered to pet-sit if I ever needed, I owed her honesty. "Stinky and loud."

Her smile was charming. "That's all boxers," she said over the whooshing of the espresso machine. "They suck in so much air with those flat faces." She tipped her head at the cups. "Who's the second coffee for?"

"Both for me." I knew the proper gesture would be to smile back, to lighten the mood since she'd made me confess to being a pig. I was too tired. I glanced out the window instead.

And sucked air as the shabby vagrant from last night strode by in his red scarf.

I was halfway to the door, heart racing, when I realized it wasn't him at all, was in fact a woman about his size wearing a similarly colored scarf. Fear had a way of messing with our eyes, rewriting memory. The woman was staring at me weirdly. Wasn't she? I must've been gaping.

I returned to Alexis, accepting both coffees with a tense thank-you and left, head down.

I'd managed to get only as far as firing up my computer before the knock came.

"Come in."

Harry entered my cramped office looking like an ad for Savile Row. He managed to keep his expression neutral as he surveyed the row of empty take-out cups on my desk, but I could tell it took an effort.

"Did you know that a clean office reduces stress and increases productivity?" he asked.

His tone made it sound like he was making random conversation. I'd lay money he'd rehearsed the line all the way down the hall. "That seems unlikely."

His shoulders drooped, and he switched subjects. "I ran the features of last night's homicide through the records." His arctic-blue eyes met mine. "I think I found a cold case match."

The heat in my chest caught me off guard. Rather than go home after the scene, he'd dug for cold cases, which was exactly what I should have done—and *would have* if the entire evening hadn't kicked me in the taco, one horror after another, *boom boom boom.*

Harry looking out for me made me wildly uncomfortable. "Great," I said, the word coming out garbled. I cleared my throat. "You have a file?"

"I do." He raised the folder he held. "I'll send over a copy."

That could cross one very big problem off my list. "It's a good match?"

He gave a tense nod. "I'm afraid we have probable reason to believe that a serial murderer from the late '80s may have resurfaced."

I placed my hands flat on my desk, the situation with my ID suddenly very small potatoes. While I would have connected any case to get in, that wasn't how Harry operated. There was something dark and real going on. "Give me the Cliff's Notes."

His mouth cramped. "It'll have to be while we walk. Chandler called down, said he'd like to speak with both of us about the Emily Barris case." His expression remained troubled. "He sounded upset."

Comstock must have told. Rat bastard.

I stood. My words came out measured and tight. "Then let's get to it."

CHAPTER 17

Van

Deputy Superintendent Ed Chandler's office was located on the BCA's top floor. It had a low-rent Oval Office feel, down to its massive desk with two dusty ficuses in place of the American flags. Chandler sat behind the desk wearing his characteristic black suit, the color contrast making his shaved head resemble a boiled egg. Despite his appearance and a fondness for working British sayings into his speech to remind the world he'd studied abroad, he was a keenly intelligent man.

It would be a mistake to assume otherwise.

Harry and I were seated in the two chairs across from him. He wasted no time getting to the point. "What the hell was your ID doing on scene, Reed?"

"No idea, sir." I held his gaze. If there was an upside to being raised by a megalomaniac, it was that I'd learned how to hold an even stare no matter what churned inside me. "I haven't seen it in two years. I tossed it after I left the MPD."

I let the lie sit between us. Better he think I'd been careless a couple years ago than in Emily Barris's apartment last night.

He didn't blink. I was having Humpty-Dumpty thoughts when he finally opened his mouth. "Where'd you toss it?"

"I don't recall, sir." I kept my face serene.

He broke off the stare contest, leaning forward to rest his elbows on his desk and his chin on his steepled fingers. "That's rookie bollocks, Reed. You should've turned it in same time as your gun and badge."

"That wasn't a requirement."

"That's why I said *should have*." His eyebrows came together like boxing caterpillars. "I've seen your office. It doesn't surprise me one whit that you'd misplace your ID, hell, your *head* if it wasn't attached to your neck."

Flames scorched up my spine. I was an excellent agent, no "despites" about it. But I'd discovered long ago that allowing a superior to complete his man-o-logue uninterrupted was the quickest way to move the situation forward. Sure enough, after a few more minutes of chastising, including making me agree to keep all surfaces in my office clean—*good luck with that*—Chandler tapped the computer screen facing him.

"Enough with all that. Tell me about the potentially connected cold case, Steinbeck."

Of course Harry had already informed Chandler. Good. Saved me a step.

Harry opened the file that lay on his crossed legs. "Three sixteen-year-old girls died in central Minnesota within five days of each other in August of 1986. Gina Penchant, Robin Seer, and Lulu Geldman."

"Cause of death?" Chandler asked.

"Unknown." Harry was skimming the file, though I'd bet good money he had its contents memorized. "The only notable feature was the *risus sardonicus* on all three girls' faces. Due to their age and otherwise good health, they were processed by a county coroner. The examinations were cursory, all three deaths ruled suicide."

In the '80s, similar to now, every Minnesota county was required to employ either a medical examiner or a county coroner. MEs were appointed by a county board, were always physicians, and were usually also forensic pathologists. County coroners, on the other hand, were laypeople more often than not. While MEs performed autopsies, coroners provided more of an administrative role: declaring time of death, positively ID'ing the victim, informing next of kin, processing a death certificate. A county coroner assigned to all three cases likely meant there'd been no autopsies unless the coroner had had reason to bring in a medical doctor.

Chandler leaned back in his leather chair. "But you don't think they were suicides."

"Emily Barris had a rictus grin," Harry said, pleating his top pants leg.

The horrific image played against the backs of my eyelids, her face leather stretched over stone.

"I searched the system for deaths with similar features," Harry continued, "and got a hit on Penchant, Seer, and Geldman." He cleared his throat. "The media coverage, such as it was, labeled them the Laughing Dead."

I winced. Those girls had had families, friends. *Identities.*

"You think poison?" Chandler asked.

"Oenanthotoxin specifically," Harry said. "It derives from hemlock water-dropwort plants, which grow in Minnesota. Accidental or intentional ingestion results in common poisoning symptoms—dizziness, nausea, convulsions—and quickly leads to a death with one uncommon quality: a muscle spasm which freezes the face into what looks like a wide smile. I've advised the medical examiner to test Emily Barris's body for it, along with other poisons."

"You think someone could eat this accidentally?" I asked. I felt Chandler's eyes on me.

Harry nodded. "The aboveground plant resembles parsley, belowground parsnips. Those who've survived ingestion say it has a sweet flavor." He lifted a shoulder, dropped it. "It could potentially have been growing in central Minnesota back in August of 1986, when the three girls died, but not this time of year. It's a swamp plant, as the name implies. April is too cold."

Chandler's squint said he was taking all this in, processing it. "1986, eh? I won't find any of your stuff on *those* old scenes, will I?" he asked me.

"Doubtful, sir." I smiled tightly. "I wasn't born yet."

"All right," he said, making up his mind. "The cold case is yours if you want it, Reed."

My jaw locked shut. "I do," I managed to squeeze past.

"Good," he said. "Call in Kyle to assist if you need it."

Kyle Kaminski was a good agent. A little ambitious for my taste, but he took orders fine. "Will do, sir."

Chandler tapped his desk with his pointer finger, adopting his teacher voice. "Remember what breaks a cold case. New eyes, new tech, or new leads. But don't give this one too much rope. If it doesn't have legs and a past, you let it go. We've got other cases knocking down the door, and all signs point to Barris being a domestic." He kept pressing his desk like he was pushing a down button. "Steinbeck, you're point man on the science."

"Yes, sir."

Chandler smiled grimly before returning his attention to me. "You can start by reinvigorating those MPD connections, Reed. I want you checking in with Detective Comstock regularly, starting today, starting right now. You need to convince the bloke you're playing nice. Good?"

I nodded, keeping my expression smooth.

I should win an Oscar.

CHAPTER 18

Van

Harry was itching to come along to visit Comstock, I could tell. Too bad he was equally desperate to be in house when the medical examiner sent over Emily Barris's autopsy results, though it could take days before they were processed. I told him I'd fill him in if there was anything new on Comstock's end.

We both knew there wouldn't be.

I stopped by my apartment on the way to the First Precinct. Owl took to the air like a kangaroo when I walked in. If humans could harness the power of boxer wiggles, we'd be well on our way to solving the energy crisis.

"Cool it, girl," I said as I clipped on her leash and led her outside, but I couldn't help smiling. She was just so *enthusiastic* about everything. I wondered how long until I'd have to return her to the shelter. If the MPD even learned Emily had owned a dog, they didn't have the resources to track down the animal. From Animal Haven's perspective, when an owner didn't check in on their pet being fostered and the shelter couldn't get hold of them, they'd wait a decent amount of time before putting the animal up for adoption.

Which meant maybe Owl could live with me permanently.

She glanced back at me over her butt, tongue lolling, like she could read my mind. I immediately shut down my train of thought. The woman I was fostering for had been murdered, and I was already claiming her dog?

When Emily had shown up for our first meeting, her appearance had been largely unremarkable. White, late twenties. Hazel eyes, curly brown hair peeking out from beneath the cap she'd worn all three times. A couple inches taller than my five-foot-four, with wide hips and broad shoulders. She'd walked through fire, you could spot it if you knew where to look—the way her shoulders never relaxed, how she seemed to be constantly scanning her environment even as she embraced Owl. Trauma recognized trauma. But she'd also had one of those rich, deep laughs that invited everyone in.

She hadn't deserved to die.

"C'mon, girlie," I told Owl, patting her muscular shoulders. "We need to head back to the apartment so I can get to work."

I sat in my car outside the First Precinct cop shop, studying the building. The dread I felt at the thought of walking through the front doors had lessened in the past two years, but it still left a slick glaze in my throat.

I'd poured my soul into the MPD job, embraced the shadows with Bart Lively by my side. A decade of my life dedicated to homicide investigations and they'd run me out like Typhoid Mary. The day I walked away, I'd clutched one lousy cardboard box, the only proof of the years I'd spent there. It held my ID, a pack of gum, a handful of end-chewed pens, and trinkets from Bart.

"Here, kid," he'd say after returning from one of his solo trips. "I got you a pack of lime candy. Everyone in Key West eats it." Or: "Thought you'd like this snow globe."

I smacked my steering wheel. *Screw Comstock and the horse he rode in on.* I stepped out of my car and strode into the precinct. The echoes of my past immediately filled the air—the stink of burnt coffee, a decade's worth of heartbeats, the whispers of inside jokes. The first time I'd returned after Bart's death, I'd shuffled in with my head down, adopting the same posture I'd had working here at the end. Not this time. Chin up, gaze straight ahead, I marched past the front desk, up the stairs, and directly to office 217. It'd been Bart's when he was alive, so of course Comstock had slunk his slimy self into it the minute it'd opened up. I'd known Comstock had been jealous of Bart's and my clearance rate, but the more distance I got from the situation, the more I wondered if it was actually *Bart* that Comstock had envied.

They were both quality investigators, but Bart happened to also be kind and decent. It was hard to hang on to your soul in the job, forget your fissured heart, but Bart'd remained true blue his whole life. I could see how that would have eaten at a guy like Comstock. Hell, it would have gotten to me if I hadn't loved Bart. He was the closest thing I'd had to family. But to work alongside someone who not only did a good job but was also a good man? That would have parked square on Comstock's nuts. It explained why he'd turned on me so hard and why he'd claimed Bart's office, like maybe Bart's leftover essence could rub off.

I arranged my face and knocked on the closed door.

"Yeah," Comstock said.

I stepped inside like I owned the place, flopping into the open chair. Comstock sat behind his gray metal desk wearing the same charcoal suit he'd had on at last night's crime scene. I tipped my chin at it. "You skip your bed?"

He rubbed his face, his jowls hanging lower than usual. "Unless you're here to confess that you murdered that woman and accidentally left your ID behind, I'm busy."

He was joking, which didn't sit right. It suggested maybe he hadn't planted that ID. "We have a cold case that's possibly connected. Three girls in '86 died with the same smile on their face."

He shuddered, the motion exaggerated but with a solid center. Exhaustion must be grinding him. "Like looking at a goddamned human jack-o'-lantern. Who laughs as they croak?"

"Like I said, three girls." I crossed one leg over the other. "All were sixteen at time of death, all of them located in central Minnesota."

That piqued his interest. "They know each other?"

I shrugged, fighting to maintain my relaxed posture. I couldn't spook Comstock. I needed him to let me in. "Haven't had time to look into the cases other than preliminaries. Ed Chandler ordered me to come straight over, let you know we're at your disposal."

He scowled. "Stop blowing sunshine up my skirt, Reed. You want to know what we've got on the Barris case, and in the spirit of our continued détente"—he gave the word three syllables—"I'm happy to share that Emily Barris's ex, one Otto Pusch, has a solid alibi if Steinbeck was right about time of death being between ten p.m. and midnight."

My gut spasmed. If that's what Harry estimated, I'd bet my skin he was right. "Alibis can be faked."

"You don't say?" Comstock snorted. "Next thing you'll tell me, the sky is blue and water's wet. But here's the thing: Pusch says he was running an Alcoholics Anonymous meeting from eight to ten p.m., and then on and off the phone with a woman he was sponsoring until three a.m. this morning. Apparently, she was in crisis. He says his phone records confirm."

My airway shrank. "You have the records?"

He screwed up his mouth. "No, Reed, I don't. My butler took the morning off, so I've been *remiss* in not having all my receipts prepared for your unannounced visit." He glanced over my shoulder, probably trying to will me to leave. "What I do have is the footage from his building security cameras. Was looking at it when you waltzed in. They clock him coming in at the time he says and not leaving until eight a.m. this morning."

"You'll let me know when you confirm with AA and the woman he says he's sponsoring?" I asked.

"If you give me a damn minute," Comstock grunted, waving me out of his office.

"Thanks." I stood, my legs tight. "I'll let you know what I uncover, if anything, on those three girls."

Comstock had already returned his attention to the security footage. "If you want to help," he said, his computer's sick yellow light reflecting off his face, "make sure you don't talk to Otto Pusch without me." He turned away from his screen long enough to yank a photo from his pile and slide it across his desk. "Oh, and keep an eye out for Pusch's dog. He claims Barris stole it. Says that's why he wormed her address from a friend and went to the shelter yesterday, though of course they never let him inside."

My pulse stuttered. I was looking at a photo of Owl.

CHAPTER 19

Just Judy

1989

The new place wasn't as nice as the last one, but who liked moving? Though in the last three years, she'd grown used to the peculiar rhythm of his world. Upheaval, relocation. New faces, new places. She almost couldn't remember the girl she'd been when he first swept her away, a sad little broken thing who'd had the audacity to cut her hair.

She hardly ever thought of Gramma Anne anymore, sometimes went a whole day without remembering her laugh, or the caramel-sweet taste of her pineapple upside-down cake, or the way she'd tuck Judy in on the couch with a can of 7UP, a sleeve of saltines, and the TV's remote control whenever she was sick.

As for the classmates she'd left behind in Sauk Centre, the more she thought about it, the more she decided she'd never had any close friends. It was just the glue of being young in the same small town that'd held them together. And to do what? Chug plastic cups full of Kool-Aid and Everclear in some field, listen to Duran Duran, and make out with another kid who was as lonely as you?

No, he'd brought her to a better place, taught her to be devoted. She'd never regretted it.

It went a long way that he valued her mind as well as her femininity. After their wild ride through central Minnesota, he'd put her in charge of mixing all his tinctures. Picking the plants, processing them, extracting the essence. She was proud he trusted her with it. And nobody, *nobody*, listened as well as he did. When he was around and wasn't pulled in too many other directions, he acted like everything out of her mouth was breaking news. She'd never had that kind of attention her whole life. It felt like the sun rising in her chest.

Plus, look at this gorgeous bedroom that was all hers. It was huge, much bigger than her room at Gramma Anne's house. The sound of children playing outside drew her to the window. She stepped to it, smiling at the sight of three kindergarten-age kids playing Ring Around the Rosie.

When she touched her pregnant belly, her smile grew wider.

CHAPTER 20

Van

I sleepwalked to my car, observing rather than feeling my jangling nerves. As if I needed another reason to find out who'd killed Emily Barris. No way was I giving Owl back to the man who'd broken her ribs.

Make sure you don't talk to Otto Pusch without me. That's what Comstock had said.

Nothing about not going to his place of work to get a feel for the creep. That's how I justified pulling up outside the elegant business a block off Bde Maka Ska, Minneapolis's largest lake. The place reminded me of a French country home, the tasteful sign out front reading PUSCH PERFUMERY.

It was one of the most successful bespoke businesses in the city.

The media often tied domestic violence to poverty, giving the impression that the two went together like peanut butter and chocolate. That was misleading. The poor might have more day-to-day struggles, but in my experience, those with money were more dysfunctional. The rich had the resources to hide their shortcomings better, was all.

In the case of the locally famous perfumer Otto Pusch and human resources manager Emily Barris, my guess was he'd shrunk her life down to nothing, whittling away her sense of self. It was an old story: alienate her friends and family, build her reliance on him, and make her doubt her own experiences and feelings until she had nowhere to go but the shelter when things became unbearable.

I stepped out of my car and strolled past the perfumery, adopting a casual pace. Based on the little she'd told me, Emily had been lucky to escape with her life and Owl. Her ex kicking her, she'd grown accustomed to. The dog, though? That had been the straw.

"It's not so scary inside."

I turned toward the voice. A short, silver-haired older man—late fifties or early sixties if I had to guess—was walking up the sidewalk. His eyes were a little too far apart, his ears too large, but rather than make him appear odd, the features gave him a gentle quality. I smiled at him.

He smiled back, something predatory flashing in his gaze. I tensed as he held out his hand.

"Otto Pusch." He nodded toward the building. "That's my lab and storefront. I'd be happy to show you around. It's not as fussy inside as it looks from out here, I promise."

I could see why Emily had fallen for him. His brown eyes were innocently wide, his mouth curved in gentle hope. I'd caught the briefest glimpse of his sinister side, and only because I'd been watching for it. I knew I shouldn't be here. Comstock could kick me off the case if he wanted, and I needed his good graces. Come to think of it, I should have kissed ass back at his office, though that likely wouldn't have worked with Comstock. He'd never liked pretend groveling, only the real thing.

"No thanks," I told Pusch, releasing his hand. I had nothing to ask him, nothing the police hadn't already. Comstock had never been dumb, just mean. He'd triple-check Pusch's alibi, run prints from the scene, have another set of eyes verify the camera footage. "I was just admiring your building. Hope you have a good day."

I could feel his gaze on me as I walked away, circling the block twice before I got in and drove to Pusch's apartment building. I passed two churches between his office and home. I parked in the lot of the second one and looked up the event calendars for both. The one I was parked in front of offered an AA meeting last night and every Tuesday night from eight to ten p.m., just as Pusch had claimed.

But last night's meeting had been canceled.

CHAPTER 21

Van

Could I possibly get lucky? Did Otto Pusch poison Emily Barris? Was my ID being on scene some cosmic pull-my-finger? My apartment was on the way back to the BCA, more or less, so I dropped by to walk Owl while I tried to recall more details from the vision I'd had of Emily's murder.

I'd witnessed a shadow climbing through her vine-painted window.

Creeping across the living room and into the bedroom.

Straddling an unconscious Emily and pouring poison down her throat.

I rewound the memory, trying to see the perp more clearly, but it was no use. The shape was amorphous. I couldn't even confirm it'd been a male.

Well, Comstock was bound to discover soon that Pusch's alibi was full of holes. I might as well do my job as long as I had it. I walked Owl back to my apartment, delighted that the box of enrichment toys I'd ordered her had arrived while we were out. I set up her find-the-treat mat, grabbed a cola and a bouquet of cheese sticks from the fridge, and headed back to work.

Harry wasn't in his lab when I dropped by to update him on Pusch, so I left him a Post-it Note, which I knew would send him up a tree.

He preferred his communication neat and traceable. I only wished I'd had cheese-cracker dust to decorate it with.

At my own computer, I began what was 50 percent of my job: researching. (The other 50 percent was writing reports. I kid. Sort of.) Harry had sent over the digital file for what the media had dubbed the Laughing Dead case. The first thing I noted was that "the media" was a single article that'd run in the *St. Cloud Times* back in '86. I was grateful it had, or there would've been nothing tying these three deaths together, no reason for them to end up in Cold Case.

My pulse picked up as I read over the skimpy files on each of the three victims, imagining their lives, their vibrancy, all of it ripped away. Gina Penchant hailed from Rockville, Robin Seer from Clearwater, and Lulu Geldman lived in Maple Grove, all three towns within an hour of each other. According to their families, the girls were well adjusted, happy, though Robin's mother said her daughter had been going through a rebellious phase, and Lulu's parents had recently divorced.

Their photos—high school yearbook headshots, all of them—were heartbreaking. Big hair, popped collars, their futures written in gel-pen bubble letters in the sky. Robin Seer wore neon-blue mascara. Lulu Geldman had braces.

All three had died with a smile on their face.

Two of the victims—Gina Penchant and Lulu Geldman—had been autopsied, it turned out, their organs removed and weighed, tissue samples collected, and basic tests run. Nothing suspicious had been discovered. Gina's passing was ruled death by natural causes due to her heart being slightly enlarged. Robin and Lulu were declared suicides, suspected cause poison, though no toxin had been named.

That wasn't unexpected. With literally thousands of poisons available, testing for each would have been prohibitively expensive, especially on a county budget, especially with no reason to expect foul play. I slid my chair over to the filing cabinet, opened it, and took out a bag of chips. Forget the arty bags of angel-sliced potatoes delicately caressed by avocado oil and dusted with truffle powder.

Give me the red-and-white Old Dutch double box with two silver bags inside. Give me a chip that held its dip.

I rolled back to my computer, crunching on the way. A basic timeline of each of the girls' last twenty-four hours had been compiled. Gina had attended school, then had friends over. Neither of those friends had been interviewed. Gina's parents discovered her body when they returned from a drive-in movie.

Robin Seer had gone to school followed by a concert with her boyfriend, Charles "Chuck" Brzezinski. Charles had been interviewed. He said they'd had a good time at the show—AC/DC, according to the file—and that the only unusual activity afterward was that he hadn't walked his girlfriend to her door.

Lulu Geldman had worked the lunch shift at Chi-Chi's in Minneapolis City Center the day of her death. I took a second to wonder why she hadn't applied for a waitressing job in Maple Grove, where her mom lived. It would have saved her a twenty-minute drive and the hassle of finding parking. Investigators had interviewed her Chi-Chi's manager; he said she was a model employee, but he tossed out the name of one of his line cooks: Chris Windahl. According to the manager, Windahl had had an "untoward" interest in Lulu.

Windahl had denied it.

There was no evidence that the three girls had ever met. They weren't involved in the same sports or clubs, their parents didn't travel in the same circles. That left limited possibilities for what'd happened to them: (1) It could have been three terrible, accidental coincidences, with one or more of them having a heart condition or accidentally ingesting hemlock. (2) It also could have been a suicide train. There'd been no social media to spread stupid trends, but kids always found a way. (3) Or it could have been murder.

It appeared from the investigating officers' notes that they hadn't known about the other similar deaths happening just across county lines. LE on each scene would have assumed they had an isolated natural death or suicide on their hands. The parents would have sworn their daughters couldn't have taken their own lives, but the interviewing offi-cers would know that the people closest to the victims were notoriously bad judges of their emotional state, so they would close the files after completing only the most rudimentary investigations.

My pulse picked up. I'd come in through the back door, but there was a real case here.

These poor girls and their families had been denied justice. Even if there was no connection between their deaths and Emily's, there was still a good reason to take this cold case. From where I was sitting, it'd been fumbled from the start. Though to be fair, even if one of the responding officers had read the *St. Cloud Times* article or otherwise discovered that there had been two other similar deaths and they'd done their best to connect and solve the three, the fact of the matter was that most crimes weren't cracked. That was true even when the best cops were on the job, forget all the seat fillers who wore a badge. It was a fact no one wanted to say out loud, but the ranks of law enforcement were stuffed with dumbasses just like any other profession. I'd worked with cops who couldn't make glue stick.

Which was why I'd need to peel back all the layers and start from the beginning.

My blood fizzed as I cracked my knuckles. Reopening a cold case was a responsibility I took seriously, and also something I enjoyed. It followed a straightforward, meticulous procedure.

First, the officer accepted the case. *Done.*

Next, they reviewed the evidence and gathered it into an updated, cohesive timeline. I'd assign that to Kaminski. He loved organizing information. He was such a geek that he even sketched out his notes by hand before indexing them on the computer.

After the timeline was solid, the investigator met with the lab to request a review of the evidence, plus to check if any samples remained that could be tested using new tech. I'd shoot Harry an email on that front, though I suspected he was already on it.

Next came the heart of the investigation and the part I excelled at: interviewing everyone involved in the original case. That included law enforcement, coroner, friends and family, coworkers. The goal was threefold: find out what was missing in the file, connect dots and fill gaps, and hopefully find new leads.

Throughout it all, I'd need to question everything. Time twisted memory, but even more than that, investigators were susceptible to tunnel vision. That was true of those working the case in the '80s and could happen to me now. Once you believed you knew who or what did it, you sought out data to support your bias. It was a disease of confidence, one every human was susceptible to.

I needed to approach this with an open mind.

I needed to find out what, if anything, connected the three girls.

And I needed to do it quick, because my own mistakes were coming at me like a freight train.

CHAPTER 22

Van

A knock at my office door jerked me out of my bleary-eyed haze. Last night's lack of sleep was winning, caffeine be damned. "Who is it?" I snapped.

Kyle Kaminski poked in his close-shaven head. "I'm still waiting on the case files so I can pull together the timeline you requested." When he stepped all the way into my office, I had a moment to wonder if Harry was rubbing off on him. He wore a seriously sharp-looking pine-green suit with a navy-blue tie. The men around me were peacocks.

Kyle was a young agent, just turned twenty-six. I'd been his mentor until recently, when Chandler had decided he no longer needed one. I'd agreed, for the most part. Kyle didn't have much law enforcement experience before starting at the BCA, but he had the criminal justice degree, and he was a thorough investigator.

"I *just* emailed you that I needed a timeline." I hoped my tone expressed my annoyance. I hated being nagged.

He pretended to glance at a nonexistent wristwatch. "Yeah, four hours ago."

I started. I'd been utterly lost in research, pulling together basic facts on the families, especially the parents of the three girls, searching for any other suspicious crimes in the area during the same period, tracking down the names of the two friends Gina had been with the night she'd died. I'd even sketched out a skeletal combined timeline for Kyle to build on. First death, Gina's on August 26, then Robin's on August 29 or 30, and Lulu's on August 30 or 31. No way to be sure of Robin's or Lulu's exact date of death since their moms discovered their bodies in the morning. The parents had all been interviewed on scene with the exception of Lulu's father, who'd been living in an apartment in Minneapolis.

My eyes dropped to the time. I'd left Owl alone for hours, longer than she'd ever been without me since I'd brought her home. In a span of twenty seconds, I hit save on my work, emailed a copy to Kyle on the secure server, shut down my computer, and grabbed my coat.

"I've gotta run. Just sent you everything I have. I plan to do some basic legwork, a few interviews, before I call a team meeting." I breezed past Kyle. "Lock that door behind you."

It was everything I could do not to jog. I couldn't believe I'd left Owl to fend for herself for so long! I was moving so fast that I barreled straight into Harry coming around a corner.

"Whoa!" I pushed away from him. He appeared as surprised as I felt. "You get my note earlier?" I asked.

He straightened the front of his pin-striped suit jacket, composing himself. "The one you left in my lab saying the suspect in the early-morning crime scene had a 'weak-ass' alibi, or the email asking me to look into any bio evidence that might be available from the 1986 deaths?"

"Both. Either." I blinked. "You heard anything new on Barris?"

He shook his head. "No, and I'm afraid I haven't had time to dig into evidence storage for the '86 cases." He glanced at me shrugging into my jacket while I held my phone. "Do you want to walk and talk?"

"You don't have *anything* new?" I asked.

"No." A pair of agents appeared at the far end of the hallway, their voices a whisper.

"Then I can't." I pulled my jacket on the rest of the way.

His forehead furrowed and his voice dropped, the tone infuriatingly kind. "Are you okay?"

"I'm good." I couldn't tell him—couldn't tell anyone—about Owl, not with Emily dead, so I reached for the most obvious lie. "It's just that . . . I'm seeing someone."

"Oh." Harry's cheeks pinked. It would've been funny if not for the circumstances. "I'm sorry. I didn't mean to pry."

"You're good." I walked away, calling over my shoulder, "We'll meet tomorrow?"

"Of course," I heard him say.

Owl had shredded her stuffie. I couldn't understand how she'd managed to spread the fluff so widely without an air compressor, but I could hardly blame her, given how long the poor thing had been alone. She managed to look both twisted with remorse for destroying her toy and over the moon to see me. At least she hadn't gone to the bathroom anywhere.

"Sorry to leave you alone, girl." I kissed her noggin and then clipped on her leash so we could head straight outside into the cool April evening. She did her business the second she reached a patch of icy grass. I looked away to offer her some privacy and noticed that the setting sun was painting Loring Park as eerie as an X-ray, like shadows had frozen inside the air molecules. I shivered. At least the late-season snowstorm we'd had two weeks ago—Minnesota wasn't for the weak—had melted, turning the ground sloppy.

The memory of the storm made me think of Duluth, the place I'd been when it hit. I'd met Harry's mother and visited his childhood home, a mansion on the shores of Lake Superior that looked like it'd been outfitted by a set designer for *Dynasty*—all 1980s fussy wood, stiff furniture, and tapestries—and never updated. The place perfectly suited his mother, Myrna Steinbeck, all except for his sister Caroline's room, where the walls were covered with whimsical hand-painted white clouds.

"I'm surprised your mother allowed this," I'd said to Harry.

"Caroline painted them." His striking face had kicked with pain. "She loved clouds. Mom would hire someone to cover them up, and Caroline would simply draw new clouds over that."

Owl growled at a squirrel, bringing me back to Loring Park. I thought I should really follow up with Jobber, tell him he needed to dig deeper and faster. Every day that passed without me telling Harry about the potential connection between Frank Roth and his sister was a step across the bridge of no return. I'd already established that she hadn't been one of my Sisters.

Still, as I studied the photo, something nagged.

Before I could put my finger on it, someone rammed into me, throwing me off balance. I caught myself on the edge of a park bench.

"Watch where you're going!" the guy who had clipped me hollered.

I spun on him, ready to fight, and was startled to see him smiling, smiling too wide, exposing yellow teeth. It was not the man from the other night, but he wore an identical red scarf. It appeared hand knitted.

My throat constricted. "Who are you?" I demanded.

His piggy eyes flickered before he turned and ran toward the nearest corner. I tried to follow, but Owl was on top of a good scent and wouldn't budge. By the time I finally got her to move, the guy had vanished.

CHAPTER 23

Van

Despite being bone tired, I was too antsy to go home, too wall-crawling to be holed up in my tiny apartment, so I piled Owl into my Toyota and took us both to a burger joint drive-through. I never bought her crap—I couldn't do that to both of us—but I made an exception to order her a pup cone, which she tractor-beamed into her gullet before lying down in the back seat, beginning to snore almost immediately.

That left me in peace to eat my double cheeseburger with one hand and steer with the other. The restaurant's burgers were uniform meat disks, but they were juicy on the inside and crispy on the edges. Pair that with oozy orange cheese, tart mustard and sweet ketchup, and a couple crisp pickle slices, slam it between a butter-toasted sesame bun, and you had the food of the gods. When I washed it down with a fountain root beer, I might have moaned a little.

I didn't need GPS to find my way back to the church where Otto Pusch most likely attended his AA meetings. I discovered its parking lot empty, so I motored to his apartment building, counting the windows across and up until I located the one that was most likely his. The light was on inside. I saw no movement in the time it took me to finish off my fries.

After balling all my garbage into a single bag and tossing it to the floor to join the rest, I drove to the last known residence of Patty Devries, the woman who could put me in prison for murder if she ever wanted to. The home she'd lived in with her pedophile husband had sold a few months after she and her daughter, Gwen, disappeared in Costa Rica. I'd kept a bead on the situation—my freedom depended on Patty staying quiet and staying gone—so I knew that her sister had handled the sale.

I felt nothing as I sat outside, watching the sickly light of the TV flicker across the new owner's face as he stared at a screen nearly as large as the bay window. There wasn't even a hint of unease as I recalled slipping in through the back door, going straight to the kitchen, and forcing Randall Devries to drink sugar-sweet poison.

No regret, except that I'd been caught.

Guilt, well, that was a different story. I saved guilt for my darkest moments, when I could wallop myself without mercy.

Owl stirred in the back seat before letting out an eye-watering fart. I cracked my windows—I'd known the price of the pup cone—and took off toward Patty's sister's place in Minneapolis's Armatage neighborhood. The area was a mix of renovated craftsman homes and enormous, gaudy new builds. Diane Peterson, Patty's sister, lived in one of the craftsman bungalows, the house modest but well kept.

All the shades were drawn.

Patty had surely told Diane she hadn't killed her husband. Had she revealed who had?

If so, everything I'd worked for my whole life would disappear.

I'd deserve it if it did.

I'd murdered three men.

I rubbed my hands across my face. Patty was going to do what she was going to do. It was out of my hands. But those girls, Gina, Robin, and Lulu? Someone out there knew what'd happened to them. Finding out who, *that* I could control. *That* I could fix. Tomorrow,

I'd start the interviews, and I'd work fast, because I didn't know how much time I had.

Tonight, though, I needed something else.

I drove away from Diane Peterson's and parked in front of a place I never thought I'd end up.

CHAPTER 24

Just Judy

1993

He was angry, and the world shuddered when he was angry.

This was the first time he'd struck her, though. She'd felt the snap of bone beneath his fist, felt the hot starshock of pain, fallen to her knees, but even at the risk of further violence, she remained between him and the children, shielding them. Only one was hers, but she protected them as if they were all her babies. That was natural. Healthy. It was what she would want if someone babysat *her* child.

"I don't think I heard you right," he said. His eyes became the color of hate when he was this mad.

Judy rose shakily, her hands out on each side to keep the children from stepping forward. She needn't have bothered. They were as scared as she was.

The swelling was already visible when she glanced downward. She couldn't visit a doctor. In the seven years since she'd gone with him—yes, it had been her choice, she reminded herself of that when it got hard—she'd never left whatever property he claimed for them, not even to give birth. She'd have to mend her broken cheek on her own.

"It's just that . . ." She was too afraid to say it again. She'd rehearsed the words all morning, hoping to line them up just right, but they'd only been good once. And what had she thought he'd say in response? *Of course I'll stay home for you, Just Judy. That's how much I love you. I don't need to go out and hunt anymore.*

Hunt. That's what she'd begun calling it when she first realized what he was doing. Hunting was common in the Midwest. Hunting deer, anyhow. Or ducks, or geese. So she cloaked what was really happening in comfortable language, and mostly she managed to not think about it, earning her keep by cooking, cleaning, and watching other women's children.

He'd be gone for weeks at a time—he said his second life was vital to their greater plan—but he provided, didn't he? There was always food, and she was a good-enough seamstress to keep their clothes together. Thank God for that high school home ec class.

Then came her little one, and it was like the world bloomed for her. Sure, she had thought she was going to die giving birth at home, but it was all worth it in the end. She finally knew what it felt like to really, truly, selflessly *love*. She'd kiss her little girl's tender seashell earlobes, put her finger inside the baby's chubby fist and squeal when she squeezed it. Her baby fit in perfectly with the others. She taught them all to read and write, to say their pleases and thank-yous. Wasn't it better than the kind of babysitting she used to do in Sauk Centre, when she'd plant kids in front of the TV and heat cans of food for dinner?

He'd fallen in love with their child, too. She knew it because he stayed home at first. Started fixing up things, building stuff. Began planning for a better life for all of them, and not just with his words.

With his *actions*.

It'd been bliss, until today. Months of a perfect life, and then out of the blue, he'd asked her to mix more tinctures.

He didn't say it, but he was going hunting again.

He'd couched the request in kindness, reminding her how much he loved her skill, how good she was at baking, cooking, making medicines.

She'd stalled, told him she didn't have the ingredients. That was a lie, but it bought her time to rehearse what she wanted to say. When he showed up just now with a basket full of sleepy henbane and hemlock—a plant so poisonous she wore gloves and allowed no one else in the room when she processed it—she recited her short speech, the one she'd practiced over and over again until she could say it without her teeth chattering.

"I don't think you should use the tinctures anymore," she said. "I think you should stay home."

Her voice had wobbled, but she'd said the words. And he'd snatched them out of the air, twisted them until they screamed, then shoved them back in her face with the power of his fist, his eyes murderous.

I don't think I heard you right.

She realized she didn't have it in her to repeat herself. She'd never been a bold woman (other than running off with two different men, and look where that'd landed her), and the pain in her face was so powerful she worried she'd pass out.

"I'm sorry," she whispered, grateful the children had remained motionless behind her. She didn't want his rage focused on them. "I don't know what came over me. I . . . I haven't been sleeping well. Of course I'll make the tinctures for you."

He was quiet for so long that she risked lifting her eyes and looking at him, her fear so great she feared she was going to wet herself. His gaze melted with love, his face glistened with tears. He held out his hand and cupped her chin. The pain was razor white, but she managed to smile. At least she hoped it was a smile.

"That's my girl," he said.

The children stopped whimpering. The storm of his anger had passed, and he would now shelter them.

He bundled her into his arms, oblivious to her injury. He smelled so masculine, like sawdust and sweat. As he kissed the top of her head, he murmured into her scalp, "You're glad I brought you here, aren't you? You're happy?"

Judy nodded into his shirt. "Yes," she murmured, the tears falling.

She mostly believed it. What was the alternative? Graduate high school, become one of those girls who worked at the gas station until she landed a husband? Her whole life would have stretched out for miles in front of her, not a curve in sight.

At least with him she was never bored, and that was almost like being happy.

She let him squeeze her tighter because the strength of him was all that was keeping her upright.

She knew she was lying to herself.

Why else had she been so desperate to keep him from doing to other girls what he'd done to her?

CHAPTER 25

Van

"Evangeline?"

Harry stood in his doorway wearing honest-to-god golden paisley pajamas beneath a deep-blue silk robe and fur-lined slippers. His chiseled face was fuzzy with concern.

"Hi, Harry. Mind if we come in?"

Bart and I used to talk through every case. Sometimes I'd drop by his place with a pizza and a six-pack, or we'd meet up at a bar, or we'd jaw it out over the crusty coffeepot at work. My best ideas came when I had someone to bounce them off, and I missed that.

So I'd driven to Harry.

I'd never visited his house before.

"What?" He was staring at Owl. She sat primly, doing a passable imitation of a good dog. "Is that?"

I patted Owl, realizing the lie I *should* have told Harry earlier today. "I'm watching a dog for a friend."

His forehead squirreled up. Before Duluth, we'd kept our personal lives separate from work. That case had blown the paper door right off. There, I'd discovered the secret he kept buried beneath those sharp clothes. Today he'd learned—incorrectly—that I was seeing someone *and* that I had a friend close enough to watch their dog.

I smiled and took a step forward.

"Kinda chilly out here," I said.

He stepped aside immediately. "I'm so sorry. Please, come in. Can I get you something? Tea? Wine?" Owl was sniffing his feet like they were made of tuna. "A dish of water for your . . . friend?"

"We're good." I dragged Owl into Harry's den. It was austere to the point of severe, the furniture all clean Scandinavian lines and muted colors. It looked like if chloroform were a room, but it was his place and he could decorate as he liked. Clean flames flickered in the gas fireplace. The air smelled like Harry, faintly—cedar and metal. A mug of tea steamed on his coffee table next to a book that lay open, face down.

Poison Throughout the Ages by Dr. Christine Hollermann.

"Researching?" I asked as I unclipped Owl's leash. She did a down dog before padding over to the fireplace, dropping in front of it with a tender groan.

"Yes." Harry stood between the door and me, his arms crossed. I could no longer read his expression. "You sure I can't get you anything?"

"I'll take a bourbon, if you have it." I wasn't in the mood for a drink, I just wanted him moving. His watchful energy had me tense all of a sudden.

He strode over to a drink cart that I hadn't noticed, stuck as it was between a record player on one side and a beautiful wooden record holder on the other, hundreds of albums stacked inside. "You prefer ice?" he asked, his back to me.

"Yep." I hadn't yet sat down. "You really listen to those records?"

He offered me his profile. "I prefer them. The analog sound . . . reverberates."

"Show me."

He paused, smiled faintly, then reached for an album. I couldn't see which. He gently removed the record from its jacket, placed it on the turntable, and then returned the jacket to its spot, leaving it extended an inch so it'd be easy to find. When he guided the arm onto the record, Dean Martin's velvet voice filled the room.

A delighted grin broke across my face. It really did sound great, and when he brought me a lowball full of clinky ice and caramel-colored bourbon, I relaxed for the first time that day.

Harry waited until I dropped onto the couch to take the seat across from me. He reached for his mug and indicated the book. "I was following up on my theory. Hemlock is still my top pick for what killed Emily Barris, though I haven't received confirmation from the ME."

"It's also your pick for what killed those three girls in '86?"

His tea went down wrong, and he started coughing. Owl leaped up and hurried to the end of the coffee table, equidistant between Harry and me, like she wasn't sure which of us needed her more. She rested her head on the glass and glanced back and forth between us, her eyebrows lifting comically.

"No evidence was preserved from those cases." He set his mug on a coaster and wiped his eyes before leaning back, crossing his legs. A fit of sneezing overtook him. He removed a monogrammed handkerchief from his robe pocket—of course he did—and wiped his nose.

The ice hadn't had time to unlock the bourbon, but I took a sip anyhow. The alcohol went down like a warm elevator. "Tell me more about hemlock."

He nodded like he'd been waiting for me to ask. "Its use as poison has been traced back to Sardinia, now a part of Italy, where the citizens used it in ritual killings. The corpses all seemed to be smiling. Homer coined the term 'sardonic grin' from that."

My interest deepened. "Who were the victims?"

"Criminals and the elderly who could no longer care for themselves. They'd be drugged with hemlock to sedate them and then dropped from a cliff or beaten." Harry grimaced, the ancient brutality hanging in the air. "While history recorded the deaths, the plant they used remained a mystery until a Sardinian shepherd recently—in the last couple decades—took his own life by swallowing hemlock water-dropwort. His corpse had the death grin described by Homer." Harry showed his hands, palms up. "Mystery solved."

I leaned forward, absorbing the creepy details. "Why use hemlock?"

Harry's nose twitched, like another bout of sneezing was on its way. I suspected he must be allergic to Owl. "The plant is devious. It smells fragrant and has sweet roots—called dead man's or devil's fingers, because of their color and shape—making it especially dangerous. Most poisonous plants repel, but this one lures you in."

"So that's why the Sardinians used it," I said, "but why'd the guy who murdered those three girls choose it?"

"*If* they were murdered, and *if* it was a male perpetrator," Harry corrected. Owl let out a whine so I didn't have to. I leaned over to stroke her head as Harry continued. "But if they were in fact killed, for someone who knows their poisonous plants, it's not a bad choice. It's readily available, quick acting, easy to disguise in food or drink, and unusual enough that the average county coroner wouldn't think to test for it."

I took another sip, pleased that his drink cart had housed ice. The bourbon was perfect. "So I need to track down someone who either gardened or had a connection to botany who would've known all three girls as well as Emily Barris."

"Don't forget chemists." Harry rubbed the bridge of his nose. "But not only do we not know the girls were murdered, we also don't know that their deaths were connected."

It was true. The death grin was the thinnest thread linking all three. I wouldn't have been running with it if not for Comstock finding my old police ID on the scene. "I'm worried, Harry." The stroke of bourbon had loosened my tongue. "Comstock could make things hard for me."

Harry nodded. He'd witnessed Comstock's hostility toward me during the Taken Ones case, knew the man had it in for me. "A clean investigation is your best protection."

I should have known he'd say that. He probably believed it, too. I sighed. Sucked on an ice cube. Glanced around the room. Spotted the framed cloud painting on the far wall, its blues cartoonish in their brightness. "Caroline paint that?" I asked.

I felt him nod, though I kept my eyes on the painting. "My mother let me take it," he said.

"How's Myrna doing?" I asked.

I turned to see his posture had changed. He appeared guarded. "Fine," he said. "She might be visiting in the next couple weeks."

His gaze traveled to the painting, his expression softening again. "Caroline was always so brave," he said. "She was born that way. Did I tell you about the time she wanted me to explore the abandoned mansion at the end of our road?"

He knew he hadn't. He'd only recently mentioned Caroline to me at all. I let him keep talking.

"We passed it on the way to and from the bus stop. I don't know what got into her one day. Maybe the spring weather, maybe some dare at school, but after years of not even seeming to notice the place, she suddenly begged me to explore it with her." The side of his mouth twitched.

"'Pleeeaasse, Harry,' she begged. 'Don't be a stick-in-the-mud.'"

He straightened his already-straight pajama leg. "I told her it was a boring old house. She wasn't deterred. I can still see her skipping toward the leaning thing, all its windows broken out." Regret settled like dust across Harry's features. "I called her back before she made it halfway. Forbade her to take another step, told her it was too dangerous. You should have seen her face. It was like the light ran out of her. She listened, but she wasn't happy about it." His eyes locked onto mine. "Why didn't I just go with her?"

"Because it *was* unsafe," I said without hesitation. "Because you were her big brother."

He shook his head. I couldn't take the rawness in his eyes, so I changed the subject. "Do you sleep on a futon?"

That snapped him to attention. "What?"

I shrugged. "The rest of your place looks like I imagined. Like a priest with a big can of beige paint lives here. It's your *bedroom* I can't visualize." Was that a wicked grin I felt at the corner of my mouth? "I've decided you either sleep on a single bed pushed into a corner or on a futon because you don't ever want to be too comfortable."

A mix of emotions duked it out on his face—embarrassment, humor, confusion. Watching it was the most fun I'd had in days. Finally, he said in a voice so serious it was all I could do not to laugh, "It's a regular bed. Queen size, I believe. Box spring below the mattress."

"Enough room for two." Was I still baiting him? It felt like we were in different territory.

His eyebrows lowered, his expression unreadable. "It's unlikely I'd have time for that."

I suddenly felt as uncomfortable as he looked. To distract, I held up my drink in a toast. "Almost as unlikely as three girls dying with the same smile on their face."

Harry was still watching me. I held his gaze.

Owl saved us both by whining.

"Does it need to go out?" Harry asked, breaking the spell. He sounded stuffed up. He was definitely allergic.

"We both do," I said, standing. "Thanks for the bourbon."

He looked at my glass, still half-full. "You're welcome."

I leaned over to clip Owl's leash back on. "Tomorrow, I'm going to interview the friends and family of those girls. Some of them still live in the area. I'm hopeful we can crack this one."

Harry nodded. He wanted life to go well for me, I knew that. I allowed myself a moment to consider how it would feel to confess to him that I was a murderer, to let him in closer than I'd ever let anyone.

It would cost everything we were building.

CHAPTER 26

Van

The sun is beating down, but the air is cool. *Spring.* I can hear the rhythm of work all around me—hoes hitting dirt, the clang of buckets, murmured prayers under labored breaths. Brothers and Sisters, heads bowed, keep their gazes low to the ground as they move in synchronized lines. I should be helping, should be in the fields preparing them for planting.

But I can't stop watching her.

The dark-haired woman moves gracefully toward the Mothers' house, her back to me. Her bare feet hardly touch the ground, her long skirt sweeping through the grass. She doesn't look back. I take a step toward her, then another. It feels like I'm being pulled, like gravity has shifted just for her, and I'm helpless to resist. My fingers twitch. I just need to reach her.

I hurry, my heart thudding in my throat. I catch up to her at the porch. I still can't see her face. My hand stretches. I'm almost there, fingertips inches from her shoulder.

"Evangeline."

Father's voice freezes me. I turn, and there he is, standing in the yard, cradling a girl in his arms. My breath catches. The girl . . . her body is familiar—thin limbs, a white dress. But her face is wrong. It's pixelated, jagged at the edges like a bad transmission.

I realize it's Caroline's face, or at least the photo from the newspaper. I try to scream, but nothing comes out. The world starts to warp, the air turning thick like molasses, pulling me back, pulling me down. Father's eyes bore into mine, and I can't move.

The lights go klieg bright and suddenly I'm back in Emily Barris's bedroom, the painted window vines crawling toward my ankles. I know they mean to kill me, so I scurry backward, falling onto Emily's icy, smiling corpse. I scream, and Harry appears. I think he's going to save me, but then his face splits into a gruesome grin that mirrors Emily's.

"Father knows best," he says, before aiming a gun at Emily. "Let's make sure you killed her right."

My bones turn to wax. The gunshot echoes inside my skull, and for a moment, I quiver in the gauzy envelope that divides sleep from wherever my nightmares take me.

Then I land.

My heartbeat was a giant's footsteps in my ear.

I was cramped, cold, except for a warm spot in my lap.

Have I wet myself?

The warm spot grumbled and stretched. *Owl.* I rubbed my face, blinked. We were in my car, parked outside Otto Pusch's apartment building. I'd driven here straight from Harry's. I hadn't meant to fall asleep.

Owl licked my face, and I hugged her.

I am safe. I am grown. I am free.

I wanted it to be different. I wanted to not be haunted by nightmares and visions, to not have killed three men, to not have a father who may have abducted my only friend's sister. I wished I had a mom, dad, siblings like regular people, but that wasn't for me. I was a murderer, a liar, an orphan.

Owl growl-whined, turning worried eyes on me.

I patted her flank. "Should we go home?"

I started the car, my fingers stiff from cold. When to tell Harry about my suspicions about Frank Roth abducting his sister was one more problem I'd save for tomorrow, my life devolving into a tightrope walk over lit dynamite, flame racing down the fuse toward the cap.

CHAPTER 27

Van

The Bark Barn looked as stupid as its name. It was a giant square block of a building on the edge of Minneapolis's North Loop. At least its sign was friendly, all bright-yellow, loopy letters and cartoon dogs with their tongues lolling out.

"You ready?" I asked Owl.

She gave a muted butt wiggle. She'd been uncharacteristically mellow all morning and glued to my side, even following me into the bathroom as I showered. I told myself it had nothing to do with the fact that I was boarding her for the day.

"It's for the best," I said as we stepped inside, greeted by a cacophony of growls and yips and the meaty smell of dog food overlaid with a sharp zing of sanitizer. "You can go bananas, make new friends."

She tossed me a doubtful look. I ignored the sour feeling that I was betraying her and strode to the front counter. "Van Reed. I have a reservation to leave my boxer here for the day." I reached down to cover her ears. "And maybe overnight."

My day was filled with cold case interviews across the state. No way could I let her out at lunch like she'd grown accustomed to. The Bark Barn had been sending me ads ever since I'd started ordering dog toys online, and they were near enough to Loring Park.

The twentysomething behind the counter wore a headband with dog faces balanced on springs like misshapen horns. They bobbed when she smiled at Owl. "What a cutie. What's her name?"

"Ow—" I caught myself just in time. The fewer tracks I left, the better. "Auld Lang Syne," I said. "I call her Auldie for short."

"Well, Auldie," the worker said, her voice going high as she switched into baby talk, "we're going to have the very best day, aren't we? The very, very best day."

Owl was hunched over in a submissive posture. I needed to get out of there, quick, before I found a way to justify keeping her in the car with me all day. How did parents do this? I handed over her new favorite stuffie plus a plastic bag of dog food, enough for two days in case I had to work late, patted Owl on the head, and hurried out.

The 94W entrance ramp was near the Bark Barn. My plan was to start at the farthest location—Gina Penchant's childhood home in Rockville, seventy or so miles northwest of Minneapolis—and work my way back to Clearwater, where Robin Seer had grown up, ending in Maple Grove, a suburb on the edge of the Cities, where Lulu Geldman's mother still lived.

All three towns were within an hour of each other as the crow flew, and all were within ten miles of the highway, which had given nest to a theory: If the girls had been murdered, the person who'd killed them might be someone who traveled for a living.

In the early 2000s, the FBI had launched the Highway Serial Killings Initiative to address the murders of hundreds of hitchhikers, stranded motorists, and sex workers believed to have been committed by long-haul truckers. While most truckers were law-abiding, the solo nature and mobility of the profession—not to mention access to potential victims—also appealed to serial killers. The HSK's map of where nearly a thousand victims had been found showed them as red dots along the country's major highways, joining together to make bloody arteries.

The three girls' deaths predated HSK's creation by more than two decades, but I'd have Kyle deep dive into their database anyhow and see if there were any records of other victims wearing the death grin. I'd also have him set up formal interviews with all the folks involved in the original investigation as well as those—friends, family, and coworkers—who *should* have been questioned.

But today, I wanted to visit the three families unannounced to put a human face to our investigation. I didn't want them to learn over the phone that the BCA would be looking into their daughters' deaths. They deserved a presence, someone who could offer them resources or at least a listening ear if needed.

Plus, their initial reactions might tell me something important.

I thought about Gina Penchant, the first victim, as I drove. Sixteen at the time of her death, no driver's license. She'd been in track, 4-H, and theater and had no boyfriend, at least as far as her parents knew. Her file included both a school photo and a crime scene snapshot. In the school pic, her hair was long, brown, and sprayed in the uniquely '80s feathered-claw bang style. She wore little makeup—strict parents?—but had shaved the space between her eyebrows, turning them into two short hyphens. Her collar was popped. She wore a cherry stud in each delicate lobe. She was achingly young, and—if I was correctly reading her lopsided smile in the school shot—a bit of a class clown.

I wouldn't have recognized her as the same girl in the crime scene photo if not for the cherry earrings. Gina's medium-brown hair had been streaked with highlights. Any sign of carefree youth was long gone, her eyes half-lidded, her face stretched with the horror-show grin.

What had happened in the time between the school photo and her death?

That was what I needed to find out.

Classic rock and cruise control brought me to Rockville in under an hour. Another ten minutes and I was pulling down a gravel driveway to a modest farm. The egg-yolk April sun beat down on the farmhouse, fading its blue paint. The porch held a trio of mismatched chairs, but they weren't facing the yard. Rather, they'd been stacked as if to store them away.

Two red outbuildings stood shoulder to shoulder off to the right, leaning like they'd also seen better days. When I stepped out of my car, my attention was drawn to the nearest barn doors creaking gently in the breeze. The animal pens looked empty. Same with the chicken coop.

A chill sluiced down my spine. I'd grown up on a working farm; I knew what an abandoned one looked like. Robert and Jill Penchant were listed as the property owners, but it seemed deserted.

I was walking toward the faded blue house when an older man stepped through the front door and onto the porch. I instinctively assumed a defensive posture. His matted gray hair and beard were unkempt. He wore a yellowed T-shirt and pants that were so dirty they reflected the sun.

His expression was wild-eyed and angry.

And he held a shotgun.

CHAPTER 28

Van

"I'm not looking to buy anything." His voice was raw and hoarse. The shotgun pointed toward the ground, but his finger was threaded through the trigger, his knuckle white.

"I'm not selling." My hands were raised but low, nearer my waist—and my weapon—than my shoulders. I hadn't given Kyle my itinerary for the day. It shouldn't have been necessary.

He squinted. "You law enforcement?"

"Agent Evangeline Reed with the Minnesota Bureau of Criminal Apprehension."

His mouth jerked. A smile? His finger relaxed on the trigger. "That's a mouthful."

"I can show you my badge. It's inside my coat."

"No need. I could read your job a mile away." He used the gun to point at the Blue Lives Matter flag hung on the door behind him. "Son's a deputy."

I dropped my hands slowly. "I work in BCA Cold Case. We're looking into your daughter's death. Is now a good time to talk?"

Something unreadable crossed his face as he scratched his scraggly beard. "Sure. Come on in."

I was still on high alert. "S'okay if we have a seat on the porch? It's such a nice morning." It was pushing fifty, one of the warmest days we'd had since winter, but more importantly, I needed to establish he was stable before entering his home. He struck me as the kind of guy who liked to set booby traps, maybe keep a few folks tied up in his basement.

"Suit yourself." He rested his gun by the door, butt down, and grabbed the top two chairs off the stack. They were both bright plastic, one red, one yellow. Their newness was jarring against the splintered porch.

He dropped into the yellow one and started speaking in a disaffected way, almost like he was reciting a monologue. "What do you want to know? How my Gina lit up every room she walked into? How my wife started drinking right after our girl passed, then up and left me, dying alone in an apartment in Rochester? Or maybe you want to hear about my son, who never visits."

I stepped onto the porch, considered remaining on my feet for a quick escape but landed on sitting to put him at ease. Robert Penchant smelled sour up close. The candy-apple-red chair creaked as I adjusted it to face him. "Looks like you used to have cows and chickens," I said, indicating the barns. "Working dairy farm?"

"What gave it away?" he asked bitterly.

I didn't think it required a response. He waited a few beats before filling the silence. "Used to be I produced the best milk in the county. Now I got nothing but CRP payments—and the bottle, but I suppose you don't care about none of that."

The Conservation Reserve Program checks meant he was paid to *not* farm on environmentally sensitive land. That explained the abandoned look of the place.

While Penchant was older than Frank Roth, something about him reminded me of my father. It took me half a beat to realize what: This was what Frank would've been like without a farm full of acolytes to shine him up. There was a very specific timbre to men who required fawning women. When they had at least one, they presented as arrogant and unapologetic, like Frank. But when they couldn't trick a girl into staying, they reverted to their baseline state: miserable victims.

At least that was the swamp I suspected Frank had emerged from and devolved back into after his commune broke up. None of us kids knew about Frank's childhood. Questioning his status as the absolute head of the Family had been forbidden. We were taught he was holy, guided by God, and impervious to human failings. He needed to wield power, and if it was taken away from him, I suspected he'd become someone very much like Robert Penchant.

I bit the inside of my cheek. I was judging the man too quickly. I knew little about him except that he'd lost his daughter. That would twist anyone.

"I bet this was a glorious farm in its day, Mr. Penchant," I said, drawing out my notebook and pen. "Can you tell me more about Gina? About what kind of person she was?"

"She was a good girl," he said defensively. "And hardworking." His face grew gentle, and then so did his voice. "And funny as the day was long. I used to call her Gina the Jester. She could make the pope laugh."

His sudden vulnerability sat heavy on my shoulders. "You loved her very much."

His eyes scanned my face, as if looking for evidence I was making fun of him. "Want to see her room?"

Against my better judgment, I said yes.

CHAPTER 29

Van

I followed Robert Penchant into the farmhouse, making sure the location setting on my phone was on. The first room was the living room. Dust danced in the dim light filtering through the faded curtains, and the musty scent of fried food clung to the wallpaper. The space was dominated by a brown chenille couch with a shellacked look to the cushion directly in front of a surprisingly large flat-screen television. The only other piece of furniture was a chair draped with a yellowed sheet.

The wood floor creaked as I let Penchant lead me down a hall. The kitchen we passed had so many dirty dishes stacked in the sink that there couldn't possibly be any clean ones left in the cupboards. I knew what that was like. Still, there was more going on here than decay and messiness. As we moved through the farmhouse, a sense of unease crept into my bones.

"Where did all your animals end up?" I asked.

He stopped in front of a door, his back to me. His posture became suddenly tense. "You know, here and there. These days, I just tinker. No more animals relying on me."

His voice sounded strange, and I realized I couldn't see his hands. I moved my jacket away from my weapon as a cold shiver needled up my spine.

"Mr. Penchant?" I asked. "Can you please turn around?"

"But I'm about to show you Gina's room." The words were low, choked out.

My arm hair stood up. "Mr. Penchant, I'd like to see your face."

His shoulders twitched. I had my hand over my gun, ready to undo the holster. Penchant opened the door he stood in front of, and my finger popped the snap.

He turned. Flicked a glance at my weapon. His face was slack, not a hint of surprise or aggression on it. "I don't get a lot of company."

No shit. "That Gina's room behind you?"

"It is."

"Hold on," I said. "I need to text my partner where I'm at. Standard procedure." I snapped my holster closed and reached for my phone, firing off my coordinates to Kyle.

"Probably shoulda done that before you came," he said in a twisted whisper.

"I'm doing it now." I finished and tucked my phone back in my pocket. Robert Penchant was a man stuck in the grief cycle, turning like a twig in a whirlpool. He was likely not dangerous, but I'd been stupid for not taking all the necessary precautions. Now that Kyle knew where I was, I could focus on my work.

I stepped past Penchant and into a slice of the 1980s trapped in amber.

Decades-old movie posters lined the lath-and-plaster walls, heavy on the Tom Cruise, their edges curled. A boom box sat proudly on top of the dresser, ready to blast the latest cassette-tape hits. Next to the stereo lay a pile of neon scrunchies and bows. Homemade shelves like you'd see in a dorm or a first apartment held the sorts of treasures I would've loved to collect in my childhood: marbles, stones, brightly colored dolls, a half-solved Rubik's Cube. The bed was draped with a handsewn quilt.

I imagined the air carrying the sweet-sharp tang of Aqua Net.

"Haven't touched a thing," Penchant said from the doorway. He pointed at the bed. "That's where I found her, wearing the devil's smile. She loved school, had a good job babysitting neighborhood kids, even managed to get her prize pig all the way to the state fair." He rubbed the back of his neck, scaring up that sour smell. "She had everything to live for, and then she was gone."

"How do you think she died?" I asked.

He twitched as if he'd been shocked. "Oh, I know for a fact who killed her, and no way on God's green earth was it an enlarged heart."

CHAPTER 30

Just Judy

1998

Judy thought back to how young she had been when she'd first come with him, before she understood what he was doing. Such a child, so naive. She'd known he was hunting, of course, but why, and what he did with his prey? That took longer.

When she finally realized his ultimate goal—years too late—she fought him. She even tried to escape, but he found her and forced her back. He swore he'd track her down no matter where she went, track her down and kill her and their daughter.

She believed him.

And so she began to do what trapped and traumatized women have done since time immemorial: She rebuilt the story of who he was, explaining away the bad and shining up the good.

After all, he worked so hard. He was the smartest man she knew. Sometimes he'd bring her wildflowers for no reason. The world saw his professional face, respected him so much, but he came home to her because he *loved* her. If she couldn't always tell by his actions, she'd know it by his words.

It was what he called her, for Pete's sake: *love*.

Hey, love, can you make that split-pea soup again? It's so good. Hey, love, you sure are good with kids. Hey, love, we need to move again.

He trusted her, too, and that was worth its weight in gold. He even shared parts of his childhood as they lay in bed. His own mother had sexually abused him, and his stepfather had beaten him. That's why he'd never force himself on a child, he said, why he never hit Judy other than that one time, no matter how much he wanted to. He was a better man than what he'd been raised to be, and wasn't that the measure of character?

Plus, he was self-made, taught himself carpentry, wiring, all of it.

That would have made him a man worthy of respect, but not a messiah. It was his ability to know things no one should that exalted him. Her secret dreams, the exact number of berries she'd eaten when she discovered the bramble patch even though he hadn't been around that day, the fight she and another woman had had over childcare even though they were alone in the foyer, their voices lowered. He knew it all, could relate it word for word, and it wasn't just with her. She saw him do it for others, and she believed him when he told her he could read minds and tell the future.

But there was more.

The widow-maker branch that should have killed him? It hadn't been a fluke. Some of his children had the same ability. She wouldn't have believed it if she hadn't witnessed it with her own eyes, his daughter leaning out a second-story window, waving, giggling, being a child, and then, suddenly, losing her balance and plummeting to the earth.

Judy had screamed. She'd run toward the girl, certain she'd find her spine snapped, a leg twisted beneath her. The child was weeping, sure enough, but it was from fear, not pain. Judy helped her to her feet and could not find so much as a bruise on her.

It was clear: He was holy, and so were his offspring.

So it'd been easy to not only support him but want to protect him.

At least until he brought home the latest one. She fought too much. The others had been docile, or resigned, some of them even excited, like Judy had been before she realized what he was doing.

Not this one.

"Can't you just let her go?" she asked as she smeared homemade arnica salve into the long scratch marks the girl had made across his cheek. His bones were God, but his flesh was man. "She's already so much trouble."

She hadn't said anything against his wishes for months and months. She hoped she had enough goodwill in the bank, but when his eyes grew focused and hard, she knew she'd overshot.

"Does it hurt to be that stupid, *Just* Judy?"

She'd told him once, when she was feeling close to him, the mean nickname she'd been called in high school. He trotted it out when he needed to put her in her place, like now.

He continued. "Does it cause physical pain to be a medical idiot?"

She wanted to apologize, wanted it nearly more than anything, but her words surprised her. "This one will be the end of us," she said. "I feel it in my gut."

His hand flew to the air. While he'd never hit her since that once, he'd come close many, many times. She flinched. He held his hand there, his words like razors. "*You* are the man of the house? *You've* been gifted with an understanding of the future?"

"No, it's just that—"

He mocked her, his voice singsong. *"It's just that. It's just that."* He dropped his hand and stood, his voice low and dangerous. "I'm in charge, *Just* Judy. If you can't honor your commitment to me, you should leave."

He'd begun flinging that threat only after realizing she never would. The point had been reached last year. He'd brought her to town with him, left her in the car while he ran into the post office, didn't even lock the doors behind him. She suspected he was testing her, seeing if she'd run, but it didn't matter. She was no longer someone who could go back to a regular life. She was entirely his.

He'd been chosen by God, and she'd been chosen by him.

CHAPTER 31

Van

"It's no secret how my Gina the Jester passed." Robert hadn't moved from the bedroom doorway. "My wife and I weren't God-fearing at the time. That particular night, we'd gone out for dinner and to see a movie. If it'd been a weekend night, we would've gone dancing."

A light flickered in his face for a moment and then was extinguished. His clothes were so dirty they could stand on their own, but he used to be someone who *danced*. Grief had broken this man, it was clear, flattened him with its palm and held him there for decades.

Ten-plus years working homicide and then cold cases, I'd seen my share of sorrow. Some folks were able to build a new life after tragedy, though they never would've believed it at first, not when the horror of loss first blasted them. When someone close to you was murdered or died by suicide, rather than carry your pain, you *became* your pain. But eventually it turned into a wound that pulled when you stretched too far, and then that wound became a scar, which became one more ache you carried, sharper and larger than most, but still.

But others went Penchant's route, never finding an identity outside of the pain.

One person wasn't smarter than the other, kinder, more deserving, not as far as I could tell. The difference was that those who were eventually able to separate their identity from their loss—through luck or hard work or bewildering courage—were the ones who stayed connected to others, to trust that the devastating tragedy that had just befallen them wouldn't happen again, not right away at least, if they continued to love.

We walked into grief alone; the only way out was together. It was a cruel truth.

Penchant must have closed himself off and stayed closed after Gina died. As a result, he was the picture of a life devoted to misery. No judgment, only observation. I couldn't say how I would have reacted if I'd lost a child.

"We let her have a couple friends over while we were out. Local girls," he continued, catching my gaze. "They rented a movie. Back then you had to rent the VCR, too." The ghost of a smile appeared on his face. It quickly disappeared, his eyes dropping to the bed. "When Jill and I got home, we found her in here."

"With the other girls?" I knew what the report said. I wanted to know what he remembered.

Penchant shook his head. "She was alone. Lying on her grandma's quilt. The girls said Gina kicked them out, that she wasn't herself."

He took a step closer. I tensed, but he was going for the bed. "When I told you I didn't change anything in here, that was a lie, but one the Lord'll surely forgive." He pointed at the quilt. "Gina was holding a Ouija board." His face was agonized. "We hadn't even baptized her. What chance did she stand against the devil coming into her own room? We turned to God after that, but it was too late." He blinked rapidly. "For my daughter *and* my wife."

"Your son?" I asked.

"He'd already moved out." He was so close that the funk emanating from him pressed against the back of my throat. "The police who took Gina away said it looked like she scared herself to death." He shook his head. "It was the cops who were scared, with that smile on her face. The devil left it there when he took her soul."

119

I felt both compassion and annoyance. "You think *the devil* killed Gina?"

"I know it."

I kept my face neutral. "Can you give me the names of the two girls who were with her that night?"

"I can." He shuffled back into the hallway, a spirit biding his time until he was called home.

CHAPTER 32

Van

Robert Penchant had no clue where Lindy Bell ended up, but he thought he might know what had happened to the other girl, Prudence Carter. He wasn't sure if she'd married into a different surname, but last he'd heard, she was a mental health counselor at St. Cloud Technical & Community College.

It wasn't uncommon for people touched by trauma to end up in a helping profession. Most folks either punched up or punched down after experiencing horror, nothing in between. With their whole world rearranged, a middle-ground walk through life was no longer an option.

Again, I found myself thinking of Frank Roth. What had he experienced in his early life? Because I knew no greater example of someone who'd dedicated himself to controlling and terrorizing others, though he wouldn't have seen it that way. Abusers never did. They were too busy running from their pain, making up stories about why everyone else was the problem. That didn't explain why the Mothers had tolerated his behavior, though. None of us knew which woman had given birth to us. Our upbringing had been truly communal, which meant not a single one of us felt special or protected. We were there to build Frank's congregation.

Not that he ever evangelized outside of the commune. Like many sociopaths, he saved his crazy for his family. To the rest of the world, he was a successful businessman. His all-natural preserves, fruit spreads, pickles, and handcrafted breads were a staple at every local farmers' market in central Minnesota. His smiling face adorned each label, his seemingly warm gaze peeking out from beneath a straw hat.

He was a genius marketer, I'd give him that.

Before long, a nearby grocery store began stocking our locally famous plum jelly, not knowing that the fruits had been harvested and processed by Frank's many, many children. Soon, a major retail chain picked it up, and eventually, commercials featuring Frank's products aired throughout the Midwest. You've probably seen one, probably thought to yourself how nice it was that this gentle, friendly-looking man was crafting healthy foods on his family farm. You'd have no reason to suspect that Frank chose which Mother could live in his house—the only building with a television—week to week, that he'd sired dozens of kids.

The "factory" shut down when the rest of the commune did. Nobody'd tasted that plum jelly in years, but thinking about it now made me hungry. Saint Cloud had plenty of chain restaurants on the main drag. I pulled off a side street in search of something better and ended up in front of a sandwich shop called Bo Diddley's. While they made my ham and turkey sub, I looked up the SCTCC website.

Only a single counselor was listed. How was that possible, for an entire college? Her name was Prudence Kramer, and based on her apparent age—her smiling headshot showed a woman in her fifties with a feathered bob and vintage-looking tortoiseshell glasses—plus that unusual first name, she had to be who I was looking for. I inputted the college address into my phone, grabbed my warm sub, and headed back to my car.

My plan had been to drive and eat, but when I opened the sandwich, it was too drippy for that. I wrapped it as well as I could to catch the liquid and took a bite.

My eyes almost rolled into the back of my head, it was so good.

The meat was standard cold cuts. The lettuce, banana peppers, oozing mayonnaise, melty cheese, and Italian dressing elevated it, but it was the bread that hit the sub out of the park. Soft, warm, with little kernels of some grain giving it a texture. I took a big draw on my fountain soda, mowed off another large bite of the sandwich, and asked my phone to dial Kyle while I finished the feast.

"Hey, Van." Kyle's voice came out of both speakers. "You done at Penchant's?"

"Yup," I said. "The guy's basically a shut-in. Kept his daughter's room preserved. Thinks the devil killed her."

A moment of silence. "Are you talking with your mouth full?"

I took another bite. "Sure am. I'm outside a sandwich shop in Saint Cloud. Bo Diddley's. You need to try it if you're ever in town."

He made a noncommittal grunt.

I sucked down some more soda. "I'm heading to the local community college to talk to one of the two women who was with Gina Penchant the night she died, see if she has anything to add to the file." I swallowed. "I need you to do some research in your spare time."

"*All* my spare time?" he asked, but there was no malice.

"I need you to track down a Lindy—I think that's her full first name—Bell, who would've attended Rockville with Gina Penchant. Plus, can you look for anything with a similar ring occurring on the interstate highways?"

"You thinking HSK?"

I smiled. I knew Kyle was smart, but sometimes I forgot just how quick he was. Of course he'd have considered the Highway Serial Killings Initiative. "Yup."

The sound of pen scratching paper came through the speakers. "Anything else?"

"Nope." I wrapped up what was left of my sandwich. My hands smelled like pickle juice and onions. "Thanks."

"You got it." His phone clicked off.

I scrubbed my hands as best as I could and took off toward the college.

CHAPTER 33

Van

St. Cloud Technical & Community College resembled a '70s bomb shelter from the rear, but once I parked and walked around to the front, I spotted its striking lobby, all sculptures, windows, and modern lines. Students funneled in and out of the many doors, and one optimistic group tossed a Frisbee on a swampy stretch of spring-thawed lawn. Chirping birds provided a background to the thrum of conversation.

The chatter grew louder inside as I found my way to a bespectacled, Scandinavian-looking student worker at the information desk. He directed me to Prudence Kramer née Carter's office. "She might be on her lunch break," he said, "but the desk worker in her section should have a better idea."

Classes must have just let out. I swam upstream, sticking close to the brick wall. I'd always loved school, probably because Frank Roth never allowed us to go, other than the one ill-fated experiment that ended in Sister Veronica's maiming. He'd chosen ten of us to attend. We didn't know who'd put the bug in his ear, who had convinced him that his "human garden" needed to spread beyond its current acreage. Maybe it was one of the Mothers. Maybe God really had spoken to Frank, like he said. All we knew for sure was that our divine task was to carry his message of patriarchal communal living into the world.

Our time at school lasted only a few short weeks, and we'd loved every second of it. School lunches with *dessert*. A whole room full of books with bright covers. Music, gym, teachers who smiled at us.

No physical labor for hours at a time.

But when Sister Veronica wrote the essay that innocently shared the truth of Frank's Farm—boys forced to leave when they turned eighteen, women traveling in and out of Frank's bed, the punishments for disobeying Frank—the school had called him, alarmed. He pulled us out immediately. If there'd been any follow-up, any social workers interested in visiting the Farm, I never heard about it.

The Mothers had done a fair job of basic homeschooling, I discovered when I passed my GED. When it came time to attend the University of Minnesota, though, I found great gaps in my knowledge, mostly in literature. I was surprisingly gifted at history, though. Frank had insisted we learn about the terrible decisions made by governments throughout time.

Obviously, I'd been a complete outsider when it came to the social aspect of college. Being raised with a Laura Ingalls Wilder lifestyle under a Charles Manson leadership did not garner one a lot of party invitations.

But I'd loved the learning.

When I reached Kramer's office, a second student worker, this one appearing to be of eastern African descent, told me Mrs. Prudence was in and that I could head straight back to her office.

"Knock knock," I said at her open door. "Prudence Kramer?"

She glanced up from her computer and smiled. The photo on the college website must have been taken in the last year or two. She was identical to it, her hair worn in the neat bob, her funky glasses signaling her as someone who liked to take risks, at least with fashion. "Pru, please," she said. "Can I help you?"

I stepped into her cramped office. "Agent Van Reed with the BCA. I was hoping I could ask you a few questions about Gina Penchant."

Something flashed behind her eyes—concern?—but her expression stayed pleasantly bland, a skill she'd likely fine-tuned on her job. "I didn't *think* you were a student. You look too centered." She indicated the empty chair in front of her desk. "Close the door, please."

I squeezed into the chair, my knees almost touching the metal of her desk. "This is where you meet with students?"

She nodded. "Space is at a premium here. Hopefully we'll get funding to expand, but until then, this is it."

I felt my brow furrow. "And you're the only mental health counselor?"

Her smile was rueful. "Again, funding. Education is the priority here. Everything else takes a back seat."

I tugged out my notebook. "Hard to concentrate on an education when you're struggling."

She held up both hands. "Preaching to the choir." That look again. "Why do you want to know about Gina?"

I held her gaze to see if it would waver. It didn't. "We're reopening her case."

Her shoulders slumped. "Thank God. You don't think it was suicide?"

Her tone indicated where she fell on that spectrum. "There were two other girls who died in the same fashion, the same week."

She twitched like she'd been cattle-prodded. "What?"

"You didn't know?"

"I was sixteen." She shook her head. "Gina's death shattered me, shrank my already-small world until I mostly lived in my head through all of high school and even for the first year or two of college." Her face puckered. "It destroyed Lindy, too. Have you spoken with her yet?"

I shook my head. "No. I was hoping you could tell me where I could find her."

"We're not in touch anymore. My fault, probably." She pursed her lips. "It was like we switched lives after high school. Before Gina died, Lindy was on the fast track to college. Was going to be an attorney. She always did love to argue." The corner of her mouth lifted. "My dream was to head to beauty school, meet a nice boy. But after Gina?" She shrugged, the movement rusty. "I couldn't see that life for me. And Lindy was no longer interested in college. Last I heard, she was working at Fingerhut here in town. It's a processing facility."

I scribbled that down. "I have a basic sketch of Gina's last night. I was hoping you could fill it in. You and Lindy were at Gina's house?"

Pru's smile widened. "We bleached our hair. Every girl was doing it in 1986, but the three of us girls had old-fashioned parents, so we had to do it in secret. Gina's mom and dad were out that night."

I nodded. "And the Ouija board?"

She flinched. "That's in the file?"

Interesting. "Robert Penchant told me about it. He's under the impression that it was instrumental in his daughter's death."

She huffed through her nose. "It was a silly game. I don't remember if we even touched it. We colored our hair, we talked about boys, Gina pulled out the game, and all of a sudden she wanted us gone." She traced her finger across her desk calendar. "Gina was as moody as the rest of us at that age. I didn't think it was a big deal that she wanted us to go."

"She didn't give a reason?"

Pru cocked her head. "I think she said she had a headache. Lindy might remember better than me."

"Do you have any reason to be suspicious of Gina's parents?"

Her eyebrows shot up. "Robert and Jill? No. Robert worshipped the ground Gina walked on. Called her Gina the Joker, or something like that. Her mom was quiet, but fine."

I glanced at my notes. Not much there. "Do you know an Emily Barris?"

"No. Should I?"

I shook my head. "Not necessarily. It might be a related case, might not."

A knock came at the door, and a curly-haired student shoved his head in. "Hey, Mrs. K. We have a crisis in the cafeteria. Student crying. Can you come?"

Pru glanced at me.

I stood. "That's all I needed." I took a card from my inside pocket and placed it on her desk. "Let me know if you think of anything else?"

"Sure," she said, but she was already heading out. "Good luck."

The hallways were much clearer this time around, only a trickle of students. I retraced my steps to the big windowed lobby, thinking about what Pru had said about not hearing about the two other victims. There'd been only that single article in the Saint Cloud paper tying the three deaths together. It wasn't surprising that a sixteen-year-old girl would have missed it. Her parents might have even deliberately shielded her from it. In any case, I hadn't learned anything new except that asking about Gina had alarmed Pru.

Maybe I'd simply brought a bad memory to the surface.

Or it might have been something else.

I stepped into the cool hand of a blue-sky spring, thinking about the nature of crime, of how at any moment, our lives could be upended.

The most terrible things happened on cloudless days.

I was exploring that thought, running my tongue over it, when something to my right caught my eye, a flash of red from behind the giant granite sculpture on the front lawn. My blood slid sideways. *A red scarf.*

"Stop!" I yelled.

I charged forward. The man wearing the scarf turned, his hands in the air. I must have used my cop voice. He looked to be in his midtwenties, white, blue jeans and black parka, his expression a mixture of shock and defiance.

People were staring. I didn't care. "Your scarf," I barked. "Where'd you get it?"

His hands dropped a few inches. "Target, man."

I nodded as if that were the answer I'd expected and took off toward my car, my shoulders hunched.

I needed to cool off. Digging up Frank Roth, hiding the potential connection from Harry, Emily Barris's murder and then my ID showing up on the scene, the red-scarfed man I'd run into that night . . . add it all together and I was jumping at shadows.

The only way out was a good night's sleep and for the Barris case to be closed. Then I could come clean with Harry.

With that in mind, I made the worst possible decision on the walk back to my car.

I called Comstock.

CHAPTER 34

Van

In the hopes of persuading him to move quicker, I was gonna confess that I'd followed up on Pusch's alibi and that it looked like the AA meeting nearest him had been canceled the night he claimed to be there. It was pure grace that Comstock didn't answer. I hung up, ants under my skin. I shouldn't have called him. I *should* solve the case in front of me.

When I rang Fingerhut and told them who I was, they informed me that Lindy Bell wasn't working today but was scheduled first shift for the next four days.

A text from Kyle came in during the call:

Found Lindy Bell.

Shoot. I should have told him I'd tracked her down. I kept reading.

Did you contact Seer and Geldman parents to schedule interview?

Nope, I texted back.

Figured. Teresa Seer is expecting you today, remarried but kept last name, at same Clearwater house, will send address. Tomorrow is Mrs. Geldman in Maple Grove, then Lindy Bell in St. Cloud.

I grinned at my phone. Kyle wanted to be assistant deputy, but he'd never get there by being this generous. I was willing to bet he'd made those calls much warmer than I ever could have. Me, I could only connect in person.

THX, I texted back, and then I got into my car and drove to Clearwater.

I cruised down I-94 East, leaving Saint Cloud behind. The highway stretched ahead, flanked by black-dirt fields. Probably corn or soybeans. The scent of freshly turned soil perfumed the air, soothing my farmer's blood, and the rhythmic thump of my tires created a steady background noise that freed my mind to go over what I'd learned. I hadn't expected revelations today, though I'd been open to them. Mostly, I was corroborating what was in the file before I decided what direction to take the investigation.

I glanced at the odometer, noting the distance ticking away. Thirteen miles, give or take, separated Saint Cloud from Clearwater. Had the killer driven this distance once? Multiple times? When I exited the highway, the shimmering Mississippi River meandered to my left, all the ice melted off weeks ago.

It brought to mind the robust creek running through Frank's Farm. On hot days, if we'd completed all our chores ahead of schedule, we were allowed to dive into the icy-cool water, refreshing as a laugh. Well, most of us were. Frank had designated some of his children Watchers at birth. Those kids—Brothers and Sisters—were not allowed to swim. He said it would sully their holy spirit. Another control-freak move from

Frank Roth. The irony was that my towheaded Sister Veronica had been a Watcher, never allowed to cross the rickety bridge spanning the river and dive into water as crisp and sweet as watermelon. She couldn't so much as stick a toe in.

Then in the end, he'd essentially drowned her.

I shivered and shook my head to clear the memory, glancing at my GPS. The Seers lived near the Mississippi, and I'd need to drive through downtown Clearwater to reach their home. It resembled any other Minnesota small town, population not even cracking two thousand, according to the sign on my left. I passed a Travel Plaza, a Dairy Queen, and Victorian-style houses mixed with apartment buildings and new builds.

The Seer home turned out to be a little box—one story with beige siding and white trim—with a million-dollar view of the Mississippi. I'd bet good money that their place had started as someone's river cabin, maybe passed down through the family, and that the property taxes were killing them. Buildable land abutting water went for a pretty penny. Blame biology. We liked to be near trees to hide in and rivers to drink from.

I parked by a garage nearly as big as the house, got out of my car, and walked to the front door. It opened before I reached it. A woman in her late sixties, her hair bottle red, her eyes bleary, stood on the other side. "You Van Reed?"

I nodded. "Teresa Seer?"

"Yep. Kept my maiden name when I married Ted." She wrapped herself in her own arms. "You being here means they finally admit my girl was murdered, doesn't it?"

CHAPTER 35

Van

"They told me that she died of an overdose, though they could never tell me what exact drugs she was supposed to have taken."

Teresa Seer reclined on a rust-colored couch. I sat across from her in a matching chair. The living room was modest, the walls adorned with velvet paintings. There was a deep-backed television from the early 2000s, a grandfather clock out of scale to everything around it, and not a book in sight.

The view of the wide and winding Mississippi was unparalleled.

"You sure I can't get you anything?" It was the third time she'd asked. She seemed both nervous I was here and afraid I was going to leave.

I shook my head. "How do you think Robin died?"

"Not from drugs, I can tell you that for sure." She wrung her hands. "My girl didn't so much as try a cigarette. We were close. I would've known."

That was statistically unlikely. Parents were often the last to hear what illegal activities their babies were up to. "She wasn't acting weird leading up to when you found her?"

Teresa shook her head so emphatically that her glasses slid down her nose. She pushed them back up. "She was happier than she'd ever been.

High school was behind her, and she had a plan to move to Alexandria with her boyfriend. Well, not *with* him. Ray—that was Robin's dad, he died of bladder cancer a few years back—and I didn't think it would be seemly for the two of them to share an apartment before they were married."

Her tone made clear she was seeking approval for her parenting. "It sounds like the two of you loved her a great deal," I offered.

She nodded, smiling. "We sure did. And we wanted to raise her right. She'd been dating Chuck—Charles Brzezinski—since grade school. He's a good boy."

I noted the present tense.

Teresa stared off. "They were at a concert the night she passed, you know. Some rock and roll band, but that didn't mean they took drugs. They were old fashioned, both of them."

I wanted her to keep talking. "Do you know the name of the band they saw?"

"No, but Chuck would. He still stops by, you know. Brings me flowers every year on her birthday." Her eyes gleamed. "I can give you his contact information. He lives up the road in Elk River now."

"I'd appreciate that." I scribbled *Elk River = Chuck B.* in my notepad. "How about Robin's high school friends? Do any of them still live nearby?"

"She only had one good girlfriend, Mary Hedberg. I think she lives in Uptown, Minneapolis, these days." Teresa pursed her lips. "Robin was kind, you understand, but when you have a boyfriend that young, you tend to build your life around him." Her eyes brightened. "Would you like to see a picture of her?"

"Of course."

I didn't think it would help the case, but this was a mother who'd lost her daughter. She wanted to talk about her girl. I moved to the couch to sit alongside Teresa when she returned with the album. It was organized chronologically, Robin going from a generic baby to a button-nosed ginger to a striking young woman. The photo in her file didn't do her justice.

"She was stunning," I said honestly.

Teresa smiled softly. "She didn't think so. That girl was so humble." She glanced at me sideways. "I read about the other two girls." Her mouth worked, but it took a few seconds before words came out. "The Laughing Dead, that's what the three of them were called. If you all knew there was a connection, why'd you tell me she died of a drug overdose?"

She had every right to ask the question, but I couldn't speak for how the case had been handled. I could only be with her now. "I'm committed to finding out what happened to Robin," I said. "Is there anything else you can tell me about her, anything that stood out in the days leading up to her death?"

Teresa glanced at the floor. "It was so hard after she died, like my heart had been augered right outta my chest. It erased the details before it, I think. Wiped my memory clean. If Ray was still alive, he could probably tell you more. He was the smart one." She smiled apologetically.

When the grandfather clock in the corner struck the hour, she jumped. "Oh my, time has gotten away from me." She closed the photo album and set it on the coffee table. "You probably need to be going."

"I can stay," I said, wondering at her abrupt mood change. "If you'd like to talk more."

She stood. "Ted is coming home soon. He's my husband?"

She phrased it as a question, kept glancing at the clock like he'd step out of it. I didn't think I'd like Ted if I met him, and I'd only just learned about the guy.

When I didn't say anything, she continued. "It's just that he doesn't like me to dwell in the past. Says it's not healthy for me. That's why there's no photos of Robin out. Ted wants me to focus on the happy stuff." She tried smiling, but her mouth had gone stiff. "He's a good man that way."

Sounded like a selfish dink to me. I grabbed my coat and walked toward the door. I didn't want to add to her anxiety when she clearly wanted me gone. "Did you know Ted back then?" I asked as I walked. "When Robin was still alive?"

"Oh, you bet I did!" Her voice was bright, though her face was still worried. She was all but herding me out. "He was Robin's science teacher. Said she was his star pupil. Do you know that he thinks I look like her?" She laughed, an uneasy trill. "Fifty years ago, maybe!"

She held the door open. I stepped onto her porch, handing her a card, wondering if it would be worth my time to dig into Ted. "Call me if you think of anything else."

She snatched the card out of my hand. She started to say "Will do," or something like it, but she'd shut the door before she finished.

I suddenly felt so tired.

I made the drive to Minneapolis on autopilot. I planned to get Owl, snuggle her, pick up supper for both of us, and go back to the apartment to try to piece together what, if anything, I'd learned today. But then the strangest thing happened. The closer I got to the Bark Barn, the happier I grew. It felt good to think of seeing Owl, to know that someone, at least, would be thrilled to see me. I caught myself walking fast through the parking lot, remembering some new-to-Owl treats I'd passed in their entryway. I'd buy her a package on our way out.

The end of the workday meant there was a line for pickup inside, doofy mutts and aloof poodles and yappy chihuahuas all shades of ecstatic to see their owners. When I finally reached the front, I was imagining the feel of Owl's fur beneath my hand. "I'm here for—"

"Auld Lang Syne," the woman said, her expression grim. She was the same one who'd accepted Owl this morning. Her bobbing dog faces were drooping. "She's in our time-out room. I'm afraid she's had a very bad day. We won't be able to take her back."

CHAPTER 36

Van

"I can't believe you almost got yourself kicked out of doggy day care," I scolded Owl as we drove to the Loring Dog Park. Bringing her there was one of the concessions I'd made to convince them to give her one more chance.

Apparently—very much like me—Owl didn't play well with others.

The front-desk worker told me she'd plowed across the big-dog playroom like a kindergarten bully on a sugar rush, mowing through easygoing golden retrievers, knocking down shy greyhounds, verbally harassing any terrier that looked at her sideways. Her behavior was so egregious that the animal trainer took her aside for thirty minutes to teach her basic manners, but the minute he let her back into the playroom, she pinned a pit bull and snarled into his face.

"I don't think she meant any harm," the worker told me. "She just doesn't know how to behave around other dogs."

"What do you recommend I do?" I'd asked in my best grown-up voice. Owl needed to go *somewhere* while I was in the field.

The worker suggested we visit the dog park at least twice a week plus take training classes on top of going on more frequent walks. I didn't tell her the dog already had three walks a day. I needed them to allow her back so I could hit the road again tomorrow. I could probably find another place to drop her, but if she was being a dick to other dogs, the problem would simply repeat. Better I leave her someplace where they knew what they were dealing with.

Owl and I'd passed the dog park many times when walking but never gone in. My bad. It was just that all the owners seemed to know each other, or at least enjoy small talk, and I had no interest in either. Again, something Owl and I seemed to have in common.

"But we're going to do better, aren't we, girl?"

She smiled at me, her tongue lolling out. She'd been relaxed on the drive. A day of harassing others had worn her out. Still, I kept her on leash as we crossed through the dog park double gate, didn't unclip her when other dogs came to sniff her. Her posture remained subservient, head down and butt tucked.

"Good job pretending." I patted her on the head and began walking her around the perimeter, both of us trotting like we were in the Westminster Dog Show. I heard my name on the second round.

"Alexis," I said, recognizing the Magnolia's barista. "What're you doing here?"

She grinned, revealing dimples. Her dark-brown hair peeked out of a white cap with a snowball top. "Zoso and I are touring the city dog parks, finding our favorite."

"Zoso?"

An enormous black hound came bounding over, half Lab, half grizzly bear. He slowed just before he hit Alexis's legs. She patted him on his flank with a solid thump. "I adopted him last year." She looked over at Owl. "How's your foster doing?"

Owl was straining at the leash and whining, desperate to get closer to Zoso. "Not great," I said, trying out the hand gesture for *sit*. Owl ignored it. "She almost got kicked out of day care today. Apparently, she's an asshole around other dogs."

Alexis squatted so she was level with Owl. "Is this true, missy?"

Owl licked her face madly, her butt wiggling so furiously that she'd have taken to the air if she had propellers attached.

"All right, then," Alexis said laughing, pushing Owl's tongue away. She looked up at me. "You want to head over to the smaller fenced-in area to see how she plays with Zoso?"

"Thanks," I said, "but she pinned a pit bull."

Alexis stood. "Zoso is really good with other dogs. I'm comfortable giving it a try if you are."

It was one thing to hear Owl was poorly behaved. It'd be a whole other to witness. Still, it was what I was here for, and I did enjoy Alexis's company. "It'd probably be a good idea to give it a try before I drop her off tomorrow," I said reluctantly.

We walked side by side to the small-dogs' park, fenced in like the main one but currently empty. I let Owl off leash. She rocketed to the far side of the fenced-in area, her butt almost beating her head. Zoso ran along behind her, and soon they were frolicking.

"See?" Alexis said. "Owl's fine. She just needs an alpha dog to show her the ropes."

Tiny pockets of stress released all along my muscles. "Thanks."

Alexis smiled. "How's work these days?"

I tried to remember if I'd told her what I did for a living. I expected she served a lot of BCA agents at the coffee shop. "Good."

She watched the dogs play. "You never made it to yoga."

"I didn't." Owl tried to pin Zoso, and Zoso gave her a friendly nip.

"I have another class this week," she said. "It'd be nice to see you."

"Yeah, maybe. I need to get going." I whistled for Owl. She ignored me. I didn't know why I wanted to get away all of a sudden. Alexis was being friendly. It was fine. Too fine. I tugged a bag of treats out of my coat and held them up, whistling again. This time Owl charged over. She looked so happy. I leashed her and thanked Alexis again.

"No problem." Her smile wasn't calling out the dimples anymore, but it was still there. "If you ever need a dog sitter, remember I'm happy to help. Want my number?"

I studied her sweet, pretty face. She'd probably been raised by a normal parent, maybe even two, gotten to attend public school, had friends, gone days without thinking about murder, either ones she was solving or ones she hoped never got solved.

Still, I might need her in a pinch. I handed over my phone. "Put it in?"

She nodded and programmed in her number. When she handed my phone back, I accepted it and walked away. It was my signature move, after all. I'd done it to my Sisters, Mothers, Brothers. Left them behind. When I'd fled the commune, it'd felt like breaking bones, that pain of becoming a different creature, wild to human. *Snap.* I went from being an interchangeable female at Frank's to a world teeming with choices. It'd been exhilarating and terrifying.

I picked up speed. I was almost to the exit gate when Owl scooped up a tennis ball and started prancing with it.

"Excuse me?" someone asked, sounding mildly offended.

I turned to the voice. It was a woman in her late sixties just on the other side of the fence. She wore a red sweater the same color as the unhoused guy's scarf. My throat locked.

"We must be careful of assumptions, mustn't we?" she continued, her smile sly.

Father knows best.

I took an aggressive step toward her. She held her ground.

"The ball," she said, pointing at Owl's mouth. "It doesn't belong to her."

"Drop it," I told Owl. It was the one command she followed consistently. The ball fell with a soft plop. "Sorry," I told the woman.

I could feel her eyes on my back as I walked away.

One of my favorite college reads had been Shirley Jackson's *The Haunting of Hill House.* I hadn't thought of it in years, but a quote from the book inexplicably came to mind.

Am I walking away from something I should be running from?

CHAPTER 37

Just Judy

2001

The sun hung low, a hot lemon bathing the farm in golden light. Judy stood in the yard, the summer breeze teasing at her skirts as she hung damp linens on the clothesline. The fabric rippled in the wind, and the scent of wildflowers—sweet clover, milkweed, bee balm—mingled with the clean, crisp smell of soap. Chickens clucked lazily in the distance, and children's laughter, shrill and joyful, floated through the air from the fields beyond.

Judy's hands moved automatically, pinning up a shirt, a sheet, another shirt. Her mind wandered. She thought of the tincture, how carefully she'd prepared it—measuring, mixing, boiling until it was perfect, a deep pine green. She imagined his approval, though he never spoke of such things directly. She could sense it in the way the air would shift.

A sharp scream cut through the warm, lazy hum of the farm. Her head snapped up, the clothespin slipping from her fingers and falling to the dirt. Her heart pounded as her eyes darted toward the sound.

It had come from her lab.

No one should be in there.

Judy was moving before she fully registered the fear. She ran, her bare feet slapping against the hard-packed earth as she rounded the corner of the house. The world blurred—green fields, the red barn, the distant woods. She stumbled to a stop at the porch. There, lying on the rough wooden boards, was a girl, one who'd only been here for three years, who'd seemed to cry the whole time. They'd given her the name Catherine, but she refused to respond to it, no matter how close it was to her given name. Blond hair fanned out beneath her head, her blue eyes wide open, staring at the cloudless sky. And her face—her face was twisted into a terrible grin, lips pulled back over her teeth in a way that didn't belong to the living.

Judy's stomach lurched, and for a moment, the world tilted.

It was her worst fear.

A boy stood over the body, his face pale, his eyes wide, still trembling from the scream that had torn from his throat. His small hands were clenched into fists at his sides. "It was a dare," he whispered.

Judy knelt beside the girl, her fingers brushing the child's cold cheek, tracing the horrible smile. The truth washed over her like ice water. *She* had made that face. The tincture was her creation—her work, her sin.

Her legs trembled as she stood, her chest tight, her breaths shallow. "Tell no one," she hissed. "If you do, I'll drive you far away and leave you by the side of the road. You'll never see your family again."

The boy's face twisted in fear, but still, she had to be sure. She gripped his shirt collar and dragged him close. "I'll know," she said. "I'll know if word of this ever leaves your lips." She shoved him off the porch. "Now go. You should be doing chores anyhow."

He ran away with small, hurried steps.

As Judy dragged the girl into her lab, she understood that she'd become just like him. The one she served, the one she fed with her work. Now, she'd also killed.

She closed her eyes for a long moment, her heart aching with the weight of it all. When she opened them again, nothing had changed.

Judy was left alone with the dead girl and the unbearable truth. Well, at least the girl's true parents would have made peace with her loss years ago. They must know any child who disappeared for this long wasn't coming home.

Judy tried to remember the day the child had shown up—it had been 1998, she was sure of that, sometime in the spring—and what she'd been like while here, but all she could recall was the steady weeping. Probably for the best the child was gone; she was never going to adjust. The wind blew gently, rustling the trees, carrying with it the scent of pine and fresh-cut hay.

Judy glanced down at the body, at the cruel grin that twisted the girl's features, and for the first time, she wondered if he was watching. He always seemed to be. Would he be pleased? Or would he punish her for allowing this to happen?

She decided it didn't matter, when it came to next steps. She had to bury the girl.

CHAPTER 38

Van

Owl and I motored past Harry's house. I couldn't bother him two nights in a row, so we kept on driving until we reached Otto Pusch's workplace and then his apartment building. Not a single answer dropped out of the sky at either place.

I was parked in front of the Animal Haven, the shelter I'd gotten Owl from, when my phone rang. The number looked vaguely familiar. "Yeah?" I said.

"It's Jobber." The former classmate I'd asked via email to track down Frank Roth. He'd lost the Minnesota accent but sounded just as punchable. "You didn't answer my message."

Owl crawled into the front seat and wiggled her head onto my lap. It was awkward with the steering wheel, but she mostly made it work. I stroked her velvet ears. "The subject line was 'No Luck,'" I told him.

He snorted. "What happened to your curiosity? That was the name of the vitamin company Frank Roth worked at."

My pulse pounded in my ears. "What?"

"Frank Roth, the guy you had me research? He started a vitamin company out in Florida. Their tagline was 'No Luck, All Love.' It's a shit motto, if you ask me, but I'm no marketer, so what do I know?"

I tried to calm myself, but I was being ripped in a hundred different directions. "You found Frank Roth?"

"Trailed him from Minnesota." Jobber's pride was evident, even through the phone line. "Wasn't easy, not the way he traveled. First time he popped up after jail was in Key West. He led tours. Food or fishing, depending on who you asked."

Frank Roth leading fishing tours? I didn't know he could swim—I'd never seen him in water—which was the stupidest thought to have as my world tipped sideways.

Jobber remained oblivious to the effect of his words. "He did some photography, too, before word of mouth dried up his business. Seems the locals didn't trust him." He cleared his throat. "Next he popped up, he'd married a woman from Daytona Beach, a Marian Vermillion. This was all in the email, if you'd have read it."

"Keep going," I snapped. Knives were singing through my blood, traveling toward my heart. *He'd found Frank.*

Jobber cleared his throat. "I see you've held on to your singularly warm personality." My silence spoke for itself. He continued without my input. "He used her last name, became Frank Vermillion. It was her vitamin company he took over, rebranding it. I guess it did pretty well."

"Roth stayed in Florida?" My voice shook.

"He did," he said, "until he didn't."

It felt like the air in the car had been replaced by dirt. I was drawing it deep in my lungs, choking on it. "What does that mean?"

"I been tryna tell you. Frank Roth is dead."

CHAPTER 39

Van

A terrible memory wormed its way into my brain.

I was on the Farm doing some chore or another. Frank Roth appeared, towering over me. His jaw was broad and clenched, his eyes—one brown, one blue—sparking beneath his bushy brows.

He cocked his head. "Do you think Cordelia was happy here?"

My bones turned to ice. I didn't know Cordelia well. She'd shown up with a Mother one day, her hair a warm chestnut, her eyes always moving. The way she carried herself—secretive, self-contained—made her seem more like a Mother than a girl. She slept in the bed next to mine, or had before she ran away.

That's why Frank was asking. Cordelia had defied him. Hardly anyone ran away, maybe a Brother or two right before he was banished, and there was a big deal when Mother Esther disappeared and brought two girls under five with her, but there'd never been a Sister who left on her own. Why would anyone flee their home?

"She never should have gone," I said. I didn't consider whether it was true. It was just something I knew.

He nodded, the move slow, dangerous. "What did she say to you before she abandoned us?"

My eyes slid to the girls' dormitory before I could stop myself.

"She *did* say something," he crowed.

I swallowed dust. Cordelia always kept to herself, doing her chores without complaint but never laughing, never playing. The night she ran away, though, she'd tiptoed over to my bed after lights out and told me Frank wanted her to become a Mother.

Then she'd slipped into the night.

I still hadn't answered Frank. I wasn't sure why not.

"You're trying my patience, child," he said. "What did she tell you?"

Something bubbled in my belly, something new and upsetting. I didn't know what it was until it reached the surface: Frank, who was our Father and Savior, was *worried*.

"She didn't say anything," I said. It was a lie, and I could tell by the way his eyes spit fire that he knew it. I prayed he'd only take the belt to me. It hurt, but it was over quick.

"Take your clothes off and begin in the kitchen," he commanded.

Every cell in my body shrank. He was giving me the naked punishment.

Through sheets of tears, I stripped. I watched him pick up my dress and my drawers. Naked and burning with shame, I went directly to work, vowing to get the kitchen cleaner than it had ever been, trying to escape my body, pretending it wasn't exposed for all my Family to see. I was on my knees scrubbing the wooden floor when one of my Sisters ran in to tell me everyone must gather in the compound immediately.

When I stepped outside, there was Cordelia, her dark hair reflecting the sun. When she spotted my nakedness, she began weeping quietly, her shoulders shaking. She must have guessed she was the reason I was being punished, but it wasn't her fault.

"I want to apologize," she said. Her voice was quiet, but I heard it. "I want to apologize to you all. I am lucky to be betrothed to Frank. When I turn eighteen, I will become a Mother. I will move into their building immediately so I can better prepare."

Frank was watching her, exultation in his eyes. When he noticed me on the perimeter, shivering and unclothed, he ordered me back to the kitchen to clean.

Current me shook my head violently, trying to leave behind that terrible memory. Frank Roth was gone. The abusive bastard was dead.

Why couldn't I feel anything? No joy, no sadness, just numb.

"Are you sure?" I asked Jobber.

"Yup. You remember Flight 515? Leaving Cancún, headed to Atlanta."

It took me a few seconds. "Crashed in Florida. One of the deadliest accidents in recent aviation."

"Hit the Everglades." He made a nose like a missile crashing to earth and exploding. "Frank and Marian Vermillion were on it, along with 124 other folks. Only body parts were recovered."

The information felt slippery. "Cause of crash?"

"The pilot had some medical emergency, as far as they can tell."

It still wasn't making sense. "How do you know Frank Roth was on it?"

"Besides the ticket charge made on the missus's credit card, the passenger manifesto, and the official body count?" Jobber laughed, a dry sound. "Some woman, a daughter of two of the people who died in the crash, filmed them boarding. Guess it was their first time on an airplane. But yeah, Frank Roth can be seen going through security, clear as day, and then boarding the flight, along with his wife and the other victims. Talk about no luck."

When I didn't respond, he clearly thought it was because I'd missed his lame joke. "Get it? His vitamins were called No Luck, and then his plane crashed."

"Send me the footage." My mind should've been shutting down. Instead, it was running angles like I was playing a video game. Detached. Cold. "What do you know about Marian Vermillion?"

"Before she died? Not much." Paper swished in the background. How like Jobber to keep printing out stuff in the digital age. I should introduce him to Kyle, and the two of them could trade off Rolodex tips. "Married rich with her first husband. The vitamin company she started seems like a vanity project, but it really took off when Frank came on board."

Frank must have seduced her like he had so many of the Mothers. He was a monster, but he could also be charming, charismatic. That was how he lured people in. But why did they stay? Frank Roth would never have been able to do nearly as much harm if he hadn't had all those enablers.

"Did Marian have children?" I asked. I dearly hoped not.

"An adult daughter," Jobber said. "Lizbet Vermillion. She took over running the vitamin company after Frank and her mom died."

I suddenly wanted to see that footage so bad I couldn't breathe. "You went by his house?"

"Yep. Yesterday, in fact. Lizbet lives there now. No signs of a commune, just a single woman running a business." He coughed. "From what I found out about your father, the guy needed attention like most of us need oxygen. At least he got to die with an audience."

Jobber wasn't wrong, but . . . I still couldn't believe that Frank would be gone like that, that I wouldn't know, wouldn't feel a rip in the fabric. Frank had been my dark sun for eighteen years. How could he have slipped into hell without me sensing it, without feeling some great sense of relief?

I realized Harry was the one I wanted to talk this through with, but I couldn't, for obvious reasons. My thoughts coiled back to all the Mothers who'd allowed Frank to get away with his abuse. Sure, he'd messed with them, just like he had with us, but when did a victim stop being a victim and start being responsible for what they allowed to happen to others?

It was a trick question.

They were always a victim, and they were always—once they became an adult—responsible for the harm they permitted.

CHAPTER 40

Van

After a quick stop at the Lotus to grab spring rolls, tofu with sweet and hot peppers, and an order of chicken lo mein, I drove home and got Owl settled in her dog bed before I fired up my computer. Now that we were home, she stuck to me like Velcro, like she was afraid I'd leave her with strangers again. The fact that I couldn't explain to her that I would always return as long as I was alive and free hollowed me out.

Watching her person leave must feel like heartbreak every time.

I fridged the spring rolls and lo mein for later and ate my stir-fry out of the white box, using the plastic fork they'd supplied. It was a good thing they'd included it because all my dishes were dirty. I knew I should probably clean again. I had after the Taken Ones case, but it hadn't stuck. Turned out I liked to nest, and Owl didn't seem to mind. More piles of stuff for her to snuffle into.

The sourness of the banana peppers perfectly complemented the earthy creaminess of the tofu and the broccoli's crispness. Harry'd probably lay an egg if he saw me consuming this many vegetables, which was why I never ordered anything like it in front of him. Didn't want to give him the satisfaction. The truth was, I loved to eat anything with complex flavor. Sure, a lot of the time it was junk food, but it was also good pizza, and Vietnamese, and Mexican—anything forbidden on Frank's Farm was a must-eat for me. Our diet growing up had been healthy but bland and unchanging. Porridge for breakfast. Homemade bread and salt-free soup—vegetable or barley—for lunch. Dinner was always boiled vegetables with bread and a protein—chicken or beef, both raised on the farm—and again, no salt.

I didn't know what I'd been missing until I escaped and ate my first fast-food burger. I almost came in my pants. I'd sampled every cuisine I could since, though I gravitated toward Vietnamese.

I checked my email while I chewed. I had only one, from Jobber. The subject line?

Frank Roth video

I clicked the file open, growing distant from myself, my mouthful of broccoli turned to ash. I swallowed and leaned forward.

The ribbon-whip sound of flags in the wind announced the video's start. The person filming—a woman whose parents were presumably about to die in a fiery crash—had a traveling vision, her focus flitting from the sky to the crowd ant-lining up the airplane stairs, finally focusing on an elderly pair, their dark hair shot with white. Except for the outdoor boarding, the plane looked like any other passenger jet I'd ever seen.

Frank Roth wasn't there, and then he was, appearing at the end of the line.

The sight of him was a bell ring of shock that struck me momentarily blind and deaf. He was larger than life, silver-haired but otherwise exactly as I remembered, wearing a wide "everything is better than fine" grin. I felt myself shrink, regressing in age until I was a teenager, then a child, and then *gone*. It'd been trained into me. With Frank, you didn't exist as a person. You were a servant, a prop, a machine that required a bed and food and nothing else. I ground my knuckles into my eyes until I saw stars, then forced myself to keep watching.

A woman stuck to his side, nearly invisible. She looked out of time, resembling a 1980s Nancy Reagan, helmet hair and all. That must be Marian Vermillion. The camera zoomed in on the elderly couple and then swung back to Frank. He was helping the woman accompanying him onto the bottom step. He was in public, after all. He had to pretend he was human.

Once she climbed up, he followed. What had he been doing in Mexico? Vacation? The elderly couple had already disappeared inside the plane, but their daughter kept filming, likely to capture their takeoff. The woman who was probably Marian Vermillion stepped into the plane. I thought Frank was going to follow her, but instead, he turned to the airport and held up what looked like a towel. He shook it. It slapped right and left, a struggling snake, and then unfurled.

It was a banner.

No Luck, Only Science—Vermillion Vitamins Save You

I choke-laughed.

He'd gone to Mexico to sell vitamins and intended to advertise to the bitter end. No half measures for Frank Roth, no "clearer skin" or "better sleep." If he couldn't control your very soul, why bother? These dark thoughts still limned my body as he folded up the banner and disappeared into the plane. I watched until the end of the video even though there was nothing more to see, just Flight 515 taking off, where it would stay airborne for one hour and forty-five minutes before receiving a distress call from the pilot and then plummeting into the Everglades.

Jobber had been right. Frank Roth was dead.

My nerves crackled.

How had the earth not shuddered, letting me know that the devil had passed? I watched the video three more times, scanning for loops, evidence of tampering, photoshopping.

It was real. Frank was no more.

How should I feel? The question had no meaning, because I couldn't feel a thing.

My brain was racing, though.

Frank Roth was confirmed dead. That left only my Mothers and Sisters to help me learn the truth about Caroline. Good thing I'd submitted DNA samples into a genealogy website as soon as Harry and I returned from Duluth: one of mine and one of his, a tissue I'd nabbed from his hotel garbage.

I hadn't yet been able to bring myself to check if the results had been processed.

I wasn't a woman given to flights of fancy. With Frank Roth dead, I knew there were only two possible outcomes for the DNA tracking. The first was the least hellish, though it still made my blood run cold: DNA would connect me with my actual birth mother or one of my Sisters. I'd find them, show them photos of Caroline, and ask if they remembered her from one of the trips they'd been on with Frank. He usually went alone, but sometimes he included a Mother and, even less often, a Sister. I think he enjoyed the power of it, reminding us that he was our only doorway to the outside world.

While I liked nothing about that option, the second possible outcome was far, far worse: I would stumble across a child who shared both Frank's and Caroline's DNA. That person would also share significant DNA with me—Frank was my father, too, after all—as well as with Harry, who would be their uncle, confirming that Frank had abducted Caroline, kept her in a separate enclave, and forced her to bear his child. But where was the enclave, and might it mean Caroline was still alive? That there was a chance to reunite her with Harry and Myrna?

My stomach felt queasy. I pushed away the carton of food. Owl was still leaning against my leg, staring at me with her forlorn boxer side-eye, like she was worried I was going to ask for the money she owed me. I was suddenly overcome with a blazing warmth for her.

"No point in putting it off any longer, is there, girl?" I asked, scratching her behind the ear.

She raised her eyebrows and smiled.

I logged into my genealogy account before I could talk myself out of it.

The information came like bullets.

My DNA had been processed.

There were two hits.

CHAPTER 41

Van

The stir-fry scrabbled back up to my throat. I barely made it to the toilet in time. Even after there was nothing left in me but dry heaves, I stayed on the cold floor, hugging myself.

I'd had no choice but to leave the commune to survive, that was what I kept telling myself. I'd been too brainwashed, and the harrowing visions were crushing me at that point, forcing me to watch the most depraved horrors while I slept, like some *Clockwork Orange* experiment.

But that wasn't the only reason I'd run, was it?

I'd also been a coward. Ashamed of who I'd been, what I'd let happen. I wanted to leave it all behind and start over with people who didn't know I'd been raised by wolves, that I'd scrubbed the floor naked, that I'd never watched TV, that I'd let my Sister be destroyed in front of my eyes.

That explained why I'd fled, but not why I'd never looked back. I could have helped my Sisters after I ran away. Not immediately, but once I found a good therapist and a career that made sense. I could have tracked them down and made sure they were okay.

But I never had.

Not until now, not until I needed something from them.

I lifted my head from the bathroom floor. Glanced at the thin drawer on the front of my vanity, the one that looked like a decorative front but hid a shallow lip for a toothbrush and toothpaste. My pulse choked my veins as I imagined opening it to get at the three tiny bags I'd tucked inside, the ones that held the hair of the men I'd murdered.

I reached toward the drawer, not sure what my plan was. Punish myself by looking inside? Lean into what an awful person I was? Use them like a gruesome rosary? That's normally how it played out.

Owl padded in and curled up next to me, her mopey eyes traveling from my face to the drawer, the drawer to my face. *Don't open it,* her expression said. *There's nothing in there for you.*

I buried my face in her fur. I believed her, at least enough to stand up, at least for tonight. That was the magic of Owl. She protected me from my worst self.

Screw putting this off any longer.

I went to my computer—the genealogy page still open—and tucked away my warm and vulnerable parts so I could read the report like a machine would, simply processing information.

The results were black and white: Two of my Sisters had been found.

I blinked, my lids scraping my eyeballs, and clicked the "More Information" link.

The genealogical site allowed users to upload photos of themselves as well as contact information if they were interested in hearing from relatives, so I was looking at two of my Sisters' faces for the first time in well over a decade. I recognized them immediately. Sister Grace and Sister Hannah.

Time twisted, turning the world momentarily upside down.

They'd aged, as had I, but in Sister Grace's faint smile I recognized the twinkle of the girl who liked to doctor the farm kittens, and in Sister Hannah's fierce gaze the child who once fought off a neighbor's dog with a stick rather than let it carry away a lamb. I hadn't been close to either, not like I'd been with Veronica, but I'd seen their faces every day for nearly eighteen years. It was the oddest sensation, gazing at close family I no longer knew. Such a tender, painful numbness.

With shaking hands, I cut and pasted the email address Sister Grace had provided, composed her a brief message saying who I was and that I wanted to meet, and then I hit send.

It felt like sending a vital organ, or a secret, or a bomb.

To a stranger I'd called Sister.

CHAPTER 42

Van

I woke up with breath that could kill a ghost. A night of hospital-quality sleep did that to a person, especially if it was threaded with nightmares of murder and abusive fathers and communes. If all the patches of actual rest I'd carved out were added up—at least according to my app—they wouldn't come to three hours.

I checked my email. No response from Sister Grace, though had I really expected she'd respond in eight hours? I tried to tell myself it was okay. The mystery I intended to solve was as cold as ice. There was no urgency, that was the lie I was choosing to believe. If Frank Roth had abducted Caroline, she was safe from him now.

I knew that train of thought was gold-plated bullshit, by the way, even without the sad, judgy look Owl kept tossing me as I got us ready for the day.

"You keep that up," I told her, "and this morning's walk will be short."

But of course it wasn't. There were infinitesimally small specks of earth that Owl had not yet rubbed her snout over. For all the reasons there were to be miserable, I had to admit that it was nice to have an excuse to get out and walk before the sun came up. The glowing blue-black of a city starting to wake, the crisp scent of damp earth mingling with the promise of blossoms, the rhythmic percussion of Owl's paws on the pavement, the sensation of being cozy warm in my parka and cap.

It was all so peaceful that I jumped when my phone buzzed in my pocket.

I tugged it out.

The incoming call was from Animal Haven. My gut kicked. I considered not answering it, bundling Owl up in my car, and driving south until we hit Mexico. Instead, I sighed and clicked the green button. "Van Reed."

"Hi. You're awake! Figured I'd leave a message. This is Katy at the animal shelter. Is everything going well with your foster?"

Owl whined. I realized I'd stopped walking. I started again.

"Totally," I said, my voice tinny even to my ears. "She's a great dog."

They must have heard Emily had died. What if Pusch had tracked Owl down to Animal Haven and requested her? They wouldn't tell him who was fostering her, though.

Owl is mine now.

"So glad to hear it," Katy said. "We just like to check in with our fosters and offer any help they may need. Do you have enough food?"

I'd been holding my breath. "Plenty," I said, exhaling. Matter of fact, I'd bought a large bag of the most expensive breed-specific kibble the pet store sold. The shelter provided what they could afford or what came in through donations, which was barely better than nothing.

"That's wonderful. No behavioral issues?"

"None," I lied.

I needed to bring down my blood pressure. They weren't taking Owl away from me, they were checking in on her. I'd continue my foster as scheduled so as not to raise any red flags, and then I'd give the mucus monster back at an appropriate time, letting them know I'd be happy to keep her permanently if necessary.

Animal fosterers got first pick when one of their charges went up for adoption.

"So wonderful! We'll give you a call if we hear anything from the dog's owner, but until then, you know where to reach us should you need anything."

"Thanks," I said, my breath sticky in my mouth. I was hanging up when I saw the text come in from Harry.

Can you come in? I have something.

Well, wasn't today already turning into a rock tumbler of dogshit. I'd been planning to bring Owl directly to doggy day care for her second chance and then head to Maple Grove to continue where I'd left off with interviews yesterday, but I couldn't blow off Harry forever, especially if he had something relating to the case. I'd drop Owl off and then swing by the BCA before heading out.

Be there in 30.

CHAPTER 43

Van

Harry's lab smelled chalky, like inhaling baking soda. I held the door so it'd close softly, allowing me to quietly study him. He was bent over what I assumed was a flux capacitor filled with medical tubes. He wore casual wear, for him: brown leather shoes, navy pants with a faint pinstripe, crisp white dress shirt, a tie pinned in place. His shirt was rolled up to his elbows, revealing surprisingly muscled forearms.

When we'd shared adjoining motel rooms on the Duluth case, he'd rushed into my room one night wearing only pajama pants, thinking I was being attacked. I'd been so disoriented from the violent vision he'd woken me from that I'd almost missed the burn scars across his chest. Self-inflicted, most certainly, as a way to deal with the misplaced guilt he felt for not preventing his sister's abduction.

It was a human truth that we all needed someone to blame. Too often, we chose ourselves.

I reminded myself it was for Harry that I'd tracked down Frank. For Harry, I was reaching out to meet up with two of my Sisters for the first time since the feds had raided the commune. For Harry, I had to. I didn't know a better man. I didn't have a closer friend.

"Evangeline?"

My mouth snapped shut. I'd been standing in his doorway, gaping at him like some potato farmer. I shook the bats out of my skull. "Sorry. Bad sleep last night. You wanted me to drop by?"

The concerned line between his eyebrows stayed for an extra moment and then smoothed out. See, that was Harry. He'd never push it. He grabbed a sheet of paper from the counter. "Thanks for coming in. The ME sent over Emily Barris's tox results."

He walked over, his strong, safe smell leading. "It's poison," he said, offering me the paper.

I scanned it. Most of the information was indecipherable to a layperson, but I recognized the important word. "They found your oenanthotoxin?" I asked.

His mouth thinned. "It's the one I recommended the ME test for, though I suspect she would have landed there herself, given the victim's appearance."

"You told Comstock?"

Harry shook his head. "That's my next phone call. Wanted to tell you first."

I held up the paper. "I need to talk to him anyhow. Can I bring this printout?"

He wanted to say more, I could tell, but he was giving me a long leash. "Let me know his reaction, or if there's anything else you need." He paused, his ice-blue eyes scanning me. "For the case."

I nodded. "You got it. I plan to call a cold case team meeting soon. Just need to do a few more field interviews."

And talk to my Sisters. See if they know what happened to yours.

He reached around me to hold the door open. I walked out without saying a word. It was often how we ended our interactions. No goodbye, just going our separate ways. As I walked down the hallway, I realized why.

I knew he was someone I'd see again. I liked that feeling.

As I paced outside and crossed the street to Magnolia's for some coffee, I found myself thinking about past coworkers, landing on my previous supervisor, the MPD chief of police. Chief Longman had been more like Bart than Chandler, an old-school detective who'd been forced into the role. But he'd mostly stayed out of our way in homicide, and I'd appreciated that. I say fire the folks who suck and let the rest of us get to work.

It was my turn at the cash register. Alexis was nowhere in sight, and I didn't recognize the twentysomething behind the counter with a green pixie cut and septum ring.

"Cinnamon mocha, please," I told them.

They studied me for a moment, their head cocked. They really did look like a pixie, or some other forest creature. "Oh, hey!" they said, as if realizing something. "You work at the BCA, don't you?"

"Yep."

They leaned back to dig beneath the counter and came up with a red scarf. "You dropped this last time you were here," they said cheerfully.

The hairs on my arms stood up. "No, I didn't." My voice sounded harsh, aggressive. I tempered it. "Who said I did? A customer?"

They shrugged, their sparkle fading as they picked up on my mood. "I dunno. Some guy handed it over. Said it belonged to the BCA agent with white hair."

"Is he here?" Because the red yarn was a message, wasn't it? I *wasn't* being paranoid. Someone was messing with me. I just didn't know who or why.

I whipped around to take in the café.

Everyone and no one was watching me.

CHAPTER 44

Van

The pixie barista said the man who'd left the scarf was a middle-aged white guy wearing a yellow or tan Carhartt jacket. No one fit that description in the coffee shop or out front. The scarf I was handed bore no tag and appeared to be hand knit.

I walked out of Magnolia's in a daze, straight into Otto Pusch.

If I were a cat, my tail would have gone fat. "What are you doing here?" I demanded, stepping away from him.

Several expressions rolled across his face, all of them moving too fast for me to get a read. He landed on a smile that lifted his large ears. Did it have a calculating edge? "The woman from outside my perfumery. We meet again."

I held up the scarf. "Did you leave this?"

His eyebrows reached toward the sky and then dropped. "Excuse me?"

My brain swirled. I *should* calm myself down. I *should* walk away. Instead, I shoved the scarf in his face. "This. Is it yours?"

His nose wrinkled, and then his gaze sharpened. He reached forward and plucked something off my jacket, holding it between us. If I weren't wound so tight, and so aware that any physical alter-cation between us would have gone straight to Comstock and cost me the case, I would have clocked him. Still, it took effort to cool down enough to focus on what he was holding.

I was looking at a short tawny hair.

One of Owl's.

He let it drop. It immediately disappeared in the bright sunlight. "You're covered in them," he said, cool as a lizard.

He was right. Boxers didn't shed as much as most dogs, but they still lost fur regularly. My black jacket was a showcase. "Sorry," I said, too late, my brain pinging.

There were two possibilities why he was here, outside Magnolia's, a whole city away from his neighborhood. The first was he killed Emily, planted my ID on the scene, and was continuing to mess with me, motive TBD. The second was that he was coming for a cup of coffee, just like I'd been.

Either way, I'd played it like a fool.

I planted my most disarming grin on my face and shook my head. *I'm such a dummy.* "The barista told me some guy forgot their scarf and pointed through the window at you. Didn't mean to be so intense."

He was still studying me with his reptilian gaze. "It happens."

No sweet disguising his bitter anymore, no sun-shaming grin to convince me he was a nice guy. He'd placed me in a different column and was no longer going to waste his good moves on me.

"Thanks for being so understanding. Sorry again." I was laying it on a little thick, but it was all I had left after how poorly I'd played this. I held up the scarf. "Guess this is mine now."

He blinked, nodded, and ducked into the coffee shop.

I wanted to burn the damned scarf, but instead, I tossed it in the back of my car and drove to the First Precinct, vacillating between fuming that someone—the good money was now on Pusch—was messing with me and being unsettled by how well it was working. Or was all the red a coincidence? Sometimes, when my visions got bad, reality and nightmares blurred together, giving the waking world a weird hallucinatory cast. But that wasn't what was happening now. Someone was making people wear red to mess with me.

Why?

I joggled my head to dismiss the question. That mystery needed to play with itself for the time being. I had one Detective David Comstock to deal with, and I wasn't looking forward to it. I cursed the fact that he still worked for the department. He was in his sixties. No one would blink twice if he retired, but Comstock was one of those guys who identified heavily with his badge. Who'd give him the respect he thought he deserved if he didn't carry a gun? He was the type who hung on to his shield long after its expiration date, spending less and less time in the field and more behind his desk.

My bad luck that Emily Barris's death had gotten him off his butt.

"Comstock?" I said, knocking on his open door. "Got some news from the ME on the Barris case."

He stared at his computer screen a few more beats than was polite, in case I'd forgotten he was a dick. "They have you doing personal courier service over there at the BCA?" he finally asked, sliding his reading glasses up onto his head.

I stepped into his office, handed him the sheet of paper I'd taken from Harry's lab, and dropped into the worn pleather chair across from his desk. "I was in the neighborhood. Thought I'd stop by and see if you had any updates on her murder."

"Huh." He leaned forward on his elbows, his hands crossed like he was praying. "Thought you were on cold case."

I'd witnessed his ethics up close the last time we'd worked together. He could step down off that pedestal. "You know my case might intersect yours."

He made a huffing noise, dropped his glasses back on his nose, and scanned the paper. "ME already sent this over, and I already read it. Barris was poisoned, and we have every indication she did not drink it willingly. So if you're here to earn my good graces, that train has left the station."

I'd swallow a little shit if it helped my case, but not an indefinite amount. "You already found out there was no AA meeting the night Otto Pusch claimed he was at it, right?"

Comstock frowned. "You sleeping in my bed?"

It was embarrassing how much I relished annoying him. "No reason to get starchy. My ID was found on the crime scene. You can understand why I'd have an above-average curiosity here."

He was searching for a way to get at me, I could see it in his watery eyes, but he either couldn't find one or he was tired. "Yeah, we know Pusch lied about the AA meeting." He removed his glasses and began polishing them with a blue scrap of cloth. That's when I noticed how gray he looked, how his face seemed swollen.

"You okay, Comstock?" My concern was genuine. He'd done me dirty—twice—but he'd also been responsible for some good work in his career, saved some lives.

His eyes softened. I thought for a moment he'd get vulnerable with me, tell me what the deal was. Not Comstock. His face buttoned right back up. "I got a bad case of the Van Reeds, that's all. Think there's a cream for that?"

I scowled, about to let loose, but to my surprise, a laugh erupted instead. It wasn't the worst joke I'd ever heard. I stood and started toward the door.

"Reed," he said.

I turned. His glasses were back on, his face staring at the computer screen. I wondered for a second if I'd imagined him saying my name.

He cleared his throat, still not looking at me. "It seems as though Pusch is also in an intimate relationship with the AA sponsor he claimed to have been on the phone with helping all night, so his alibi couldn't hold a feather even *if* there'd been a meeting that evening."

Then he began typing.

I nodded and walked out, feeling much lighter than I had walking in. Comstock might despise me, but he wasn't going to let it interfere with his job, at least not this time. That was good news on top of good news because it really looked like Pusch was the killer, which meant I needed to dig quickly into any possible connections he had with the three poison victims from 1986. He was old enough to have been around back then. Maybe Comstock and I could put him away for all four murders.

My heart gave a little kick. Once the Barris case was closed, I could bury the fear that somehow I'd started sleepwalking during my visions, killing again. It must have just been the research on Frank and my family that had me all sorts of triggered.

I am fine, everything is going to be fine.

CHAPTER 45

Just Judy

2007

When he entered the bedroom, Judy's stomach plummeted through the floor. His face was twisted in anguish, his posture passive, like a toddler rather than the leader she knew him to be. He dragged himself to the bed and collapsed.

She'd been knitting, enjoying a few quiet moments before her day began. She immediately dropped her yarn and threw her arms around him. "What is it?"

He sounded as if he were choking. It took her a few seconds to realize he was weeping. She'd never heard it before. He was squeezing her so hard it hurt. She'd learned in health class a lifetime ago that a drowning person could pull you under if you tried to save them. That's what this felt like.

"It is time." His voice was hoarse, gasping. He turned his wet face to hers, and she felt like she was looking back at herself. He didn't allow mirrors, so his features had taken the place of her reflection in the twenty-plus years they'd been together. She loved that face, touched it gently.

"You know I had to sacrifice three girls the same year you joined me."

She nodded, her mouth going dry. Of course she'd guessed. She hadn't witnessed it, but after he'd asked her in the car that first night what the most poisonous plant she knew of was—back when he was courting her, making her feel like the smartest girl in the world—and she'd said hemlock, he'd begged her to show him what it looked like. That was easy. Gramma Anne had shown her some so she could avoid it. That was just country knowledge. So they found a few plants, and then he begged her to mix a tincture of it, even rented them a hotel room with a kitchenette so she could process it. She hadn't witnessed him giving the poisonous tincture to any of the girls, but she'd seen his face when he came back, glowing with reverence.

But they'd never spoken of it, until now.

He was bigger than her, but he burrowed his face into her neck like he was a small boy and she his mother. "It was so long ago that I'd nearly forgotten," he said. "They defied the path they were destined to walk, and so there was no choice." He moaned into her skin. "When you decline the Lord's kingdom, he demands a tithe in flesh."

She rubbed his head, struggling to make sense of this. "The Lord is *you*."

He pulled back, his expression liquid rage before his face knit itself over the anger. It'd been quick, but the force of it made her reel. "Not me," he said, offering her his square-jawed profile as he pointed skyward. "The Lord above." His eyes settled on hers. "He wasn't happy to witness the child you killed."

Her hand went to her throat. He *had* seen her bury that golden-haired girl he'd stolen from another family. Of course he had. He saw everything. "Why are you bringing this up now?"

His eyes were pleading. "The Lord is going to ask *you* to step up soon. Are your shoulders strong enough to bear this task?"

She nodded automatically, fiercely. She'd been training for this since she'd arrived.

"Good," he said. "Everything that's passed between us must stay here." He tapped her chest gently. "You are now the keeper of the Truth. Everything that is mine belongs to you."

She beamed, prepared to tell him how excited she was to be the only one he trusted with his secrets, but a commotion outside stole her words. His eyes turned cunning for a moment—that couldn't be—and then dropped. She expected him to stand, but instead, he stayed curled on the bed.

She hurried to the window.

Men and women in black vests, thick and ugly weapons at their side, swarmed their land. She glanced back at him. The sly look was back, but this time it was naked. It turned her organs inside out to witness, but it was too late, wasn't it? The time was now. The test wasn't meant to be easy, or what sort of test would it be? He'd been living a double life for decades, and now the two worlds were colliding. They couldn't lose what they'd built, couldn't allow those girls he'd killed or the ones he'd taken to be for nothing.

It was *her* time to shield *him*. That's what he'd been trying to tell her.

She strode downstairs, out onto the porch. Her children had already been led outside. They were weeping. Were those *television* cameras amid the chaos?

"Remember your names!" she yelled at the girls. "Remember who you are!"

And then she stepped off the porch, her hands held in front of her, wrists together, awaiting the cuffs.

CHAPTER 46

Van

An image of Mother Mary crept into my mind. I hadn't thought of her in years, but this past week, she'd felt so close. First there was the nightmare featuring her the evening Emily Barris died, and now, as I left the First Precinct, came a perfect memory of her bandaging my raw knee.

I think I was five or six. My chore that day was cleaning out the calf pens. I didn't particularly mind the job. The baby cows were soft, and when you got too close to them, they'd hop in the air like popcorn, their tiny hooves clacking. On top of that, our farm cat had recently birthed kittens in a corner of the barn, and I hadn't had a chance to meet them yet. Veronica said there were two gingers and two calicoes, that they were the sweetest things.

Distractions weren't allowed, but would anyone find out if I stopped mucking the stall to sneak a quick look-see? I glanced out the open barn doors, spotted no one, set down my kid-size pitchfork, and raced to the rear of the barn. I swore I'd only peek, maybe touch each one, and I held myself to my word. They were so cute, but I only set my pointer finger gently on each tiny fluff—one of them mewed, raising its bobbing head—before I hurried back to my station.

But I hadn't closed the calf pen, and a baby cow had run loose.

Even now, I could call up the icy terror of Frank Roth finding out I'd been careless. I charged so fast toward the open door that I fell hard, scraping both knees bloody. Mother Mary appeared, leading the calf into its pen before I'd even gotten back to my feet, her lips tight in reproach.

I'd immediately spilled the truth. I'd been looking at the kittens when I should have been watching the calves. I'd betrayed the Family. She glanced at my knees, the blood and watery serous fluid seeping through the raw skin.

"At least you got your punishment right away," Mother Mary said. "It's always better to pay your dues in this lifetime than the next." And then she'd cleaned off my knees.

She never told Father.

I still believed what Mother Mary had told me about paying my dues in this lifetime, probably for different reasons than she had intended. We all needed to face the consequences of our actions. It wasn't about religion. It was *right*.

I held that thought close as Martha Geldman, mother to victim #3, Lulu Geldman, buzzed me up to her second-floor apartment in a blocky three-story building tucked behind one of the clots of chain stores that riddled Maple Grove's arteries.

She was waiting in the hallway when I arrived. She wore comfortable-looking exercise pants and a matching sweatshirt, her hair piled into a messy bun atop her head. Her face was heavily lined, and the smell of cigarettes hit me before I was close enough to shake her hand.

"Thanks so much for seeing me, Mrs. Geldman."

"Martha," she said, her hand fluttering in the air. "I kept the last name but not the donkey who gave it to me." Her chortle turned into a phlegmy cough. "Come on in."

The apartment was neat, with a wide view of the parking lot below. The cigarette stench was stronger here, accented by the treacly perfume of a plug-in air freshener, but the ashtray was empty, the beige couch pillows perfectly arranged, and the magazines on the coffee table fanned out.

"I'd offer you something to drink," she said, "but I think we both want to get this out of the way quickly. Am I right?"

My smile was genuine. "That's up to you. Agent Kaminski told you why I'm here?"

She dropped into an easy chair, tucking one leg beneath her, and indicated I should take the couch. "He said you were looking into Lulu's death. Tell me: Is Agent Kaminski as attractive as he sounds?" That wet, chortling laugh again.

"Depends what you find attractive." I pulled out my notebook. "Can you tell me what you remember about Lulu's final days? The file notes are brief."

Her mouth twisted, her "carefree divorcée" mask slipping. Talking about Lulu must cut at her, it had to. Grief like that never expired, it only lay in wait. Judging how or when it would show up was a fool's game.

"Can't say as I'm surprised about the skimpy notes. I'm a nurse, as I imagine you know." Her hand indicated the general direction of the ashtray. *Despite what it may look like*, the gesture said. "I know how depression shows up, and I know what poisoning looks like. Lulu wasn't depressed. She may have accidentally ingested poison, or someone may have given it to her intentionally, but she didn't take her own life. I tried to tell the police that, but I saw the looks they gave each other." She shrugged. "I didn't think they'd investigate much, and I know why. I've seen firsthand how delusional people can be when their children end up in the ER, getting their stomachs pumped or their wrists bandaged."

Her eyes shot to the coffee-table drawer.

"I don't mind if you smoke," I said.

She glanced out the window, blinking rapidly. A P.F. Chang's was visible. She leaned over, withdrew a pack of Marlboro Lights from the drawer, extracted one, lit it. Her eyes closed as she drew deeply. "Lulu's dad had an apartment in downtown Minneapolis."

"You think he might have poisoned her?"

Martha's eyes shot open, landed on me. "No. He was a terrible husband and a mediocre father, but he was no killer. Too much work." She cackled, but there was no energy in it. "Last I heard, he moved to Chicago with a new wife. It's so easy for men to find love again, isn't it? The whole thing's set up to make them seem like the prize, make marriage look like a good deal, but it's only a good deal for men. You couldn't get me to start dating again for a million bucks." She blew out a long white cloud. "I'd rather get a public bikini wax."

I glanced down at my notepad. "Lulu worked a shift at Chi-Chi's her last day?"

Martha went still, and then her head swiveled toward me so robotically that I could almost hear the clicks. "Chris Windahl," she said.

"Excuse me?" I found myself leaning forward.

She copied my posture, tapping her cigarette in the ashtray. "Chris Windahl. He was a cook at her job. She never mentioned him, but after she died, I read her diary." She grimaced and then continued. "She wrote that he creeped her out."

"In what way?"

Martha's cheek spasmed. "I think he was paying too much attention to her. The bad kind. A woman knows the difference." She sucked in another drag. "I still have her diary. You can borrow it if you think it'd be helpful. I've taken photos of every page, saved them to my computer plus a jump drive, emailed them to myself." Her smile was sad. "I used to be certain the police would somehow crack the case. Didn't want to risk losing any evidence, even after all this time."

"I'd appreciate borrowing it," I said. "If you're all right with it, we can scan it at the BCA and get you the original back."

She stood. "Whatever works." She disappeared down the hallway and returned with a notebook, a fat orange Garfield the cat on its cover.

I accepted it, opened it to the first page. "Lulu Geldman" was written on the inside cover in bubble script, READ AT YOUR OWN

RISK sketched on page one with a bubblegum-pink gel pen. It hurt to look at it.

"Thank you," I said, closing it. "Can you think of any reason Lulu would have traveled to Rockville or Clearwater, Minnesota?"

Martha shook her head. "None. Lulu was 100 percent a big-city girl." She stamped out her cigarette, accordioning it into the ashtray. "The animal exhibit at the state fair was the closest she came to farm country. She loved those baby lambs."

Something about her comment snagged my brain, but I couldn't get a handle on it. "Is there anything else you can tell me?"

She glanced off toward P.F. Chang's again. "Not really," she muttered. "Not anything except that she mattered, she mattered a whole lot. Not because she was going to win a Nobel Prize, though she might have, nothing like that." She held her hand to her chest. "She mattered because she was alive. Because she was mine."

Her profile was proud, desperate. Something about it locked onto my heart so hard that it made me angry. "She did matter," I said. "She *does*. I'm going to find out what happened to her."

Martha's mouth twitched. "If you say so." She sounded tired. "Okay if I call if I think of anything else?"

She no longer believed there would be justice for her girl. Why should she? "One more question. Do you know this man?"

I showed her a photo of Pusch on my phone. She shook her head. "No. Should I?"

"The name Otto Pusch mean anything to you?"

She shook her head again.

Frustration gnawed at me, but I told myself it was early in the case. There was time to make the connections. I stood, slipped my notebook into my blazer pocket, and offered her my card. "Please do give me a call if you think of anything else." I held up the diary. "And I'll get this back to you soon."

"Great," she said without emotion. "Mind showing yourself out?"

Our brief talk had carved a piece out of her, one I was willing to bet she'd spent years building back after Lulu's death. It was wrenching. My anger grew. Someone had stolen her daughter's life, and with it, a chunk of her spirit. I was thinking about the price murder exacted on a family, a community, as I made my way out of her second-floor apartment. I was so lost in thought that I was startled when ahead another person disappeared through the doorway leading to the stairwell at the end of the hallway.

He moved like his skin was too tight, and he wore a bloodred scarf.

CHAPTER 47

Van

I only saw his back, his clothes a nondescript brown, a red scarf trailing behind, but the way he lurched out of sight, his movements herky-jerky, showed he'd definitely been aware of me. And something about him was eerily familiar. I had an icy image of the Bendy Man from the Taken Ones case—jailed for the rest of his unnatural life, as far as I knew—before I took chase.

"Stop!" I yelled, chewing up the ten yards separating me from the door he'd disappeared through. He was nearly around the corner half a floor up by the time I'd made it to the stairwell, his rubber-soled shoes noiseless. I turned the first corner, but he was out of sight. When I reached the second, I had the choice between stepping into the third-floor hallway or going up one more half flight to the roof. I glanced out the third-floor door, saw nothing, and charged upward. I tore open the metal door.

I saw a flash of red near the roof's far edge and ran toward it. The gravel crunching underfoot was loud, but I still heard a powerful crashing sound followed by a grunt. Had he fallen? I skidded to a stop at the roof's lip and peered over.

This side of the apartment building abutted a small forest next to yet another parking lot. It held one car, a silver sedan, its license plate obscured.

A man in brown—it couldn't possibly be the man I'd just seen in the stairwell—was brushing off his pants, straightening his red scarf, and walking toward the sedan, his back to me, his walk carefree.

"Stop!" I screamed.

He got into the car, flipped down the sun visor to hide his face, and drove away, slowly, gradually, no hurry at all. By the time I reached the lot, out of breath from running down three floors, there was no sign he'd ever been there.

Maybe he hadn't.

All I knew for sure was that I was running out of time and couldn't survive much longer not knowing what was up or down, reality or a hallucination.

CHAPTER 48

Van

Lindy Bell lived in a pocket of Saint Cloud behind the downtown post office, in the bottom level of a large house that reminded me of skin hanging off old bones: front porch sagging, paint peeling, the runty brown yard pocked with circles made white from dog pee.

I stepped onto the porch, ignoring its creaks. It was easy to do with the cacophony of dogs coming from the second level. They sounded like beasts, that assessment backed up by the size of the piles in the yard. But it seemed quiet inside Lindy's apartment. No animals, no people, no movement, not that I could see when I peered inside the window. The interior was decorated in Goodwill chic—serviceable unmatched furniture, framed art on the walls in no particular style. No plants, a few shelves of paperback books. Not messy, but not neat, either.

Kyle had told Lindy to expect me, and I was on time. Where was she? More to the point: Was she deliberately avoiding me?

I wrote a note on the back of a business card and slipped it through her mail slot.

Back in my car, I checked my email. Nothing from Sister Grace. Like most people who'd grown up in a household controlled by a paranoid megalomaniac, I abhorred talking on the phone. It didn't help that I was eighteen years old before I made my first call. But I could no longer wait for Grace to respond to an email. I inputted her number into my phone, my hands so slick with sweat that I smeared my screen. I wished Owl were here. Grace had included contact info on the genealogy website because she *wanted* her family to reach out to her. Right?

Frank trained his women to stay off the grid. But now that he was gone, what if I could not only track down Caroline but also have a relationship with my Sisters? That's what had kept me away, partially. Fear of inviting Frank back into my life if I reconnected with people from the Farm. No family was worth opening the door to that monster, not even a crack.

But he was now the memory of gator food in the Everglades.

The phone started ringing. One. Two. Three rings.

Click.

"You've reached Grace Roth. Please leave a message at the beep."

Grace *Roth*. My guts churned. She'd kept his last name. "Hey, Grace. It's Van . . . Evangeline. Your sister. I'd like to see you, soon, if possible. Maybe tomorrow, if you're still in Minnesota? Give me a call back, please."

I ended the phone call and sent a text to Kyle.

Turns out there's a time crunch. Please call a meeting about the 1986 deaths. You, Harry, Deepty and Johnna, if they're free. I'll be back in 60.

Yup, all I had to do was quick-solve the decades-old cold case involving three girls who'd died wearing gruesome clown smiles, figure out why my ID had been discovered on the scene of a similar recent case, and find out if Frank Roth had abducted Caroline Steinbeck and, if so, what he'd done with her.

I'd have laughed if I didn't feel like I was drowning.

When I met Harry at his lab door to walk to the meeting Kyle had managed to convene, he looked as crisp as a lounge singer at the beginning of a set. He wore navy dress pants with a matching suit coat, a crisp white button-down, and a brown belt and shoes. I admired his commitment to the 1950s look and almost wished he had on one of his fedoras, though he'd have removed it immediately upon seeing me.

"How're the interviews going?" he asked, falling in step alongside me. It felt good, how quickly we could connect.

"No smoking guns," I said. *Not like with me. Have I mentioned I killed three men and left a witness?* I glanced at him sideways, but he was staring straight ahead. For a moment, I pictured the long prison time I'd be serving if I were busted for triple homicide, but really, what destroyed me was imagining Harry's expression when he found out I was a murderer. "Can I ask you something?"

His back straightened. "Of course."

"Is it possible for a human to drop three stories and walk away?"

His forehead crinkled. He was wondering if I was making fun of him. "No," he said.

That's what I'd figured. Of course I hadn't seen some awkward-moving guy with a red scarf run up to the roof of a three-story building and leap off, unharmed. The stress and not enough sleep were messing with my ability to tell truth from hallucination.

"Except . . ."

My gaze flew to him. "Except what?"

He shook his head. "Let me look into it."

It was such a ludicrous question I'd asked him and here he was, trusting me against his better judgment.

All that would evaporate once he discovered what sort of person I really was.

CHAPTER 49

Van

Deepty Singh and Johnna Lewis sat at the far end of the table, a laptop open in front of each of them. They looked nothing alike—Deepty in her thirties and of Indian descent, always wearing mechanic-style denim coveralls, her hair a glossy black; Johnna, a Western European–descended brunette in her fifties—but they had one of those connections that made me think of them as sisters. It was an easy, joking relationship, no matter how grisly the case they were working. Both were forensic scientists with a wide range of skills, with Deepty excelling in recording crime scenes and Johnna's specializing in gathering trace evidence without losing her lunch, no matter how decomposed the corpse.

Harry, the best forensic scientist in Minnesota, claimed the seat next to them, watching me expectantly. Kyle Kaminski sat opposite Harry, his suit coat draped over his chairback, his scarlet tie a crisp contrast to his white dress shirt. I noted the paper and pens he'd placed in the center of the table plus the multicolored markers he'd supplied at the whiteboard.

The first meeting I'd led with all four of them present, on the Taken Ones case, I'd felt like a total impostor. This was the second time, and the sensation was only marginally better.

"Thanks for coming," I said. "Deepty and Johnna, I'm not sure if I'll need you on this one, but I wanted your eyes and ears for this first meeting."

They both tipped their heads, Deepty smiling encouragingly. "Not a problem," she said.

"Gave us a break from doing boring inventory," Johnna said agreeably.

"Thanks," I repeated. I went to the board and wrote Emily Barris's name in royal blue on the far left. "The hot case involves a victim by the name of Emily Barris, found dead in a women's shelter due to oenanthotoxin poisoning. She presented with a wide death grin and bruising on her wrists suggesting a struggle." I wrote Otto Pusch's name below Emily's. "The shelter was located on the east side of Loring Park. She'd been there for fifteen days, escaping alleged abuse at the hands of Otto Pusch, owner of Pusch Perfumery."

I glanced back at them to see if anyone was going to crack jokes about male perfumers. The MPD cops I'd worked with definitely would have. Instead, all four watched me expectantly, so I turned back to the board and grabbed another marker, creating three columns in sea green. The first I labeled Gina Penchant, the second Robin Seer, and the third Lulu Geldman. "There was one *St. Cloud Times* article written about the 1986 cold case. In it, the reporter, Amos Anderson, referred to the three victims as the Laughing Dead because all of them wore similar disturbing grins."

"Suspected oenanthotoxin poisoning," Deepty said, reading off her laptop screen.

"Symptoms matching Emily Barris's confirmed oenanthotoxin poisoning," Kyle said, quoting the folder opened in front of him.

A cool stream of pleasure ran beneath my ribs. Of course they'd all come to this meeting prepared, damn the fact that I'd given them only an hour's notice. They were up to date on the slim file on all three girls as well as Emily's case. "Can you run us through the timeline, Kyle?"

He stood and offered each of them a printout and then approached the whiteboard, sketching the broad information—estimated time and location of death, when the bodies were discovered, who'd been interviewed back in 1986. It took only a few minutes. "I double-checked with all three county recorders to see if there was a tox screen run on any of the victims." He turned his hands palms up. "Nada."

Harry, Deepty, and Johnna exchanged a look, but whatever they thought about county coroners, they kept to themselves.

"Thanks, Kyle." I accepted the marker from him as he returned to his seat. I wrote Gina's parents' names, plus Prudence's and Lindy's, in the Gina column. "No suspects in the first case."

I moved to the next column. "Robin's father died of bladder cancer a few years after Robin's death. Her mother remarried, a man by the name of Theodore Tate who seems to have some control issues and used to be Robin's teacher. Teresa said he remarked on how much she resembled her daughter."

"Gross," Johnna said.

I nodded. "It bears looking into more closely. There's also Robin's boyfriend, a Charles Brzezinski, who she went to an AC/DC concert with the night she died. Teresa said he stays in touch."

"Guilt?" Kyle asked.

"Possibly." I added the new names to Robin's column. "Last is Lulu Geldman. Her mother, Martha Geldman, kept her daughter's diary." I slid it across the table to Kyle. "Can you scan it, and I'll get it back to her?"

Deepty whistled. "Save me from ever having my high school diary entered in evidence."

Harry shot Kyle a stern look.

"I'll be respectful," Kyle said, taking the Garfield notebook. "I assume you want me to read it after I scan it?"

I nodded. "Pay particular attention to any mention of Chris Windahl. He was a coworker at Chi-Chi's, the downtown restaurant Lulu worked at. She had a shift with him the day she died, and Martha seems to think he had an undue interest in her daughter. As you all read in Lulu's file, the manager at Chi-Chi's thought the same thing."

"Downtown Chi-Chi's?" Johnna asked. "The one at City Center?"

"I think so," I said.

"That place was legend," she said, smiling lopsided. "Two levels, all the waitresses dressed up like a Minnesotan's idea of a Mexican girl. Come to think of it, the whole place—food included—felt like a homebound Scandinavian's image of Mexico. Fried ice cream was great, though."

I'd never know. The chain had all but disappeared by the time I visited my first restaurant. "Lulu's father lived in downtown Minneapolis after the divorce. George Geldman. He was never interviewed. Martha thinks he remarried and moved to Chicago."

I looked at Kyle.

"On it," he said, writing himself a note. "Any other unexplored avenues with Lulu's case?"

My focus was back on the whiteboard. "Nothing more to add to any of the columns." I tapped my chin with the marker. "But it's what's *between* the columns that's going to crack this."

"Between?" Kyle asked.

"Connections with the three girls," Harry offered.

I tossed him a grateful glance. It was nice to not have to explain myself. "Gina was a farm girl, according to her dad. Raised her own animals, so dedicated that she showed them at the state fair. Robin was a townie. Lulu was pure city, according to her mom. The closest she got to the country was—"

I froze, mouth open in midsentence, as the slippery piece Martha Geldman had handed me finally clicked into place.

CHAPTER 50

Van

"Was what?" Kyle asked.

"The state fair." I scanned the columns. "What are the chances that the concert Robin had attended was also held there?"

Deepty was already typing. "AC/DC performed at the Met Center in 1986, a venue that has since been razed. But no reason Robin couldn't have attended both the concert and the fair that week."

I loved an efficient researcher. My mind was racing along the possibilities. "If we can confirm all three victims visited the state fair in '86, how difficult will it be to track down the booths they might have stopped by and people they might have met?"

Kyle held up Robin's diary. "I'll start here," he said.

"But," I said, the potential connection already crashing to the earth, "the fair is huge. It might as well be its own county."

We were all silent for several seconds. I was mentally walking a grid pattern of the Minnesota State Fair, the second largest in the country, when a new thought bloomed. "What about the one who was never found?"

I saw the confusion on all their faces. "We suspect all three girls were either murdered or coached to kill themselves," I explained. Harry opened his mouth to shut down speculation—he *hated* conjecture—but I held up a hand. "Three of them dying in the same week from the same apparent poison is too great a coincidence. I'm going to proceed, for the sake of argument, as if the deaths were connected. What are the odds that it was only three girls?"

Kyle nodded as understanding dawned. "You think there's bodies they didn't find?"

I nodded. Behavior sequence analysis had mapped the standard serial killer trajectory, and everyone in this room knew the facts. A serial murderer was frequently but not always abused as a child, often suffered some sort of head injury, and they were well known to torture animals, but unlike the stereotype, many of them lived in plain sight, sometimes building families and strong community connections.

And most operated in a geographically small, defined area.

"We need to search not only for any other similar deaths in or around the fair but also for any Minnesota girls reported missing in '86, plus a year on each side for grace," I told Kyle, before addressing the three forensic scientists. "Which of you can give me a quick rundown of a serial poisoner?"

In the white space before they spoke, I wondered what would happen if one of them described *me*. I felt something like relief when Deepty and not Harry offered the profile.

"If the poisoning victim is female, the killer is most often male. If the victim is male, it's a fifty-fifty split, give or take." She cleared her throat. "Many of them are in the medical field—easy access to poisons."

Deepty glanced over at Johnna, who picked up where she left off. "Estimates are that the actual number of serial poisoners is up to thirty times larger than those who are caught, so much of this is speculation, but on average, poisoners seem to have a high IQ, strong personal discipline, and a tendency toward manipulation and subterfuge."

I nodded. "Might be worth it to check out what medical staff the state fair employed in '86."

I saw something like pride on Harry's face. I had a strong urge to shut it down. "But we're still looking for a needle in a haystack," I said. "*Anything* turn up in the evidence room on the three girls?"

"Nothing," Harry said. "No samples, no evidence."

"Any point in exhuming the bodies?"

He shook his head. "Once the cadaver is skeletonized—which can take up to ten years—the possibility of finding evidence of poisoning is statistically unlikely."

I felt a fire beginning to burn in my belly. Whoever had killed these three girls was going to get away with it if we didn't nail them. Not only get away with it, but continue to kill, if the Emily Barris case was connected.

I addressed Harry, Deepty, and Johnna. "Thanks for bringing your science background to the meeting. If you think of anything else, please let me know." I turned to Kyle. "I need you to keep researching, tracking down Lulu's father on top of coming at the state fair angle every way you can think of, including reaching out to Robert Penchant and Teresa Seer to find out if and when their daughters attended in '86." I wanted to get back to interviews, but I had a duty to the MPD case. "I'll let Comstock know about the possible state fair tie between all three of our victims so he can investigate whether Emily Barris is also somehow connected to the fair."

I glanced at the wall clock. "I'll track down Chris Windahl, Lulu's Chi-Chi's coworker, and plan on visiting him tomorrow if he's still in the area. Then I'll head back to Saint Cloud to talk to Lindy Bell."

I was calculating how long the drive would take when my phone buzzed in my pocket. I pulled it out.

It was a text from Sister Grace.

Hannah and I are not home tomorrow. Visit the day after. We're at 1024 Woodsmen Court, Alexandria, MN. Come alone.

CHAPTER 51

Just Judy

2010

It took him going away to prison for her to realize he hadn't been a hunter all those years; he'd been a *gardener*. And the children they'd planted—their flowers—had done so well. Because they loved him like she did, and because they understood the importance of his calling, they kept the secrets.

Such good flowers.

The federal officers who'd shown up had taken him away to jail, refusing to let her go in his stead. He'd been put away for a misunderstanding, an unfairness that he should never have had to bear. Thankfully, the authorities hadn't found out about the three girls he'd poisoned, the three paving stones that'd been necessary in the laying of their path.

He'd told her their names before he was taken away: Gina, Robin, and Lulu.

She'd made them saints in his absence. He might disapprove when he was released, but she'd been forced to do her best with a lot of things after he was taken away, and that one felt right. They wouldn't be so close to having everything if not for those three girls. Wasn't that deserving of honor?

Thanks be to Saint Gina, Saint Robin, and Saint Lulu.

Because of them, all was possible. Because of them, all was true.

They'd lost some progress when he was arrested, and they'd had to scatter in each direction like seeds on the wind until he called them back. But that was part of the divine plan. She'd chosen to stay close to him, finding a tiny one-room apartment near the prison. She was rusty at being in the world, but it came back to her in fits and starts.

Lift your head when talking to people; looking at your feet makes them uncomfortable.

Leave your hair uncovered, though it feels like public nudity.

The hardest part was having hours where there was nothing to do. Her apartment came with a television, but the one time she'd turned it on, she'd been horrified at the glimpses into the homes and hearts of strangers. But with his support, she gathered the courage to take community ed classes, where she learned accounting, computer usage, how to buy real estate, and basic car and home repairs. She used this knowledge to begin to track down their scattered children and to take proper care of their land. He'd put the assets in her name before he was jailed, she discovered. He was the Messiah.

He'd known his arrest was coming, knew it all.

The only workshop not worth her time was the Basics of Botany class. She knew far more than the teacher about combining herbs to make people sleep, to paralyze them, or to kill them; she just didn't have the instructor's fancy words.

So her life again became productive, but it was lonely, as she was only allowed to visit him one day a week. He looked so vulnerable in his prison orange, but his eyes were vibrant fire. He was gardening in jail, he told her, building their flock even from behind bars. She had a start at that—did he want prison men around their flowers?—but he told her to trust him, and that was the one thing she was born to do.

Plus, the men in prison taught him things that were useful—including how to keep their names out of the paper—and were able to get her the forged birth certificate necessary to earn her driver's license. He told her that her gramma was long dead and there was no one looking for her, but he didn't like to take unnecessary chances.

And then came the best news of all: At her most recent visit, he'd told her he was getting out.

They'd till up a fresh garden, build bigger than before.

He just had a couple things he needed to check on first.

She'd never felt happier. And she didn't think he'd mind that she told some of the others where they'd be going. He'd be elated to have them all back together.

Wouldn't he?

CHAPTER 52

Van

I was beat by the end of the day, but the thought of seeing Owl gave me a second wind. I hurried inside the Bark Barn, hopeful that the day had gone well. My stomach plummeted when I spotted her back inside the time-out crate near the desk.

The counter worker fully removed her springy hair binder to deliver the bad news. This was serious. "Sorry. It's not going to work."

I glanced in disbelief from her to the crate. Did they really need to put Owl on display where everyone could see who the naughty dog was? "It can't be that bad."

The worker shook her head solemnly. "She's terrorizing the other animals. We can't have her here."

"But I brought her to a dog park yesterday. She did fine." With one dog, anyhow. I knelt next to the crate. Owl stared at me from inside, her head hung, her butt still. "Did she bite anyone?"

"No." The worker actually clucked. "But we think it's only a matter of time."

"What am I supposed to do with her while I'm at work?" I knew it wasn't their problem, but I needed help. Tomorrow, I could track down Chris Windahl, Lulu's Chi-Chi's coworker, for an interview, run home to let Owl out, then drive the hour to Saint Cloud to talk to Lindy Bell.

That was one day solved—Owl'd be fine for those short bursts—but I needed to go to Alexandria and who knew where else the day after.

"Sometimes, if there's stress at home, the dogs bring it here with them," she said, glancing at the long line forming behind me.

Does your owner being murdered count?

"Thanks a bunch," I said, opening the crate. Owl did the crawl of shame toward me, her head and butt all but dragging. I kissed her before clipping the leash to her collar. "Come on, girl, we'll go somewhere where you're appreciated."

Problem was, I didn't know where that was. The only animal she seemed to get along with had been Alexis's dog, Zoso, and I didn't want to be indebted to her. Well, I'd cross that bridge when I came to it.

It took a long walk across Loring Park for Owl to return to her cheery self—they must've really done a number on her self-esteem at the Bark Barn—but by the time we returned to the apartment, her butt wiggle was back. I fed her, microwaved myself a bag of popcorn, worked some on my laptop, and considered trimming my hair and fingernails—both of which were past due—and showering.

Instead, I fell into bed. I hadn't had a decent night's sleep in two weeks, and it'd only gotten worse since Emily Barris's death. I was thinking of her, wondering how she was connected to the three girls who'd died in '86, or maybe it was her ex, Otto Pusch, who was the connection, when sleep slipped a black bag over my head and stuffed me into the trunk.

It's dark when I open my eyes.

What woke me? I scan the room, feeling uneasy, like I've woken up on a movie set, or in a stranger's bed. Something is very wrong.

That's when I realize I can't move.

I'm fighting to lift my head when a shape in the corner that I thought was a pile of clothes shifts, peeling away from the wall and shambling toward me. My heart pumps hot. I struggle to make a noise—I've heard that if you make a sound while in sleep paralysis, your body must respond—but I'm frozen.

The shape sidles toward me, the light murky and liquid. This has to be a nightmare. I'm in my apartment that isn't my apartment. I try to focus on the figure, to blink the swamp grit out of my eyes, but the shape is shadow until suddenly it isn't.

It's Frank Roth.

I almost swallow my tongue, turning animal with fear.

He looks like he did in the plane crash video, his hair gone silver, his eyes two different colors, his jaw so square, so wide, but his skin is twisted, melted. He leans over and whispers in my ear.

"I'm going to live forever."

His breath smells like cadaver. When he drops on the bed next to me, the mattress bends to him.

Owl, I scream, or try to, but my mouth isn't mine.

Frank strokes my head. "I miss your beautiful hair, Lucky Bird," he says, smiling, using the nickname he's given me. He reaches for my hand. "But these nails are too long. You really should clip them."

He brings my hand to his face. I think he means to more closely examine my nails, but then he opens his mouth and begins nibbling at each finger, chewing off the nails with his teeth. Once they are all short, helpless tears dripping down my cheeks, he stretches his mouth even wider and swallows me whole, one appendage at a time, until I'm inside him. His interior smells like freshly butchered chicken—copper and organ. All my Sisters are already here.

I am quivering jelly.

"You're late," Sister Grace says from a pocket of Frank's inside. She appears angry. "She wasn't going to be able to wait much longer."

She points to a huddled figure I didn't notice before.

It's my best friend, my favorite Sister, the girl Frank destroyed when he slammed her head into the side of the horse trough and held her underwater. *Veronica.* She's no longer human, though. She's a puddle on the floor of him, boneless, her brain pulsing outside her head.

The horror finds my voice, and I scream as I claw my way up his throat, my Sisters grabbing at my ankles to pull me down. I climb, climb forever, never getting any closer to escape, until finally my strength is gone and I have no choice but to drop into the pit of Frank, a boneless blob next to Veronica.

Next thing I knew, it was daylight.

I was in my apartment, Owl curled next to me.

I held my hands over my head.

My nails were bloody nubs.

Never in my life had I chewed my fingernails.

CHAPTER 53

Van

My phone was blinking when I walked into my office. I considered not listening to the message. Turned out waking up with magically short nails after dreaming your dead father chewed them off wasn't conducive to restful sleep. I was tired, unsettled, and wanted only to check my work email and grab a company car before hitting the road.

But I was here, might as well listen. I jabbed the button.

"Reed, it's Chandler. Take Kyle with you into the field today."

That was it. No more details, no reason why. I groaned. Was I babysitting or being babysat? Either option felt as good—and as useful—as a G-string, but what choice did I have? After ensuring there were no urgent work emails awaiting me, I stopped by Kyle's office, half hoping he'd say he couldn't come with.

He was working behind his desk, posture as straight as a stick. He smiled as I walked in. "Chandler says I get to go outside today."

Well, that settled that. "I've really been tying you to your computer that much?"

He stood, grabbing his dark-gray suit coat off the back of his chair. "Not just you. Somehow, I've become *everyone's* Velma."

"There's worse things you could be," I said. "Shaggy, for example."

"Chris Windahl?" he said, ignoring my comment and gliding past me. "He's a chef at the Wita Waste Café these days. Works morning shift."

"I know." I'd uncovered the same information on my laptop last night. The café had been a fancy Minneapolis mainstay through the '80s, situated on Wita Waste, an island in the Mississippi walkable to downtown Minneapolis. The restaurant hadn't been updated since then, but it still carried some of its former charm. "That's a step up from Chi-Chi's. I'm driving."

"Figured."

If I had to work side by side with someone, Kyle would do. He was no Bart, all grump and comfy as your favorite sweater, or Harry, clean lines and crisp words, but at least he only spoke if he actually had something to say. He was quiet as I tooled through Saint Paul, slapping down the sun visor as we drove east. The morning felt hot, almost feverish, after the refrigerator cool of yesterday. Many of the cars we passed had their windows rolled down, the diversity of the Cities coming through in the music that leaked out—Prince, Ethio-jazz, bluegrass.

"Lulu Geldman had her day at the state fair recorded in her diary," Kyle offered. "Robert Penchant confirmed Gina attended the fair the same day. He still had her ticket stub in a scrapbook his wife made after Gina died. Says he's pretty sure Lindy Bell went with her, drove them both down."

I drummed the steering wheel. "You ask Chandler to come with me today, or did he ask you?"

I felt Kyle's eyes slide toward me. "I asked him if I could get out in the field. He suggested you."

Whether that was true, I couldn't tell. It was definitely something I'd lie about if I were Kyle. "You called Robin's mom? Teresa Seer?"

"No answer."

"I can stop by tomorrow, see if she has anything new to add. I'd like to talk to science-teacher-Ted as well as Robin's boyfriend, Chuck." The state fair angle had the most shine, but I needed to visit every corner of this case.

"Did you tell Windahl we're coming?" Kyle asked as we crossed the Hennepin Avenue Bridge. The Mississippi River glistened, reflecting the budding trees on its banks. Wita Waste—the original Dakota name, recently reclaimed, for the island—came into view on our right, an oasis in the middle of the river that contrasted with the bustling city on each side.

"Nope," I said. "I don't want him to no-show, like Lindy Bell. If he's here, we won't take much of his time."

I curved the car around until we were on the island. It wasn't even one square mile. A few hundred people lived on it, most of the houses straight out of the Gilded Age. The place had a tucked-in, storybook feel, like a time machine slice set against the downtown Minneapolis skyline.

I parked in front of the café, which was a refurbished factory made of whitewashed brick. Kyle let me lead the way inside. The front door was locked. According to the sign, the place served breakfast only in the summer months; the rest of the year, it was exclusively lunch and dinner.

"The cooks might be setting up," I said, walking around back. We passed by the manicured front and side of the building until we reached the rear dumpster. Sure enough, the metal door was propped open, the woody, bitter smell of a fresh-smoked cigarette clinging to the air. I was deciding whether to knock or poke my head in when a man in his late fifties stepped out, a lit cigarette dangling from his mouth.

"That can't be up to code, can it?" I smiled. "Chris Windahl?"

The cigarette pointed downward as the man's eyes widened, and then he took off running.

CHAPTER 54

Van

The thing about an island was you could get only so far on foot, and you were slowed considerably if you were a regular smoker. As I chased after Windahl, I considered all my options for taking him down. I took regular walks, was well trained in self-defense, and was as quick as silver.

But the easiest way was almost always the best way.

I gave a little puff of speed, enough to slip me directly behind Windahl, and knocked one of his feet behind the other.

He fell with an *oof.*

I walked around to his front, Kyle at his back. I crouched. "Like I said, Chris Windahl?"

He turned over, pulled himself into a sitting position, and rubbed gravel out of his palms, glowering at me. "Yeah?" he grunted.

"How about you take us back to the kitchen and answer a few questions."

The Wita Waste Café's dining room might be fancy, but its break room was identical to the ones in every restaurant I'd ever visited: a pop-ringed card table crammed between metal shelves, uncomfortable chairs squeezed close, a fine layer of grease coating every surface. Windahl appeared to be the only one working this early in the day.

After I pulled out a photo of Lulu Geldman, he confirmed that he'd known her but denied seeing her outside of work.

"I always wondered what happened to her," he said. His beard and mustache were a few days past a shave, and a yellow spot on his lip where his cigarette had been hanging suggested he had a poor relationship with his shower. "Left work one day and never came back."

"So, you two didn't hang outside of work?" I asked.

He snorted. "Naw, those waitresses didn't fraternize with us kitchen guys. Pretty snooty, most of them."

Kyle asked the obvious question. "If you didn't do anything wrong, why'd you run?"

Windahl scowled. "Only lost kids and girls in horror movies trust cops."

He wasn't wrong. My best guess was the guy had drugs on him, but that wasn't my problem. I needed him to take me back to 1986, show me the landscape of Lulu's last day. "What was it like working at Chi-Chi's?"

His chest puffed with a restrained laugh. "A real celebration of food, you know?"

When Kyle and I didn't respond, he kept going. "It was my first cooking gig, though it wasn't really what I'd call 'cooking.' Most everything was premade. We slopped it together and heated it, though from all the training they had us go through, you'd think we were handling nuclear secrets back there."

"Were the waitresses trained, too?" I asked.

"Yeah, I suppose. We all watched the same video on the history of the place, anyhow." His eyes sparked, like he'd remembered something. "Lulu hated that video. I overheard her telling Caesar how demeaning it was. That's the word she used. *'Demeaning.'* Figured she was a women's libber, which was one more reason I wouldn't have been interested in her. She hated the part in the video where the guy who founded the place said that he chose the name as a tribute to his wife. 'Chi-chis' are 'boobs' in Mexico, I guess, and she apparently had quite a pair." He snickered, then tried on an apologetic look, aiming it at me. "Things were different then."

"No, they weren't," I said matter-of-factly. "Shit still stank."

Windahl glanced to Kyle for support, but Kyle remained stone-faced.

"Maybe the chupacabra got her," Windahl offered, clearly trying to change the subject.

"Chupacabra?" I asked.

"Yeah." He was getting fired up at the memory. "Everyone said the place was haunted. Not a single restaurant stayed there very long. Italianni's, Chi-Chi's, Ol' Mexico, they came and went. What else could be responsible but a demon, a location that prime?"

"A demon?" I'd found that repeating someone's words back to them was often the shortest route to showing them they were an idiot.

He rubbed the back of his neck. "All I'm saying is people swore it was haunted. That's all I remember. Maybe you should track Caesar down. He was a cook, like me. Now *there* was a guy who had a crush on Lulu. He worshipped the ground she walked on."

I pulled out my notebook. "You have a last name?"

"Naw," he said. "What was that, forty years ago? You're lucky I had a first."

He had the definite air of someone trying to get the heat off himself, but I'd follow any lead. "Anything else you can tell me? Anything else you remember?"

He shifted in his chair. "When'd Lulu go missing again?"

"Late August 1986," Kyle said.

Windahl closed his eyes, the picture of helpfulness. "End of month, we would've all been stressed about the first coming. Welfare checks. We'd be slammed." His eyes flicked open. "Other than that, it was the same old, same old. Sling rice and beans, try not to burn yourself handling the hot plates, and take home as many chips as you . . ."

His head cocked, and his eyes went unfocused.

"What is it?" I asked, my blood suddenly sizzling.

"Something's coming to me." He tugged his bottom lip, reached for the photo of Lulu. "Yeah, she was a cute one. Caesar liked her, like I said. I only know because he got mighty mad when some guy came round looking for her one day, can't remember if it was her last. The dude came up to me when I was outside smoking, asked for Lulu. I went in and got her." He was nodding excitedly now, a satisfied smile on his face. "Yeah, that was the last time I think I saw her. She never came back to work after that."

My pulse was kicking. "Was this him, minus a few decades?" I pulled up the photo of Otto Pusch on my phone, turned it so Windahl could see.

"Naw." Windahl screwed up his face. "The guy I remember was maybe middle or late twenties, wearing asshole glasses. Those mirrored ones. I remember thinking he looked a little like Tom Cruise, maybe, except his jaw was as square as a stone box. That's why it stuck in my head. 'What's Tom Cruise doing at Chi-Chi's back door?' I thought to myself. Said those exact words to a buddy later that night. We had a good laugh."

The mention of Tom Cruise scratched at something, but I couldn't place it. It didn't matter. *We might have our first actual lead.* I slid Windahl a card. "You've been very helpful. Give me a call if you think of anything else?"

He nodded, but he looked at the card like it was a trap.

I was already dialing Martha Geldman on the way back to my car. "Hello, Mrs. Geldman," I said when she picked up. "Can I run a description by you, and you can let me know if it sounds familiar?"

I unlocked the car while I spoke. Kyle slid into the passenger seat and pulled Lulu's diary from his briefcase, paging through it immediately.

Martha Geldman confirmed that Lulu didn't hang out with any men in their twenties, especially anyone who resembled Tom Cruise. According to Kyle, her diary confirmed it.

"We haven't had any other mention of a Tom Cruise look-alike on this case, have we?" I asked Kyle as he put the diary back. That detail was still nagging at me.

"Not that I know of. Should we ask Lindy Bell?" Kyle asked. "See if she saw a guy like that?"

"Yep," I said, "but I need to stop by my apartment on the way out of town."

If it'd been up to me, Kyle would never have seen my place, but there wasn't time to worry about that, not if we had a break in the case. So I didn't object when he followed me up, pretended I couldn't see the mess through his eyes, told him not to touch a thing while I brought Owl on a quick walk. The more people who knew about Owl, the worse my position was, but what could I do? Leave her alone all day? It probably would have been easier to just bring Kyle on the walk, given how Owl seemed invested in sniffing every inch of him, but I didn't want to answer questions about her, so I dragged her outside, just her and me, let her do her business, and ran her back up.

Kyle had cleared a corner of the kitchen table when I returned and was typing away on his laptop. "Your apartment is gross," he said as I unclipped Owl.

I scanned his face for signs of judgment and found none. He was just stating facts.

"I'm not asking you to move in," I said. "You ready to head?"

He nodded and snapped his computer shut.

I rubbed my arms. The morning had started out unseasonably warm, but it was still chilly in the shadows, and I'd brought the cold in with me.

"You want to bring this scarf?" he asked, stopping by the door.

"What?"

He bent over, tugged something from the edge of a clothes pile, and turned. He held a red knit scarf in his hand.

My blood froze.

"Van, you okay?"

"Where'd you get that?" I choked out.

His chin jerked back. "Off your floor. Just now. You saw me."

I did. I also knew I didn't own a red scarf. I glanced at my nails, shorter than they should be, and felt hot tears push at my eyes. The room was starting to close in on me when I remembered something: I'd brought home the scarf from the coffee shop. But I'd left it in the back of my car, hadn't I?

My car that was parked in the BCA lot.

This weirdness was getting out of control. I couldn't drive there now to check for it, and what would be the point? If there was no scarf, it meant I'd brought it into the house. If there was a scarf, it meant I somehow got my hands on a second one, right? Bought it a while back and forgot about it in a pile of clothes.

Except I knew that wasn't true.

"Let's get going to Saint Cloud," I said, squatting to snuffle my nose into Owl's neck. "We don't have much time to waste."

Some of us less than others.

CHAPTER 55

Van

Kyle clacked away on his laptop during the entire ride to Saint Cloud, using his phone's hotspot to get online. An old-school detective like Comstock would've made fun of Kyle, calling him a nerd, a pencil pusher, a soft man, but connecting information from the internet to our databases was how most crimes were solved these days.

Probably Bart wouldn't have been a fan, either. I could hear him as clear as if he were in the car: *Kid, you don't know a thing about the people posting stuff online. Nothing beats looking someone in the eye when you want to know the truth.*

I suddenly missed him so much it burned my gut.

"What did Comstock say when you told him about the possible state fair link?" Kyle asked, not bothering to look up. He must have read something that'd jogged his memory.

"I left a message."

His fingers stilled, and he glanced out the window. "What do you think is the connection between Emily Barris and those three girls in 1986? It's a pretty long time for a killer to stay dormant."

The flat, brown prairie abutting 94 flew by, as boring as a plate. "It's also a pretty unique poison to use."

Kyle looked back at me. "You think the killer chose it because it makes his victim smile like that?"

I'd thought about it. It would be a memorable signature, if he was the kind of killer who was into that. "It's more likely the poison is easy to get hold of, hard to trace. My guess is the grin is an unfortunate side effect more than the goal."

Kyle snorted.

"What?" I asked, ready to be offended. Murder was not a laughing matter.

"Just envisioning Harry's face, listening to the two of us guessing at things."

My mouth twitched in response. "He's a genius, though."

Kyle stretched his fingers until they popped, the gesture deceptively casual. "You two dating?"

I swallowed wrong and started coughing. "Me and Harry? God, no. What made you think that?"

He shrugged. "Something happened between you two in Duluth. You came back different."

No lie there. "You know how it is. You work out in the field with someone . . ." I let the thought hang, then brought us back to the case. "When I left Comstock the message, I asked him to give me a ring if he uncovered any connection between Barris and the state fair. She wouldn't have been born in '86, but if our guy had a booth there every year, or worked for the fair itself, they could have crossed paths since."

A comfortable silence landed between us, so I went back to studying the terrain, wondering about the type of Europeans who settled in Minnesota. Farmers, obviously. This land was made for it. So why had Frank Roth left a familiar landscape and traveled to Florida? I'd never been myself, but a kindergartener would know the climate was a one-eighty from Minnesota. Had Frank tried farming there? It'd been such a big part of his life.

The first Saint Cloud exit loomed. I got us to Lindy Bell's without GPS. When we pulled in front of her house, a curtain twitched on the bottom floor. "Someone's inside."

Kyle closed his laptop and slid it under his seat. "Hope she's not a runner, like Windahl."

"Seems to be the opposite," I said, staring at the front porch as the door opened and a tall woman with a silvery buzz cut stepped onto it.

"Hello!" I called as I got out of my car. The second-floor dogs started barking furiously. That must have been annoying to live below. "Lindy Bell?"

She squinted, though there was no sun visible in the slate-gray sky. "Yeah. You the cops from Minneapolis?"

"Bureau of Criminal Apprehension," I said, walking toward her. I was mindful of my posture, keeping it relaxed, slow. "I stopped by to see you yesterday, but no one was home."

She crossed her arms. "Sorry about that. I went out with friends."

No mention of whether she'd done it purposely to avoid me or she'd forgotten about our scheduled meeting. "Do you have some time now?"

She tilted her head at Kyle, then looked back at me. "Sure. Come on in."

Her apartment smelled of cinnamon, and an essential-oil diffuser puffed out soft, wide clouds. The inside looked the same as it had from the window: garage-sale purchases, everything well used and clean, nothing matching, nothing manufactured in the last decade. She led us to a plain, round dining room table surrounded by four chairs, all different heights and wood.

"How long have you lived here?" I asked conversationally.

She dropped into the farthest chair and clasped her hands in front of her. Her body language was tense. *Could be having two agents in her house, could be something else.*

"A few years." She swallowed. "Prudence reached out to me. Said you stopped by her work. Haven't seen her since our twenty-five-year reunion. I almost didn't go, you know? Not much for me to brag about."

Her eyes flew to my face, then dropped to her hands. "Worked at the same place since I graduated. No husband, no kids."

I glanced around her sparse dining room, over at her living room. "Who are they?" I asked, pointing at an eight-by-ten of a boy and girl, both in their teens, resting on the table by the couch.

Her face warmed. "My niece and nephew. If you ask them, I'm not so bad."

"I believe it," I said. I did. She had the singular posture of a woman bowed by guilt. She'd never grown beyond the crush of it, similar to Gina's dad. Unlike him, though, she seemed to have formed relationships and kept steady work. "Can you tell us what you remember about the night you, Gina, and Prudence colored your hair?"

Her bark of laughter seemed to surprise her. "I forgot about that. Pru must have told you. Robert never would have. He thought Gina walked on water." A shadow crossed her face. "I always felt bad that our little act of defiance was the last thing he had to remember her by. She was a good kid. We all were."

"Is it all right if I run through the timeline we have?" Kyle asked, startling her. It was like she'd forgotten he was there.

"Sure," she said.

He opened his file and recited the facts as we knew them: Robert and Jill Penchant leave at six p.m. Lindy and Prudence pull up at six thirty. Between nine and ten, both girls go home. The Penchants return around midnight and find Gina on her bed.

"She was grinning ear to ear," Lindy finished for him, her face stark. "I don't know what time they got home, but everyone heard what Gina looked like." She glanced at me, her eyes pleading. "Is it true? She died with a weird smile on her face?"

"Yes," I said. No point in denying it. "Any idea what happened to her?"

Lindy shook her head. "No. I mean, the rumor was that she was scared to death. Everyone at Rockville was into the Ouija board that summer and fall." She leaned forward. "The thing is, we didn't even use it. It was our turn, sure, and Gina brought out the board, but then some encyclopedia salesman came by, ruined the whole vibe."

Kyle stiffened. It was nearly imperceptible, but it was there. He'd need to work on that. Most humans—especially those who'd suffered trauma—were hyper-tuned to body language, though they might not know it. Tightening of shoulders, artificial smiles—the smallest unplanned gesture could shut down a witness.

"Encyclopedia salesman?" I asked. "There wasn't anything in the file about that."

She shrugged. "I told my parents. They said they told the police."

"What'd he look like?" I asked.

She shook her head. "Pru and I never saw him. We all had plastic grocery store bags on our heads. It was part of the dye job, to protect our regular hair from the lemon juice or whatever. Gina was the only one who went to the door."

My neck was itching. "How long after that did she ask you to leave?"

Lindy picked at a fingernail. "Right after. I mean *right*." Her eyes grew glossy, like tears were building up. "You think the person came back and killed her?"

"We're just trying to fill out the timeline," I said. "Don't suppose you saw what make of car he drove?"

Her chin quivered. "No. We didn't even hear it pull up. I remember how shocked we all were when the knock came. I should have made sure the police knew about it." Her voice grew thin as she repeated herself. "I should have made sure."

"Lindy," I said firmly. "You were a kid, one who'd just lost a close friend. It was *not* your job to make sure of anything. Can you walk us through what else you remember?"

She closed her eyes, a full shudder traveling through her body. The thing about pain this deep was it didn't go away. You could do your work and shrink it, get better at identifying it when it showed up, but it was always there. Violent criminals didn't commit *an act*. They warped lives.

"Gina came back from the front door. She wasn't herself anymore. She flopped on the bed, said she had a headache, kicked us out. I thought she was being a drama queen." Lindy's eyes snapped open, sharp. "You know what the last thing I said about her was, before I knew what happened to her? On the way out, I said to Pru that Gina would rather die than give up the center of attention. Rather *die*," she wailed.

My skin grew hot. *We all needed someone to blame.* "That sounds like exactly what I would have said about one of my sisters at that age."

Kyle stirred next to me—I didn't talk about my family—but it was worth it when Lindy said, "Really?" Her expression was naked hope.

"Really," I lied. She didn't need to know that emotions hadn't been allowed on Frank's Farm. "Our prefrontal cortexes are still forming at that age. We're fiends." I reached out to touch her arm. "You're not the one who killed Gina, and nothing you could have done would have saved her. But you *can* help us to make sure we have all the information now. Do you remember going to the state fair with Gina that year, a few days before you all dyed your hair?"

"Do I *remember*? It was my first time driving in the Cities! I gave us both ten heart attacks." She relaxed her hands, blood flowing back into her white knuckles. "It was a great time, though, once we were there. The place was huge."

"Anything unusual happen?" I asked. "Did you meet anyone?"

She shook her head. "Naw, we went alone, though we could have left with a whole bunch of guys." Her cheeks pinked. "We were cute, young, and tight. That lasts for about a minute." She glanced down at herself as if to demonstrate. "Though it sure felt good to have all that attention. But no, we were there to look at the animals, eat some of the food, take a couple rides."

I glanced at my notepad. I hadn't written a thing since we'd arrived. I was about to close it when Lindy said, "There was one guy. He took a real shine to Gina."

My breath razored. "What did he look like?"

She tapped her chin. "Tom Cruise, if you can believe it."

Her words sounded like they were coming from far away as I fell down, down, down a tunnel. I had a terrible feeling growing in me, a cancer in my belly, but it couldn't be.

She continued, oblivious to my reaction. "Only a little, and only from a certain angle, but Gina had such a crush on Tom that she was lapping up that guy's attention like ice cream. I was jealous, I remember. He wore those mirrored sunglasses. Gave him a mysterious air." She chuckled. "Girls can be dumb, you know?"

Horror sealed my throat as past and present aligned with terrifying clarity. It wasn't the eerie coincidence of two reports of a Tom Cruise look-alike stalking these girls. It was the gut-wrenching realization of what had been bothering me ever since Chris Windahl described the man. Before she vanished, Caroline Steinbeck—Harry's little sister— had been telling Harry about someone chillingly similar, a man she'd met earlier, the same man who'd likely abducted her: *The dude had black hair, for-real black, not dark brown. He had a nice smile, like Tom Cruise, where the front tooth is a little off. But his eyes were weird. One brown, one blue. Can you believe it? Two different eyes. I guess it was a little creepy.*

Frank Roth couldn't have been responsible for Gina's, Robin's, and Lulu's deaths.

It was impossible.

I was losing my mind.

CHAPTER 56

Van

Windahl's reference hadn't been enough to knock it loose, but back-to-back with what Lindy had just said, the detail train-pounded me in the face. Caroline's description had spelled it out. I'd written off the reference to the actor as a girl's imagination, wanting to superimpose someone famous, someone safe, over the adult man giving her uncomfortable attention. Had it been the same for Lindy and Gina, girlish fantasy seeing a resemblance where there was none, or had the man they'd encountered been the same one who'd abducted Caroline?

I hadn't seen my first movie until college, and though I had a fleeting image of Tom Cruise from grocery store magazine covers, I'd never watched anything starring him. Did my father resemble the actor?

The thought was ridiculous.

I was grabbing at straws.

Two of the three victims, according to witnesses, had both—shortly before their deaths—interacted with someone who resembled one of the most famous men in the world. *That* was a lead. *That* was something we could follow. The idea that it was connected to Frank Roth had come simply because I was researching him, that and me succumbing to sleeplessness and paranoia. Seeing red scarves, sleep-clipping my nails, blurring my visions with reality. I was running on fumes when I needed to be operating at my peak.

Lindy had no more information to share but promised she'd reach out if she remembered anything else. Kyle hopped straight back online as soon as we were inside the car, and I was grateful for the silence. I tried shoving myself into a meditative state.

I am safe. I am grown. I am free.

I practiced the breathing exercises my therapist had given me, quietly so Kyle wouldn't notice. In through the nose for a count of eight, out through the mouth for a count of eight. When was the last time I'd seen my therapist? Weeks? That was the problem with mental health issues. When you most needed help was the time you were least equipped to seek it out.

Here were my problems in descending order of life destroying:

Tomorrow, I was meeting with my Sisters for the first time since the commune had been broken up. I'd bring a photo of Caroline, the black-and-white one every newspaper had run when she disappeared. Whether or not they recognized her, I was going to come clean with Harry about Frank Roth's possible connection. He'd hate me less if I had a lead, but he was going to hate me regardless for keeping this from him. *I'd* hate me.

My ID had been found at a murder scene. So far, I had no explanation why.

Three girls had been murdered in 1986. I'd met the families. They deserved justice. What happened to their daughters *mattered*.

Finally, I was responsible for another living creature, a dog that wasn't mine but that I loved like family.

My eyes felt clotty, my blood thick. I blinked rapidly.

"You want to hear some good news?" Kyle asked.

An involuntary noise, like a cry, came from the back of my throat. I unscrewed my hands from the steering wheel, opting for a more relaxed posture. "Sure," I told him.

He turned his computer toward me, though I couldn't read it while driving.

"I found our fourth," he said, his tone triumphant.

"Fourth what?" I asked, but I knew immediately.

"Fourth girl gone. A Judith Morsa went missing from her hometown of Sauk Centre, Minnesota, in August of 1986."

Sauk Centre, just up the road from Saint Cloud following Interstate 94. Also on the way to Alexandria and my Sisters. My brain was spinning how to use this information. "Morsa? Sounds Swedish. Don't suppose she visited the fair that year?"

"I suppose she did." Kyle tapped the screen. "She lived with her grandmother, an Anne Morsa. Anne didn't report Judith missing right away. Figured she was just having some fun. But when she received a Minnesota State Fair letter from her, postmarked August 25, 1986, she called the police. They never found the girl, but her grandma makes a Facebook post every year on the day the postcard was sent, asking if anyone's seen her granddaughter. This is last year's."

I spared a glance. There was no photo, which surprised me. Her grandmother must not have known how to scan and upload pictures. "Send me a link to that page, add all the information you found to the file, and set up an appointment for me to meet with Anne Morsa tomorrow afternoon. Alone."

He nodded. If my last request bothered him, he didn't mention it. He also didn't comment when I pulled into a coffee shop drive-through on the edge of the city and ordered two large espressos, double shots each. Good thing, because I would have ripped out his throat. Caffeine and a need to find out what happened to those girls were all I had keeping me going.

When the coffee came, the acrid scent made me realize I had only one option for Owl until I could bring myself to return her to the shelter.

CHAPTER 57

Van

Alexis answered the door the next morning looking like she'd had a good night's sleep.

That made one of us.

She knelt to greet Owl, Zoso sitting back just inside the duplex like a very good dog. Owl had none of Zoso's cool. She *vibrated* with excitement to see Alexis.

"Thanks again for offering to watch her," I said.

Alexis had been my only option besides returning Owl to the shelter, which I simply could not bear to do, not yet. I loved digging my face into the rolls at her neck, hugging her, her smell, walking with her in the park, seeing the world through her eyes. Forget that the only reason I'd been able to carve out a few hours of sleep last night was that she'd lain across my stomach like a security blanket.

I didn't deserve her, but I needed her.

"No problem," Alexis said, standing to take the dog food I offered. "She eat twice a day?"

"Yep." I told her how much, leaning over to pet Zoso when he deigned to nuzzle my hand. Owl chose that moment to lunge forward, getting between me and the black dog. In her exuberance, she knocked a bronze Buddha statue off a table just inside the door.

It fell to the ground with a clatter. Owl tossed me that look of hers, like she was permanently apologizing. This time, it actually fit the situation. I patted her head.

"Sorry," I said.

Alexis picked up the statue and set it back on the table. "No harm. She's just excited to be here."

"It might be overnight," I said tentatively, glancing at the dent now in Buddha's head. "That okay?"

I had a lot to fit in today. Chuck and Teresa in Clearwater first thing, then Anne Morsa in Sauk Centre, then on to Alexandria and my Sisters. It might have been the lack of sleep, or all the thoughts around my Father, but I'd woken up with a fatalistic feeling about meeting with Grace and Hannah, like I might not come back.

Alexis would know what to do if I didn't return for Owl.

"We're happy to have her." Alexis smiled, lighting up both her dimples. It made me unspeakably sad. I'd never been that free, that joyful. I'd had close female connections at the Farm. It'd almost killed me to lose them, but that had been a whole different world. I was an adult now, out of the commune. The timing wasn't great, but what if there was a future where Alexis and I were friends?

"Thanks," I said. I touched her arm.

Owl made a grumbling noise and walked over to lean against my leg. Did she also think this was the last time we'd see each other? The thought was unbearable, and I suddenly couldn't get out of there fast enough. "You have my number," I called over my shoulder as I hurried to my car. "And let's go for coffee sometime, all right?"

It was a coward's move, not saying goodbye to Owl, but I wouldn't have been able to leave her if I had, and I owed Gina, Robin, and Lulu better than that. Anyhow, the way Alexis's face lit up at the mention of coffee almost made up for it. I'd taken the first step toward making a new friend. It felt surprisingly good.

Robin's mother, Teresa, had yet to return my call, but Chuck Brzezinski, the boy Robin had gone to a concert with the last night of her life, had agreed to meet at the Clearwater Travel Plaza in an hour. I hoped he'd be able to confirm Robin had visited the state fair. Either way, I'd swing by Teresa's afterward. With luck, her husband, Ted, would be there, too.

The clock was ticking.

Charles "Chuck" Brzezinski was in his midfifties, with pleasant smile lines and salt-and-pepper hair feathered in a style that I hadn't seen since the movie posters in Gina Penchant's room. Whether Chuck was frozen at his greatest trauma point or simply liked the hairstyle was anyone's guess.

He stood from the booth as I approached. "Van Reed?" he asked.

"Yep. Chuck?"

He nodded as we shook hands. "You weren't lying about your hair. It's *white* white." His cheeks bloomed. Had he realized commenting on someone else's appearance wasn't cool? If so, it made me like him instantly. We all messed up sometimes; I appreciated a person who recognized when they had.

"No reason to lie," I said. *About that, at least.* "Thanks for meeting with me."

"It's not a problem." He signaled for a waitress. When she came over, I ordered a cup of coffee, though my insides already felt acidic. The travel center was hopping, a convoy of eighteen-wheelers parked out front and the booths packed with long-haul truckers.

"Teresa Seer mentioned that you still visit her."

Chuck's mouth pinched. "She was supposed to be my mother-in-law."

I accepted a cup of diner coffee, reaching for the silver pot of half-and-half. Chuck did not wear a wedding band. "She said you and Robin were planning on moving to Alexandria together."

"Not together." The crinkle at the corner of his eyes told me it was an old joke. "On the same street."

"Did you end up attending college there?"

He ran his hands through his hair. "Yeah. I sleepwalked through the whole year, but I somehow earned a certificate. Been a truck driver ever since."

"Any idea what happened to Robin?"

His glance drifted toward the window, tracking a pair of men in flannel shirts and ball caps. "I always figured she killed herself. She seemed happy, but you can't always tell, you know?" He tipped his coffee cup and stared into the bottom of it. "My brother's friend took his own life the year before. We thought he was the most laid-back guy we'd ever met. There aren't always signs."

I took out my notebook. "Had she said anything to indicate she was depressed?"

He shook his head. "No." His voice dropped. "I didn't walk her to the door that night."

The file had mentioned the same detail. It was clearly important to him. "What?"

"We went to see AC/DC at the Met Center. Damn, was that a good concert. I was on top of the world. So buzzed with just plain happiness that, for the first time since we started dating, I didn't walk Red to the door." His eyes met mine, pleading. "You think that's enough to push someone over the edge?"

"No," I said with all the certainty in the world. "I don't."

He nodded, took a sip of his own coffee. "That's what everyone says."

And he believed none of them. Like Lindy with Gina and Harry with Caroline, we all needed someone to blame. "Do you happen to know if Robin visited the state fair in 1986?"

"Sure," he said, his gaze back outside and his voice telling me he was lost in memory. "That's where we got the concert tickets."

I set my cup down hard. "What?"

My tone pulled him all the way back. "Day before the concert, we visited the fair. Robin wanted those chocolate chip cookies that come in a plastic bucket. Right outside the gate, there's this guy scalping concert tickets."

My blood hummed like an electric wire. "What'd he look like?"

Chuck rubbed the bridge of his nose. "Bald, I think. Kinda weaselly. I remember he was a little guy, shorter than me and I'm five nine."

No mention of Tom Cruise. "Did he look like this guy?" I showed him the current picture of Pusch, told him to shave off forty years.

"Naw," Chuck said. "Not that I remember."

"Anyone else at the fair stick out? Anyone give Robin undue attention?"

His eyes grew misty. "You've gotta understand that Robin was beautiful, man. Natural redhead, a smile like the sun coming out." He glanced at his coffee cup. "But she only had eyes for me. She didn't talk to anyone else that day, not that I saw."

Disappointment dug in its claws. "No other unusual activity the last week? Nobody she mentioned meeting?"

His head tilted like he had something, but I saw it slip away. "Sorry. It was so long ago."

I nodded. "How well do you know Teresa Seer's current husband?"

"Ted Tate?" He sucked on his teeth. "Robin had him for chem. I wasn't smart enough to get in one of his classes. She never mentioned him, really, not that I recall. Who talks about their teachers unless they're unpleasant or super cool? I guess Mr. Tate was neither." He shrugged. "He seems to make Mrs. Seer happy."

It was oddly charming how he referred to both of them formally. "Did you ever marry?" I hadn't planned to ask the question. It just rose to the top.

His mouth drew down at the corners. "Naw," he said. "I know what I had. I wasn't going to recruit some poor woman to be second best, you know?"

I didn't. "Thanks for your time." I stood, tossing five dollars and my card on the table. "You'll call if you think of anything?"

But he was staring out the window again, through time to the life that should have been his.

CHAPTER 58

Van

I thought I saw movement in Teresa's river cottage when I knocked, but the driveway was empty and no one answered the door. I debated leaving a note but settled on another phone message asking her to call me. If Ted intercepted it, well, that wasn't on me.

Next, I programmed the address for the Sauk Centre nursing home into the car's GPS and headed northwest. Kyle had tracked down Anne Morsa, grandmother to the missing Judith. I called him as I drove to fill him in on what Chuck had said.

"It's the state fair, isn't it?" His voice held a tremor of excitement. "It *has* to be."

I agreed. "Any chance you can track down all the 1986 vendors?"

"I sure can try." He sounded ecstatic. Nerd.

"Great. Get lists of employees and photos where you can." We were searching for a needle in a haystack, and we needed to examine each shaft. "We're looking for a Tom Cruise–ish type. Chuck said Robin wanted to go to the cookie-in-a-bucket place, so start there."

My current working theory was that the perpetrator marked all three—and maybe four—girls at the 1986 Minnesota State Fair. He could've been working there, could have simply been a spectator, could've even been there with his family. Serial murderers had girlfriends, wives, children. They hid in plain sight, and what better place than a fair? But I quickly discarded the image of him as a family man, at least while he was selecting victims. It'd make it difficult to follow his targets, forget convincing someone to visit the fair with him multiple days.

No, he had more likely worked solo, trailing the girl he'd selected from a distance, blending easily into the massive crowd, stopping when she stopped, glancing off when she looked his way. And then he either spoke with her and got her address or at least her hometown, or he stalked her to her car and then got into his and followed her home. The odds of parking in the same lot—there were dozens surrounding the state fair—were thin. Had he lost dozens of girls that way, ultimately murdering only those he'd been able to trail all the way home?

Or . . .

"Look into 1986 state fair parking lot attendants, too," I told Kyle.

"Anything else?"

"That's it." I ended the phone call.

Once the killer knew where they lived, did he lurk outside, watching the house until his victims were alone? Had he been the "encyclopedia salesman" who'd knocked on Gina's front door while the three girls were getting ready to play Ouija? The one who'd waited for Lulu in the Chi-Chi's alley? If so, it meant he checked in with his victims before killing them.

I asked my phone to call Chuck.

"Hey," I said when he answered, hating the vulnerability of talking on speakerphone, "Van Reed again. I have a quick question. Got a minute?"

"Sure." The background noises told me he was probably driving, too. "What's up?"

"Between the state fair and the concert, was there *any* man who talked to Robin that you saw? The person who sold her the cookies, a parking attendant at the fair or concert, someone while she was waiting in line for the bathroom?"

"I wasn't there when she bought the cookies." His regret soaked the phone line. "She was inside the fair for about half an hour without me. We took the bus there and back, so no parking attendants. She for sure didn't talk to anyone at the concert. We were together the whole time. I—*damn*."

His tone carried the weight of the world. "What?"

"She wanted a beer. I had the fake ID, but I was glued to my seat. She got thirsty, or she saw a friend, I can't remember because I wasn't listening. I couldn't believe I was seeing AC/DC live, you know?" I heard a sound like coughing. Might've been tears swallowed. "Whatever it was, she disappeared for a few minutes. When she came back, she was a wreck. Said some guy mistook her for someone else." His voice dropped. "He was the one who killed her, wasn't he?"

My gut said yes. "You didn't see him?"

"I didn't see anyone but Angus Young that night."

The road thrummed beneath my tires. I wasn't responsible for this man's emotional state, and I didn't know him from Adam. Did I care enough to lie to him? Turned out I did. "You were a kid. You couldn't have done anything differently, and you get to forgive yourself."

Several beats passed. A bird flew toward my car, almost hit it, swerved back into the ether.

"But you *don't* get to forgive yourself," he said softly. "That's a fib we tell children. The truth is we carry the stones of the bad things we've done. You can lighten it with an honest apology, but that rock is yours to haul on your back for the rest of your life." He sighed. "If you're smart or lucky, you figure out how to screw up less before your mistakes bury you. That's all any of us can hope for."

I ended the phone call without responding. That one hurt too much.

CHAPTER 59

Van

The Eden Valley Nursing Home did not resemble Eden and was nowhere near a valley. It was plunked just off the highway on the outskirts of Sauk Centre, a snow fence and fir trees separating it from a series of warehouses. The building itself was one level spread out, crouching beneath the weight of its 1970s design aesthetic.

Kyle had told them to expect me, so I was ushered directly to Anne Morsa's room.

It was generic, pale, and potpourri scented. Anne Morsa sat in a chair near the window, knitting with Scandinavian intensity, the sunlight turning her short, yellowed hair into a halo.

"Mrs. Morsa?"

The knitting needles kept flying, their clicking hypnotizing. Her yarn was soft pinks and yellows being transformed into . . . a scarf? I blinked. No, I spotted one sleeve, and then another. She was knitting a sweater. I stepped into the room, raising my voice slightly. "Mrs. Morsa? I'm Agent Evangeline Reed. I'm here to talk to you about your granddaughter. Is that all right?"

She kept knitting. She must have been in her late nineties, her back bowed, her fingers twisted. I didn't spot a hearing aid. I knelt in her line of vision. "Mrs. Morsa?"

The needles stopped and her eyes focused. "You're not a nurse."

I softened my voice. "I'm not. I'm an investigator with the Bureau of Criminal Apprehension. I'm here to ask you some questions about your granddaughter. Is that all right?"

Her face split into a perfect wide grin, catching me off guard. "You're a friend of Judy's? Well then, have a seat."

She was in the only chair. I leaned against the window ledge. "I'm wondering what you can tell me about her disappearance."

She went perfectly still, her eyes growing confused. People bustled past in the hallway, conversations leaking in beneath the door, but Mrs. Morsa appeared not to hear any of it. I was about to leave to get a nurse when her face cleared.

"You saw my Facebook post. My friends tell me I'm foolish, going onto the internet every year, but I'm not going to let them forget my Judy. She was a good girl." Mrs. Morsa pointed at me as she said this, like she thought I'd argue. "It skipped a generation. Judy's mother got pregnant from my no-good son. She died having Judy, and my boy ran off."

Her hands started moving again, the needles turning string into clothes. "I think Judy was trying that running on for size. What child doesn't go through a phase where they follow in their parents' footsteps?" She chuckled. "Too bad Judy's parents were both a waste of skin."

I found myself smiling. The words were unkind, but she said them with love. I bet she'd been a wonderful grandmother. There was something so soft, so maternal, about her, with a hint of steel beneath. "You think she ran away?"

"I know she did, at first," Mrs. Morsa said. "I went down to the ice cream shop where she worked, and they told me she'd taken off in a red sports car with a strange man. Can you believe it? I almost called the police, but I figured I'd let her sow her wild oats. Get it out of her system in one shot so we didn't have to go through it all again."

That'd been a terrible decision any way you sliced it. Even if Judy had returned home, she was a minor. She needed adult guidance. I rethought my opinion of Anne Morsa. "But then?" I asked.

"But then I got that postcard from the state fair, and Judy never showed up." She wrinkled her nose. "That girl was half homing pigeon. First day of kindergarten, she decided she missed me and walked the full mile home even though she'd never been at that school before. The only reason she wouldn't have come back to me is if she couldn't." The needles clicked. "I tracked down that man she left with, you know."

My spine snapped to attention. "You did?"

"Yep." She frowned at the memory. "Camped out at the Dairy Freez until he showed back up. Men who try to date underage girls are not so smart. He figured he'd already gotten one peach from that tree, why not come back and see if any more dropped out."

"Did he tell you what happened to Judy?"

"After a fashion." Her eyes grew crafty. "I had a friend work-ing at the lumber store across the street. He came over to help me convince the man." She snorted. "*Man.* Hardly. He was a skinny little punk, barely twenty. He said he left Judy at the state fair and never saw her again. And do you know what? I believed him. Didn't hurt that by that point, he would have sold his mother to stop the pounding."

I tugged out my phone and did a quick Google search. "Did he look like this?"

She leaned forward, squinting through her glasses at the photo of Otto Pusch. "No."

I pulled up a different photo. "How about this?"

She looked at me like I must be joking. "That's Tom Cruise, dear."

I nodded.

She glanced from the phone to me, then back to the phone. "No. The man Judy left with had a mustache, but even without it, he looked nothing like either of those men. If he had, I would've understood why Judy ran off with him."

She laughed again. I wondered how Chuck had been saddled with so much guilt for not walking his girlfriend to the door—even though she'd gotten inside safely—while Anne Morsa apparently felt none for not reporting her granddaughter missing.

"You *never* heard from her again?"

She shook her head. "Never. But she'll show up, just you wait. Some people just like their nest, and she's one of them. Don't care how many years have passed."

I glanced around the room. "Do you have pictures of Judy?"

"Somewhere," she murmured. She appeared suddenly exhausted.

"In this room?" I asked.

A knock at the door got my attention. An aide wearing blue scrubs poked his head in. "It's time for Mrs. Morsa's medication."

The woman in question was nodding off in her seat.

"Do you know where she keeps her photographs?" I asked the attendant.

He stepped past me, gently removing the knitting from Mrs. Morsa's hands. "If there's nothing in her drawers, then it might be in her storage locker here on-site. Can't get to that without her permission, though."

While he tried to rouse her, I searched through the dresser and the two nightstands. They contained clothes and knitting supplies. I fished a card out of my wallet and handed it to the aide. "When she wakes up, can you ask her about any photographs and give me a call if she remembers some?"

Kyle had probably already tracked down and collated every photo of Judy Morsa ever taken, but I was here.

"Sure," he said.

I gave Anne Morsa one last look and took off for Alexandria to meet with my Sisters, a newspaper printout containing Caroline's photograph in my pocket.

I am safe. I am grown. I am free.

CHAPTER 60

Just Judy

2010

He clutched his small package of belongings, the sun shining around his head like an aura as he stepped outside the prison gates. He was muscular in a way he'd never been, his clean-shaven face sculpted, his hair long and flowing. Every sacrifice she'd made, every dark water she'd had to swim through, it was all worth it.

He was a god.

She took him back to her apartment. When she saw it through his eyes, it looked small, shameful next to the Farm they'd left. But he'd carried her into the bedroom and made her forget all that. She'd missed his attention, the way he made her feel like he wasn't anywhere else, his focus absolute. Afterward, he held her while she told him everything she'd done, how she'd begun tracking down their flock.

"How many have answered?" he asked, his arm around her, his naked body warm against hers.

"More and more every day," she said. She couldn't believe her heart could grow any fuller. He was *back*. They would restart their life. She'd done all the legwork, had the location. With him at the head, they could finally finish what they'd started.

They'd grow their garden bigger than before, its roots so deep this time that no one could ever hurt it again.

CHAPTER 61

Van

If I was reading Anne Morsa right, her granddaughter had been her world. She'd responded to her disappearance by staking out the last place she'd been seen. When that hadn't brought her Judy, she'd called the police. They hadn't been able to locate the granddaughter, and so at some point, Anne had started posting to Facebook, hoping . . . what? That someone who knew Judy back in the day would respond? That Judy herself would see it?

We're all products of those who birthed and raised us. We learned to speak the language they spoke, eat the food they ate, wear what they wore. Most of us pushed back, even if it was only in our thoughts, but we stayed pretty close to home—in our values, our appearance, our geography.

I had no doubt that Anne Morsa's parents had raised her to put family above all else, which was why she'd taken in baby Judy. Yet Anne had also let a sixteen-year-old girl "sow her wild oats" with a strange man. What message had her parents given her that made that make sense? In the end, I didn't suppose it mattered. Adults constructed their own lives. Some had been raised with more tools in their tool kit, got to start on solid earth rather than belowground, but we still made our choices, just as Anne Morsa had when she elected not to alert the cops right away.

A recollection worked its way to the surface.

It must have been 2004 or 2005. Cordelia, by then eighteen, her day as a runaway well in the past, was coming toward me from Frank Roth's house, a blue pencil in one hand and a notebook in the other. She hardly ever left Frank's, so this was a rare sighting. Admiration knotted my stomach as she walked past, her dark-brown hair cascading down her back like a night waterfall. She was a Mother by then and could wear her hair as she chose, as long as she kept it long. She was the only one of them who didn't tie hers up.

When her pencil slipped from her hand, I seized the opportunity to race over and offer it back, my fingers brushing against hers briefly. Her eyes, so full of sadness and wisdom, met mine for a fleeting moment before she murmured a quiet "thank you."

I wanted to say something, to offer comfort or solidarity, but Mother Mary appeared in Frank's doorway, the weight of her disapproving gaze silencing me. We hadn't been told to avoid Cordelia since she ran away, not in so many words, but she was kept hidden from us in the Mothers' dormitory until the ceremony where she was welcomed as Frank Roth's primary Mother.

We were all envious of that, even those of us who could never be a Mother because we were Frank's kids. Frank had never given so much attention to one girl before, none except Mother Mary. As her sharp voice cut at Cordelia, commanding her to return to Frank's house immediately, I stepped away, not wanting to be associated with a rule breaker like Cordelia.

That was how we lost ourselves, wasn't it? Small moments when we should have stood up and instead, we shrank. We were all broken at the commune, bent and reshaped by Frank, and I suppose someone had first broken him. When you came from a family like that, you didn't know if returning to it would heal you or devour the bit of self you'd worked so hard to claim.

❖

My heart kicked up my throat when the GPS told me I'd reached my destination.

The two-story brown house was on Alexandria's north side, within the city limits but alongside a large tilled plot where everyone else had lawns and garages. I'd place bets that Grace and Hannah had already planted beets and lettuce. The Mothers made sure of it every spring. I could also see their influence in the lack of purely ornamental plants around the house, in its sparkling windows, in the way the wood siding appeared freshly painted.

We'd been raised to take excellent care of home and hearth, and I felt an unexpected surge of pride seeing that Grace and Hannah were clearly such good homemakers. I found myself thinking that they would have made excellent Mothers before I shut down that train of thought in horror, my scalp crawling.

The past was too close.

I would have turned tail if not for Harry. It seemed ridiculous, suddenly, as I walked up the swept sidewalk to the door, ridiculous that I thought one of my Sisters would know about Caroline's abduction. It became suddenly, blindingly clear what I'd been doing.

I'd been avoiding telling Harry about my fear that Frank had abducted Caroline not because I wanted some proof first. I'd avoided telling him because I didn't want him to see my father's crimes in me.

And being here would only make the bad worse. My head felt swimmy, the acid in my stomach churning. There was nothing to be gained. I was swiveling to return to my car when I heard the door open in the brown house.

"Evangeline?"

I would have recognized Grace's voice anywhere.

CHAPTER 62

Van

I watched myself enter the house, accept a steaming mug of chamomile tea, be led to the couch where Hannah waited, my eyes glancing off the red, white, and blue quilt draped across the sofa. I'd helped sew it a lifetime ago.

Grace took a seat next to Hannah, both of them across from me.

They truly did look like Sisters. They had Frank's dark hair—bound up in tight buns in both their cases—and large eyes. Grace had his strong jaw and solid build. They'd aged, as had I, but their faces were more familiar to me than my own. They'd been a bonded pair, not unlike Veronica and me before Frank destroyed her. It made sense they lived together now. Grace had been a Watcher, one of Frank's chosen, never allowed to swim in the creek. Had Hannah been jealous?

I was overcome by a memory of the two Sisters sitting across from me.

The sun hung high in the summer sky, its warmth spilling over the creek as the Sisters and Brothers who'd completed their chores early splashed and played. The water was a delicious, welcome escape from the blazing heat. The creek was always impossibly deep by the old wooden bridge. I floated there on my back, the water cradling me despite the weight of the dress and underclothes all the girls were required to wear. It felt like liquid silk where it touched the bare skin at my wrists and ankles.

But then I noticed Grace, standing on the bank with a sad look in her eyes. The Watchers were all bound by rules I didn't fully understand. Grace's gaze was fixed on the water, her longing evident in the way she watched every splash and ripple. I wished there were something I could do, some way to make her feel included, but the rules were the rules.

Hannah swam over to me, her eyes sparkling with mischief. "Evangeline, look!" She darted beneath the surface and emerged with a handful of smooth, flat stones. She'd always been such a good swimmer, able to dive down ten, twelve feet like it was nothing. "I found these for you."

She held up the stones, their surfaces glinting in the sunlight. Did she hand them to me? Toss them for me to dive after? The memory had gone as slippery as a fish, and I could not recall.

"You look good," I told them both in the here and now. I set the mug on the coffee table, the tea untouched. I was barely able to hold myself together. No way could I add swallowing on top of that.

"Your hair is beautiful," Grace said, her voice like chocolate. "A testament to God."

Ice crystals broke off and flowed through my blood. Were they still adherents? "Thank you," I said. "Your home is lovely."

It was. The furniture appeared hand carved, the rugs and blankets one of a kind, every surface uncluttered and spotless. That annoying pride came back. We'd been raised as pioneer women on steroids, and my Sisters had remained true to that path.

I found myself desperately wishing Harry were by my side.

Rather than respond to my compliment, they held taut smiles on their faces. I envied their stoicism. They were leaving me to cross the gap myself. My question surprised even me. "What have you two been up to since I last saw you?" I'd have howled with laughter if every nerve weren't focused on maintaining my solid form. *Seen any good movies since the feds broke up the cult we were raised in?*

"We're both nurses," Hannah said. She'd had a rasp to her voice when I knew her, and it was still there. "We work at a private clinic."

"How nice." Of course they'd gone into a caring profession. We'd been reared to believe it was our job to bury our own needs and put all our energy into raising up Frank. Without us, he could not reach his highest form. Our sacrifice was necessary, crucial, noble. Same bullshit, different religion. "It looks like you have a beautiful garden every year, too."

"Do you still work the earth?" Grace asked, using the archaic phrase from our childhood. More of the ice crystals scraped my veins.

"Nope." My voice sounded unnaturally light. "I'm a city girl."

They both twisted their lips, mirror images of distaste. I was surprised to feel the sting of their judgment. Why did I still care what they thought?

"You're not the only one who has reached out to us," Hannah said.

My whole body tensed in hope. "Veronica?"

Their eyes shutter, and my hope drowns.

When Frank finally pulled Veronica out of the trough, her body had draped like a rag doll. I knew she'd left us that night, but it seemed some part of me believed in miracles, hoped that once the feds raided, they'd done something to bring her back.

"Veronica is no longer with us," Hannah said. "Several of us took care of her after the government attack. She died peacefully."

"The *attack*?" There was no mistaking the venom in my voice.

Grace leaned forward, tapping the table lightly. "You're upset. You feel guilty because you and Veronica were close, and then you left. We understand."

How like family to dress a stabbing as a hug. It was only thanks to years of therapy on top of more than a decade of experience controlling my emotions in high-stress situations that I was able to swallow my scream. "We were close," I said through gritted teeth. When someone came for you, the best way to regain the upper hand was to agree with them. "I'm glad you were able to care for her after what Father did to her."

Their expressions wiped clean. "He did what he had to do," Grace murmured.

"He paid for our nursing school, you know, all four years," Hannah said. "He's cared for every child who's allowed him, including those who were put into foster care . . . after." Her expression tightened and began to glow, like someone had flipped on a night-light behind her eyes. "He continues to know things about us that only the Messiah would. When we graduate. When we need help, money. He sees all, and he provides."

A million insects crawled across my flesh.

Grace nodded vigorously, lit by the same internal flame. "Father Frank knew where all the children ended up. With his help, we're not only reuniting our Family, we're growing it." Her grin was feverish. "We've been blessed in our pursuit of expanding Frank's Flock. People are tired of social media, isolated. They want to be part of something bigger. The flowers are ready to reap. You'll help us, won't you, Evangeline? You'll come back into the fold? It would be such a blessing to have law enforcement on our side."

I found myself checking for a clear path to the door. I'd made a tremendous error in judgment coming here. They weren't lost souls in need of protection. They were vipers coiling to strike. "You still believe all of that?" I asked.

They nodded in perfect sync.

My words coasted out on a wave of fear-tinged fury. "Too bad Frank Roth is dead."

The secret smile they exchanged gutted me. Their bodies were free of the commune, but their hearts and minds remained imprisoned.

"Father will live forever," Hannah said in the sweet, fake-earnest voice a certain kind of woman offered as she gently shoveled gravedirt over disagreement. "You know that. It was central to our teachings."

My extremities went numb. I flexed my fingers to make sure they were still there. I considered for a moment showing them the plane crash video, but they never would have believed it. We were warned to not trust our own eyes if what we saw contradicted what we'd been taught.

I was here for one thing. I needed to address it now so I could get the hell out of there before I lost my mind.

I reached into my pocket, took out the newspaper article, unfolded it, slid it across the table to them, Caroline Steinbeck's face gazing into the camera. It was a fool's errand that had sent me here, a fool's errand encased in a veneer of immature hope that my Family would be different from how I remembered them. I'd take my medicine and drive straight to Harry, confessing my foolishness.

"Do either of you recognize this girl from our childhood?"

They shook their heads. Of course they didn't know her.

"Who is she?" Grace asked.

"I thought she might have been a Sister, one I'd forgotten about. Maybe one who was with us for only a short time."

I leaned over to reclaim the newspaper, but Hannah slapped her hand on it, making me jump. She reached into a drawer, opened it, pulled out a black marker. The squeaks of her coloring the image were as loud as a jet engine in the taut atmosphere.

She turned the image around so Caroline was now looking at me, her blond hair colored dark and made long.

"Not a Sister," she said. "A Mother."

I didn't see it at first, and then I did.

I moaned.

CHAPTER 63

Van

My skin fell away, leaving raw, glistening muscle and exposed nerves.

Cordelia.

What age had she been when she'd arrived. Ten? Eleven? I'd thought she was so much older than me, but it must have been her ways, her confidence. She'd been terrified—looking back, I could see that now—but even despite that, she was worldly, self-aware, composed in a way those of us who'd been born on the Farm never would've been.

And her white-blond hair had been dyed dark brown.

Runaway Cordelia was Caroline Steinbeck.

It seemed ludicrous now that I hadn't recognized her, but she'd kept to herself the brief time she'd been a Sister and disappeared into the Mothers' and then Frank's house after she'd run away. Besides, it was like a childhood classmate you hadn't known well appearing in the *Last Supper* painting. The context was so bizarre, your decades-earlier interaction with them so tenuous, the image of them so different from your memory, that your brain never considered the connection.

Not to mention the daily trauma that had all us kids hyper-focused on our own survival.

I was filled with shame as I recalled my childhood response to her telling me the night before she ran away that Frank was going to make her a Mother—*you're so lucky!* That poor girl. Frank's Farm was a horror show for those of us raised on it. How terrifying it must have been for an abducted girl missing her family. Missing her brother.

Harry.

I stumbled out of the weird brown house, nearly making it to my car before I was sick, heaving until empty. I wiped my mouth and glanced back at Hannah and Grace's house. They'd closed the door behind me without so much as a goodbye.

That tracked.

I threw the car in gear and aimed for home. The movements were automatic, soulless. I reached my apartment at nightfall. I could have gotten Owl. I missed her, but I didn't deserve her. I was a terrible investigator and a worse friend.

I fell into a broken sleep.

The nightmare began the moment I laid down my head.

I'm trapped in the suffocating grip of sleep paralysis as my front door opens and footsteps draw nearer, each one echoing like a death knock. A figure looms over me, a shadowy specter clutching a knife. It raises the blade overhead, holding it above my stomach. I try making a noise, moving a pinkie, but I'm trapped, buried alive.

The knife comes down.

The killer's face is in shadow right up until the blade pierces my gut.

At that moment, I see her.

She is me.

I'm finally able to scream.

The noise wrenched me out of sleep. I was doubled over, a burning pain in my stomach, flailing at an invisible attacker. My hands struck something solid. That's when I realized I was on the floor, kneeling in front of my door. I blinked, yanking up my shirt. My stomach was unmarred. There was no one in my apartment.

It *had* been a nightmare.

But I'd never sleepwalked before. I glanced at my smartwatch. I'd been out for more than three hours. Why did I feel so wasted?

I rose shakily to my feet, my arm sore from thwacking the door. I was returning to my bed when I noticed the folded red scarf on my kitchen table, a bronze Buddha statue with a dent resting on top of it.

The same statue Owl had knocked over at Alexis's house.

CHAPTER 64

Van

I broke several laws speeding to her place.

She's fine. The dogs are fine.

Those two thoughts whipped through my head, racing each other as I tore past red lights and rounded corners so fast the Toyota nearly tipped. I careened into Alexis's driveway and threw myself out of the car while it was still running.

Owl's frantic howls hit my ears before I reached the front steps.

Ripping open the front door—why wasn't it locked?—I charged into the house. The barking was coming from the right, down a hall. I flung open the first door, and Owl flew out like a bullet. The inside of the door was deeply gouged with claw marks. Zoso lay motionless in the middle of the room. I hurried to his side and checked his pulse. He was alive but barely moving.

I hurried to the next door and opened it, Owl on my heels.

A body lay on a bed, covered by a sheet.

I hovered a moment, swallowing hard, before yanking it off in one quick motion.

Alexis lay there in her pajamas. They were white flannel with blue and green jellyfish swimming across. Her hands were clutched at her side.

Her eyes were open, lifeless, a Mad Hatter grin slicing her face, a red scarf tied around her neck.

CHAPTER 65

Van

The paramedics arrived first. By the time they showed up, Zoso was beginning to rouse. Whoever had poisoned Alexis must have drugged him, too. Owl either hadn't presented a threat or had received a lower dose.

Two uniforms showed up shortly after. I filled them in on the little I knew. A woman appeared from next door and offered to take Zoso to her place, saying she and Alexis frequently dog sat for one another. One of the uniforms said that would be fine and took her contact information. I moved Owl to my car and cracked the windows and then sat on Alexis's front stoop to wait for Comstock. When he showed up, he slowed only to toss me a disgusted look before disappearing inside.

Someone was after me. The red scarves. Emily and then Alexis, my ID at the first scene, me finding the second.

I was their target. But why?

Those two thoughts flapped in my head like carrion crows, like fingers over rosary beads, like a drowning hand grasping for solid earth.

A woman stepped out of the beige townhome across the street. Her hair was mussed, and she wore a winter parka over her pajamas. She crossed the street, eyeing me suspiciously. A uniform greeted her at the end of the sidewalk just as Harry pulled up.

Comstock must have called him.

I felt nothing as Harry stepped out of his car wearing a black fedora and his charcoal peacoat. He took one look at me, his face scrunched in worry, and began walking briskly toward me until the neighbor's yell brought him up short. She was trying to get around the uniform, demanding to speak to the person in charge.

The commotion brought out Comstock. He motioned for the woman to approach. "Good evening, ma'am," he said, glancing from Harry to me. "What can I do for you?"

"I was trying to tell that buffoon," she said, jabbing a thumb at the officer at the end of the sidewalk, "that I saw this woman earlier tonight."

She was talking about me.

I was too exhausted to care. I got to my feet. "You did. I brought my dog here." I pointed at Owl staring at us mournfully from my car. I was long past pretending she wasn't mine. "Alexis was watching her."

I turned to Comstock with the lie I'd been rehearsing, because I certainly couldn't tell him about finding Alexis's statue in my apartment. Didn't matter how screwed I knew I was. The survival instinct was the last to go. "I came to pick the dog up late. That's when I found her."

"No, after that," the neighbor said, her answer implying she spent a lot of time spying out her window. "You had your hair under a cap, but I recognized you from before."

"When was this?" Comstock asked, his voice deceptively calm.

"About an hour ago," she said, hands on hips.

The world fell away as Comstock turned to me, his voice low and dangerous. "Anything I should know?"

I opened my mouth, not sure which confession would tumble out first. That I was possibly sleep-killing? That before that, I'd murdered three men? That I'd lived with my best friend's abducted sister for years and felt *jealous* of her?

But before I found the words, Harry stepped forward, standing so close that I could feel his shoulder against mine, lending me strength.

"Evangeline and I were going over our case until a half an hour ago, when she left to get her dog."

Comstock's eyes narrowed. Hell, mine probably did, too.

"Why didn't you say that?" he asked me.

"I didn't know I was a suspect." Somehow, my voice was even.

Comstock sighed, appearing suddenly five years older, which put him one foot in the grave. "Ma'am," he said, addressing the neighbor, "did you get a clear look at the face of the woman in the cap?"

She thrust out her chin. "I tell you, I know it was this one. I'm an expert at reading body language, even when someone's back is to me."

"Her back was to you, you were across the street, *and* it was dark?" Comstock asked.

She was gearing up to argue, but Comstock cut her off with a hand gesture. "Officer Senott here will take your statement. Any information you provide will be appreciated."

Comstock waited until Senott led her away before turning to Harry and me. His eyes were ice, his face iron. "I want the two of you as far away from this scene as you can get. Goddamn it, I don't even want you on this side of town. Understood?"

I didn't need to be told twice.

CHAPTER 66

Van

I'd agreed to meet Harry at an all-night diner up the road for a brief talk. I made sure Owl was comfortable before going inside. The place looked as empty as I felt, the only movement a cook passing into the back and a tired waitress scrolling through her phone. Harry and I took the booth as far from the door as possible.

"Why'd you lie for me?" I asked the minute the waitress left to get our coffee. I was surprised to find myself scared of the answer.

He placed his hands palm up on the table. "I know you had nothing to do with either killing." He said it simply, no weight to his words, his eyes clear and blue, seeking me across the table. But the sentence, the act, was anything but simple. Harry's word was his honor.

"That doesn't explain why you lied."

He studied me with compassion or regret or sorrow. Something soft. But he didn't answer.

Never in my adult life had I cried in front of someone. *Never.* But I felt the tears suddenly sheeting down my face. I didn't acknowledge them. Maybe if I didn't, they weren't happening. I'd done nothing but lie to Harry, and here he was bending the shape of himself to protect me.

"I can't sleep," I said.

He remained absolutely still. He didn't want to scare me from talking more.

"I have nightmares," I continued. "I have since I lived on Frank's Farm." A tear trembled on the edge of my chin and splashed to the table. I kept my hands flat on each side of it. I *hated* that Frank scarred me. I *hated* that I had to carry it for the rest of my life and that Harry could see my weakness.

He was watching me, barely blinking.

"And now I'm seeing *him*. Frank Roth. Out of the corner of my eye, in the shadows of my apartment, in my nightmares."

This would be the perfect time to tell him about his sister. It fit like a puzzle piece into the slot of the conversation. *It's because I'm researching him. He took your sister, Harry. My dad stole Caroline from you.*

"I think it's because I'm so strung out," I said instead, horrified at my own cowardice. "I know I'm hallucinating. Frank Roth is dead."

Harry broke his silence, though his face stayed impassive. "When did he die?"

"Last year. Plane crash in Florida. I saw the video."

He finally unlocked his gaze from mine and glanced out the window. I could see his face reflected back to me. His eyes were tense. The waitress used the moment to run our coffee over along with a pot of cream we hadn't requested before scurrying away without a word. She was earning herself a good tip.

"What is it?" I asked.

I felt him pulling away from me, and the severed connection after being alone for so long was unbearable. "I might have killed Emily Barris and Alexis," I blurted out, realizing I didn't even know her last name.

Harry shook his head, but he was still staring out the window. "You wouldn't kill anyone."

I have.

"Harry." I placed my hand on his. He looked at it, then at me. His pleading gaze sank me. I had no choice. I owed him some truth after what he'd done for me. "I have visions." The words stopped my tears. "I see crimes when I sleep. Murders, assaults, *real, actual crimes.*"

He squinted like he was trying to see me through fog. I couldn't stop now that I'd started. I'd held it in too long. "The first time I realized that it wasn't just my screwy brain was after I'd left the commune. I saw Frederick Colum being arrested on television," I said, naming one of the most notorious child sex traffickers in US history, "but before that, before I knew he was an actual person, I'd seen him abusing kids in my nightmares."

A cramp of empathy seized Harry's face, but it was replaced almost immediately by something else. Anger? Frustration?

"It wasn't just that." I swiped at my wet cheeks, then began listing the crimes I'd witnessed when I worked homicide at the MPD, how Bart and I'd solved them. I couldn't look at Harry, could only hurl the details onto the table.

When I stopped, he was silent for several beats. Then: "Those were while you were with the MPD." His voice sounded gravelly, unfamiliar. I still couldn't look at him. "What about since?"

I didn't answer. I couldn't.

"The baby in the floorboards on the Taken Ones case," he said, grinding out the words. "The man in the jail cell in Alku. What else?"

I still couldn't look up, but I found my voice. "Lester Dunne, John Wilson, and Randall Devries," I said, naming the three victims of the supposed Sweet Tea Killer. Would he make the connection? Would he know I'd killed them to stop their crimes?

"It's impossible." He sighed deeply. Waited a few more moments. Then said, softly, "But sometimes, the impossible happens."

My eyes flew up. He was reaching inside his peacoat. He pulled out a few papers that were stapled and folded in half. He laid them on the table, next to his fedora, turned them to face me, and smoothed them out before sliding them over.

CHAPTER 67

Van

I scanned the information, not comprehending. "What am I looking at?"

"A scientific study on a gene in chromosome 11. They discovered a mutation known as LRP5."

"Harry," I begged. "In normal words."

He blinked. "After you asked me if it was possible for a human to drop three stories and walk away, I started researching. I came across LRP5. Researchers had connected it with low bone density. They wondered if the mutation could also correlate with *high* bone density." He cleared his throat. "They discovered it could. That's when the research began into families all over the globe with the same mutation. They all have incredibly dense bones." His eyes flicked to mine. "A lifetime of no breaks, no injury to the skeleton at all, across generations. They've walked away from car crashes, unhurt."

I felt myself dry up from the inside out. "But not plane crashes."

Harry tilted his head to the side. "It's highly unlikely but not impossible."

A memory came to the forefront. I was on the Farm, maybe eight or nine years old. Our days were prescribed: wake up before the sun, wash our hands and faces, brush our teeth, make our beds, dress, and begin chores. Only our stations alternated. Some days we were assigned to the kitchen to cook all three meals, which included baking bread and putting up and processing food. Other times we were on cleaning duty, or gardening, or laundry, or repairs, or animal husbandry.

We became skilled at every aspect of survival.

It was exhausting, and we were allowed zero privacy. Even the bathroom door was to be left open. But there was a small, secret room in the barn that one of the boys had built before he was banished, as every boy on Frank's Farm was when they turned eighteen. Frank was the only man allowed. But this boy, Ezekiel, had managed to turn an unused bump-out at the back of one of the cow pens into a secret getaway by stacking boards in front of it. The space was barely large enough for two kids to sit in, but the important thing was none of the grown-ups knew it existed.

We'd take turns hiding in it, stealing moments of quiet when no one could see us, command us, where we could luxuriate in our private thoughts. I couldn't remember what stressor had caused me to lay claim to the secret room on that particular day, but I'd weaseled out from kitchen duty by saying we needed eggs, and then I'd crawled into the space. I was sitting there, gathering deep breaths and staring through the slats, when Frank Roth strode into the barn.

My heart seized. I'd be tortured if he caught me.

But Frank couldn't see me, I reminded myself, trying to steady my shallow breathing. I had only to stay quiet and still until he left. I hoped it was before someone came looking for me, wondering why it was taking so long to gather eggs.

Frank shuffled around for a few minutes before crawling into the overhead haymow, out of my sight. I could hear him stomping around up there, taking forever. I'd almost decided to make a run for the door—someone was going to come for me any second—when Frank fell from the sky and landed on the hay-strewn concrete floor in front of me.

Without thinking, I rushed out from my hiding spot. He had to have fallen at least twenty feet. I expected to see blood gushing, maybe a cracked bone poking out, but instead, Frank hopped to his feet. He turned around and saw me standing there, my mouth hanging open.

It was the only time in my life I'd heard him laugh. "Close your mouth, girl. I'm fine. You must be my lucky bird."

He'd patted my head, then walked away, not even limping.

That's when he'd first given me the nickname. While I loved the attention, I didn't think I'd brought him luck that day. Instead I believed I'd seen him behave like a god, exactly as he'd always taught us he was.

Had it been a genetic defect all along?

And the man who'd run up to the roof, who'd at first moved like his skin was too tight, who'd reminded me of someone? "People with this mutation," I whispered. "They don't look any different?"

Harry flipped the page in front of me, revealing a printout of an image. "Difficulty swimming because of the density of their bones, unusually square jaws, and in some cases, a bony growth on the palate."

I was looking at a cauliflower of skin blooming inside the roof of someone's mouth and thinking about the children Frank called the Watchers, the ones he wouldn't allow in the creek. Of Veronica, who was one of his chosen until she told on him, who he had to hold underwater to punish.

I groaned. "Frank had the mutation."

I told him about my father falling from the haymow, uninjured, about his offspring who likely shared the altered gene, of how I'd thought I knew the man running up the apartment stairs, even if I hadn't seen his face. The weight of the truth was crushing, and as I spoke, something was starting to come together. A horrible, outlandish theory and, with it, a light to its dark: the realization that Harry believed me.

It wasn't comfortable for him, and I was sure he was scrambling for a scientific explanation, but he believed me about my visions, and he'd believed me about the man falling from the apartment building, at least enough to dig deeper into it.

I loved him so much in that moment. I couldn't lose him, not yet, and if I stayed there one more minute, I was going to confess about his sister.

"I have to go," I said, jumping to my feet. "Owl's been in the car too long already."

Harry was sliding toward the edge of his seat. "I'll go with you," he said. "You need sleep. I'll watch over you." His eyes flew to mine, swimming in horror. "As a friend, of course."

He meant it. He wasn't going to let me leave by myself. This would not do. I put my hand out. "Give me your phone," I said.

He appeared confused but handed it over without question. I downloaded the sleep app I used, logging in with my information. "I won't be able to rest with you there," I told him honestly. "You've seen my place. It's one big room. But this is the app I use. It tracks how deep I'm out, my heart rate, all that good stuff. I'm going to walk the dog and then head straight to bed. If you see anything that looks like a problem, give me a call. Let it ring until I answer. Cool?"

He scowled, his expression telling me this very much was *not* cool. "Fine."

"Thanks, Harry." I wanted to hug him so bad.

CHAPTER 68

Van

Despite Comstock's warning, I drove past the scene on my way home from meeting with Harry. I had some vague plan I'd convince the next-door neighbor to let me take Zoso, but I came to my senses as soon as I spotted the officer working the perimeter. It was guilt driving me, a desire to somehow make all this up to Alexis.

Alexis, who *Frank Roth* had murdered to discipline me.

That was the horrible theory that'd taken root and grown ugly black leaves when Harry told me there was a chance he'd survived the plane crash. How like my manipulative, megalomaniac father to plan such a public "death." If the outlandish idea worked, it got him both an audience and a record of his demise. He'd be invisible after that.

At least, until I began to draw undue attention to him by digging around.

That's why he'd begun killing people in my orbit: to punish me for looking into his whereabouts. First, he went after Emily Barris, leaving my ID at the scene—he must have stolen it out of my apartment after spotting Emily and me together with Owl in Loring Park—and then Alexis. He'd seeded the ground around both murders with fear by hiring strangers to wear red scarves and sweaters and stalk me, drawing attention to themselves before they disappeared.

It would have been simpler to kill me, certainly, but where would the punishment have been in that? No, Frank wanted anyone who defied him to suffer extensively and publicly.

He always had.

Frank had abducted Caroline, faked his own death, and poisoned Emily and Alexis. He might have killed those three girls back in 1986, too. Yes, the more I thought about it, the more likely that was.

Frank Roth was responsible for *all* of this.

A hysterical laugh escaped my mouth. Everything finally made sense.

Owl was glum on our walk through Loring Park, the chill of predawn pressing down on us both. She and Zoso had had a terrible night, locked away while Alexis was murdered. She kept glancing back at me to make sure I was really there. To be fair, I felt half-gone, deranged from this last week coupled with the lack of sleep.

I was feeling jittery and uneven on the stairs up to my apartment. When had I last eaten? I checked the lock on my door. It looked undamaged. Frank must have picked it. He'd always been handy. Tomorrow, I'd get a new, heavy-duty lock plus a security bar. For tonight, I'd stack empty cans in front of the door so I'd wake up if he tried sneaking in while I slept.

After, I unclipped Owl, poured her kibble, and opened the fridge. I was looking at cans of pop, a half jar of pickles, and the spring rolls and lo mein noodles I'd gotten from the Lotus. I grabbed the spring rolls first because I was too tired to heat anything up. I opened the wrapper and sniffed. They'd already gone bad. I chucked them in the trash and went back for the lo mein. It seemed fresh enough. I wolfed down half the box, cold, then went to the bathroom to wash my face and brush my teeth, made sure the REM app on my wristwatch was on—Harry was about to see a woman knocked out cold—and then fell into bed.

When next I opened my eyes, Mother Mary was standing over me.

She beamed at me. "Awake, I see. You always did like noodles." Her eyes slid to the half-empty takeout carton on my table. "That's why I put the poison in them. It takes more than the clatter of cans to revive someone in your state."

I thought I saw Frank looming just behind her, but I couldn't move my head.

I couldn't move anything.

CHAPTER 69

Van

Surely this was another nightmare.

Mother Mary appeared older than I remembered, crow's-feet in the corners of her eyes, marionette lines at the sides of her mouth, her light hair gone silver, the facial disfigurement on one side of her face sunken with her cheeks.

She looked the age she'd be now.

A guttural cry escaped my mouth.

"I spiked the dog food, too," she said. "I hope I didn't go too heavy. I didn't know how much you'd feed the beast. I'm not surprised you kept the dog, by the way." Her mouth curved in disapproval. "You were always a selfish girl."

I'd never heard her speak so much. She'd been so mild, so *invisible* throughout my childhood. She sat on the edge of the bed. I tipped toward her as the mattress went down, the only movement I could make an involuntary one. Was I blinking? I was too scared to close my eyes and find out.

She leaned over, and I smelled onions.

"You didn't honor your Father, Evangeline," she murmured. "You turned away when he was jailed. The others found their way home, but not you. You kept on your evil path." She moved even closer, her mouth brushing my ear, the onion smell growing stronger. "'Whoever reviles his Father or Mother must surely die.' That's what the Bible says. It's hard because, as your Mother, I love you deeply."

Was she speaking factually now, or metaphorically? We'd thought she'd been Frank's favorite, before Cordelia, and when my fellow Sisters and I whispered about which Mother we hoped was ours, I always picked Mary. Looking at her now, I wondered if I hadn't been right. Our features were similar—the light hair, the wide eyes, the nose, though her busted cheek was her most prominent feature. Had Frank done that to her? Why had I never wondered before?

"And a parent never stops parenting, which is why I'm here to teach you a lesson. I cannot have you messing up your Father's mission. We were willing to let you remain on your own godless path, but we cannot let you interfere with our holy one. Too bad you didn't heed my warnings."

She pulled back. Moonlight fell on her red sweater and red scarf. I made the cry again. The woman who believed she'd seen me go into Alexis's house? It was Mother Mary she'd seen, slinking in to drug both dogs and poison Alexis. Same with the shadow I'd witnessed slink through Emily's window, followed by vines.

Not my Father. My *Mother*.

My heart thudded violently, careening inside my rib cage.

Mother Mary clucked her tongue. "It's better to pay in this life than the next, Evangeline. That's why your two friends had to be handed off to God. It was your penance on earth so there can be room for you in heaven." Her head tipped so she could study me. "I know you think you can escape the pain by helping people who are powerless, but that's like washing a mirror and hoping to get your own face clean. No, it's better this way."

Her eyes grew unfocused. I strained everything in an attempt to move my hand, desperate to get to Owl. It was no use. Whatever she'd slipped me had paralyzed me.

"Do you know that he let me stay in charge while he married that woman in Florida? He sent us her money so we could continue his work. Father always provides. I chose the location for our new Farm and have prepared all your Sisters to be called home, all but you." She unwrapped the scarf so it hung loose. "We've built up Frank's Farm even better than before. It's twice as big. We have sheep and specialize in knitting. We're called Crimson Wool. 'Though your sins be as scarlet, they shall be as white as snow; though they be red like crimson, they shall be as wool.'"

She smiled beatifically. "It was me who decided it would be best for you to go to prison for the murder of those two women. You'll be completely discredited, anything you say. All loose ends will be tied up. All problems gone."

I started laughing. It came out as a wheeze. Mother Mary's eyebrows pressed together. "What?" she asked, her eyes boring into mine.

You want to send me to prison for two murders I didn't commit when you could have waited for me to be caught for the three I did.

But my mouth didn't move.

She frowned and continued. "But since you visited Grace and Hannah, Father decided prison wouldn't put you far enough away, and Father knows best. That's why I'm here now." Her face cleared. "It was on my direction that Grace put her DNA into the system a few years ago. That was the easiest way to call the stragglers home, and we finally have contact with all of them. We were waiting on Rachel, and two weeks ago, she found us."

I thought about moving my pinkie. I was surprised when it responded. When I tried my toes, they also twitched. My pulse skip-thudded.

"The Mothers all stayed in contact, of course. It was best to let the children scatter, but nothing could break us up. Even Cordelia returned to the Family, and you know what a problem she always was."

Cordelia! Was she still alive?

I felt Mother Mary press something cold into my hand. My pistol. My heart splintered as she steered my hand toward my head.

"Now you can go knowing I love you." I felt the cold muzzle press against my temple as her breath heated my ear. "You really were mine, you know," she whispered. "The child of my loins."

Did the shadow behind her move? Had Frank Roth come to witness my death? Mother Mary was guiding my finger onto the trigger when we both heard the mighty growl. It was full of meat and primal rage and it echoed and then suddenly, Owl launched on top of me. She was swaying and snarling, unable to see straight but wanting to fight whatever was hurting me.

Mother Mary grabbed the gun from my hand and pointed it toward Owl.

"No," I groaned. Then, louder: "No." Finally, I screamed it. "No!"

A wave of concern surged across Mother Mary's face. She glanced behind her, toward the front door, and then leaped to my window and yanked it open, a shadow at her heels, just out of my line of vision. She disappeared onto the fire escape moments before the door flew open and Harry rushed in.

CHAPTER 70

Just Judy

2020

He raised himself on an elbow, staring down on her, one eye blue, one brown. His hand ran through her hair, soothing her. "I have a wonderful surprise for you."

"You are all the surprise I ever need."

Frank Roth shook his head, smiling beneficently. "I've been sent a new Mother. She heard about our Farm and wants to be a part of it. Her name is Marian Vermillion. She lives in Florida, and she wants to tithe to us." He cupped her shattered cheek, the one he'd broken with his fist all those years ago. "We'll never want again. Can you be patient with me for a while longer? Can you hold the Family together while I go to Florida?"

Bone dust coated her mouth, choked her throat, stuffed her stomach. She'd thought the test was finally over. They'd been through so much since he'd been released from prison, steady work rebuilding what had been lost. When their reunion stalled, she'd had the idea of Daughter Grace and Daughter Hannah putting their DNA profiles online like a clarion to call the rest of the Family home. She had thought it was finally almost over, but she'd been wrong. "Of course."

He beamed at her. It was pure sunshine after a lifetime in shadow.

"You're the only one," he'd told her when she visited him in prison. "The only woman I need."

She'd trusted him. What had she done to suddenly force him into this corner, to make him believe he needed a Mother from outside the Family? How had she fallen short? Well, she knew what her punishment would be. More time without him.

She'd survived it before.

"Do you know how long you'll be in Florida?" she asked.

His face darkened. He sat all the way up and reached for his pants. She grabbed for him but stopped just short of touching his flesh.

"I'm so sorry," she said. "I didn't mean to question you." She pulled up a blanket to cover her shame.

He stood, yanking on his trousers. "You'll keep Cordelia close?" he asked, his back still to her.

"Yes." It hadn't been easy over the years. That girl had been noth-ing but trouble. Mother Mary couldn't stand her. It wasn't the hair that required regular dyeing, or even how she'd always been Frank's favorite. Those sacrifices she could live with. It was how Cordelia had run away, almost ruined their whole operation a lifetime ago, and gotten Evangeline in trouble to boot.

She wasn't supposed to feel anything special for the only child of her blood, but she couldn't help it. Evangeline had always been so bright, so dutiful—at least until she lied for Cordelia. Of course Frank had seen right through it. Evangeline's punishment had been to clean naked, tears streaming down her face.

It had taken everything in her not to carry clothes to her daughter.

The whole awful experience was Cordelia's fault, but still, Judy had done her duty by the girl, dyeing her hair, giving up her shared bed with Frank when Cordelia turned eighteen. He never slept with girls he was related to. It was why he had to go out and pluck flowers for his garden. When he brought them back, most were meek, some of them—like Catherine, who'd accidentally drunk that poison all those years ago—to the point of uselessness. Not Cordelia. But Frank had worked his magic on her through the years, first telling her he'd kill her family if she ever disobeyed him, and then magicking her to forget who she was and what she'd left behind.

These days, Cordelia was no longer a threat. She'd gone from being a spitfire who'd always tried to escape to living with another Mother, as biddable as a lamb. Mother Mary was also a mere trace of the girl she used to be all those years ago, working at the Sauk Centre Dairy Freez.

It had been different for her, hadn't it?

Different for Judith Mary Morsa.

She shuddered. She hadn't thought that name in so long. Who even was that girl?

She was Mother Mary now, chosen wife to the Messiah, and his vision would never lead them astray.

CHAPTER 71

Van

Harry had been sleeping in his car outside my apartment when the app started buzzing.

While he fed me water and massaged movement back into my extremities—whatever Mother Mary had drugged me and Owl with, it'd begun receding before she'd fled—he told me about the alarm announcing that my heartbeat had dropped dangerously low and then skyrocketed. It had been going off for minutes before he realized it wasn't part of his dream.

"I'm so, so sorry," he kept saying, remorse tattooed across his face.

"It was my Mother," I finally got out. As soon as I could move, I gathered Owl into my arms. She licked my face furiously, her rump wiggling. I felt her all over. She seemed to be fine.

"Your *mother* was here?" Harry asked.

I nodded, my face pressed into Owl's neck. "Mother Mary. From the commune." My heart ached so bad I wanted to cut it out. "She said she was the one who gave birth to me. She also confirmed Frank Roth's still alive." I shuddered.

"Do you believe her?" Harry asked softly.

I thought of the shadow in the corner of the room. I'd felt like it had been Frank, same with the man who'd jumped off the roof. But I hadn't seen either of them, not clearly. Could it really have been Mother Mary behind everything? "I don't know anymore."

Harry had been sitting on my bed. He stood and went to the sink to refill my water glass, wading through the garbage. "What was she doing here?"

He hadn't removed his peacoat. His hair was tousled, and from behind, he looked both strong and vulnerable.

"She came to kill me," I said simply.

He stopped. Turned. His profile was gorgeous, carved of glass.

"She said Frank wanted it." Owl fit as much of herself on my lap as she could. "She said that she was the one who killed Emily Barris and Alexis to frame me, that she thought that would be enough to punish me for leaving the Family." I squeezed Owl. "And for recently investigating Frank Roth."

Harry took a step toward me. His face was exposed, so handsome it hurt to look at. For a moment, I thought how unhinged this all sounded, like the story of a woman who was covering for her own crimes. Harry hadn't witnessed Mother Mary leave; he'd only seen an open window.

"You didn't mention you were investigating Frank Roth," he said. "Why?"

My apartment was so cramped, so dirty. It wasn't fair that I had to tell him here, but what choice did I have? I'd already waited far too long. I moved Owl off my lap as gently as I could. I needed to stand, facing Harry, to do this. My legs were shaky but held. "Since you told me that Caroline's abductor had two different-colored eyes."

He went so stiff that it was like looking at a cutout of him, a Flat Harry.

"Frank Roth had two different-colored eyes," I said. "One blue, one brown. He was also on the road a lot, and sometimes he'd bring home different girls." The grief was so intense that it felt like someone had scraped away my muscle, leaving skin draped on bone. "One year, he showed up with a girl with dark hair. She kept to herself. I thought she was much older than me, but it turned out she wasn't. It was just the way she carried herself."

Harry's hand lifted, like he was touching a ghost only he could see.

"We were told the girl's name was Cordelia. She tried to escape once," I said. "But Frank brought her back. I didn't know until yesterday that Cordelia was your sister." I dragged in a breath. "Cordelia was Caroline."

His knees buckled, but he caught himself. He stepped back when I reached for him. "You suspected? Since Duluth?"

We were so near now that I could see the pain glistening on his face. I nodded.

"Do you know where Caroline is now?" he asked, his voice hoarse.

I shook my head. "No, but Mother Mary made it sound like she was still alive."

He took another step back, then another, until he was up against my kitchen cupboards. He began shaking his head side to side, slowly at first, and then faster.

"Every bad thing you think about me is true," I said.

Hatred flashed across his face before he closed it off. A terrible chill squeezed my chest. Harry was done with me, just like that. I'd known this was coming, but nothing could have prepared me for how bad it hurt.

"Lock your window," he said gruffly. "Prop something against the door tonight and change your locks tomorrow."

He strode toward the door. Stopped, his back to me, his hand on the knob. "You're medically stable?"

"Yeah," I choked out.

He nodded, opened the door, and stumbled away.

CHAPTER 72

Van

Dawn cracked through the frozen crust of night, hauling in the day on cold, rose-colored arms.

I watched it from inside my car, Owl beside me.

Mother Mary—*my mother*—had killed two women because she believed Frank Roth wanted her to, and she'd been about to murder me for the same reason. She was a serious threat, and she'd be difficult to track down. All the Mothers were off the grid, outside the system. How to find her?

But that wasn't mine to decide anymore. Today I would confess to Harry about the three men I'd murdered. It would be my last day of freedom. That was the hardest part, the cases I'd leave unsolved. My throat grew tight. No, the hardest part was losing Harry. He'd go straight to Chandler, if he hadn't already, tell him about Mother Mary, about Caroline, about Frank Roth potentially being alive. Chandler would've already assigned the case to someone else.

Not to me. Never again to me.

Movement on the other side of the door drew my attention. The Animal Haven shelter wouldn't officially open for a few more hours, but the morning caretakers arrived with first light. I got out of my car, nudging Owl to follow. She wouldn't budge. I finally had to lift all seventy-five pounds of her. I don't know how I found the strength. I kicked the door until a woman opened it. I didn't recognize her. I handed her Owl's leash.

"This is my foster, Owl," I said, my voice garbled. "She's the best dog in the whole world, but I have to return her early. I have an emergency. Her owner's name was Emily Barris, but she's no longer alive. The Minneapolis police will have the records, and once you confirm, you can put her up for adoption."

I ran away before the woman could ask any questions. I covered my ears so I couldn't hear Owl howling. They'd find her a good home, a steady one, and soon. It was the best thing for her.

Then I drove to work feeling as hollow as a fresh-dug grave.

I didn't have much time before Harry got in. I hurried to my office and fired up my computer, glancing at the clock. It was early, but I was banking on the Eden Valley Nursing Home having staff on at all hours. When someone answered, I explained who I was and the situation.

The email reached my inbox before I was halfway through writing the report.

The subject line was Anne Morsa Photographs. I clicked it open and skimmed the scanned photos the attendant had gotten from her album, three snaps of Judy Morsa in high school.

Judith Mary Morsa.

Mother Mary.

Whatever had shattered her cheek had happened after she'd been abducted. The severe injury was enough to blur the resemblance between the girl who'd run away and the woman who'd birthed me, unless you were looking for it.

That made Anne Morsa my great-grandmother.

I included that information in my report, typing from a great distance.

In my estimation, Frank Roth had hunted without a clear goal in the early years, maybe even before 1986. But in 1986, he'd been at the state fair—I put in a note for Kyle to confirm this—where he'd crossed paths with Gina Penchant, Robin Seer, Lulu Geldman, and Judy Morsa. He'd tracked them all down outside the fair and murdered the first three by having them drink poison. He'd possibly asked them to go with him, and when they'd refused, he'd killed them. Frank Roth had never handled rejection well.

Judy Morsa said yes, and so she lived.

Did she know about the other three girls, the ones whose corpses she'd walked over to stay with Frank? It was worth looking into. What I knew for sure was that she'd killed two women closely associated with me, Emily and Alexis, intending to frame me for their deaths. She'd fed them the same poison as Frank had fed those three girls back in 1986. Her plan had then been to kill me with my own pistol, making it look like suicide. Her motive? That I was digging into Frank Roth's 1998 abduction of Caroline Steinbeck, who'd been raised on the commune as Cordelia Roth.

I included every detail Mother Mary had dropped last night, including mention of a farm named Crimson Wool, and then I sent the report to Harry and cc'd Chandler.

They now knew everything I did. I trusted they would handle it better than I could.

I stood and walked to Harry's lab. Green mile, indeed. But I needed to come clean, about everything. I owed him that much.

When I opened the door, Harry was sitting facing me.

There was an empty chair across from him.

CHAPTER 73

Just Judy / Mother Mary

The Present

He was always with her, even when he wasn't. His presence, his command, it filled her. With every step she took, with every breath, she carried him. She would do anything for him, had already done so much. The way his bones resisted every blow, how his vision saw through flesh, time, and lies. He was more than human.

He was a god, and she was his disciple.

She had never given up hope, even after seeing the crash on television, knowing that he was on that plane. No impact could kill Frank Roth, she knew that in her heart. So she'd built up their empire for years, all of it leading up to this moment: the culmination of her obedience and devotion. Before he'd left for Florida, he'd promised that it would all pay off. Now, here she was, tying the final strings, her body beginning to bend but her soul burning with the anticipation of what was to come. Last night hadn't gone as expected, but just a little more effort and they would reclaim what was theirs.

He wanted Evangeline's visions, she knew that. He thought they would come to him with Evangeline's death. It gutted her that she hadn't been able to deliver that to him, but she could give him another pair of eyes.

Hers.

A flicker of doubt brushed the edge of her mind, a tiny whisper of the children she had lost, of the life she'd once lived. But his presence swelled inside her, and the doubt disappeared. She was entirely his now. Always had been. Her spine creaked as she pulled the stick out of the flames, hands finally steady. He would be pleased. He would smile that smile that made her feel young again, though she wouldn't be able to see it. She imagined his touch.

And then she drove the fiery stick into each eye socket.

"It's done," she whispered to the wind, knowing he could hear her. He always did.

CHAPTER 74

Van

The air in the lab tightened, a pressure valve seconds from bursting. There was deciding to tell Harry and sacrifice our friendship and my career, and then there was actually doing it.

But he already knew, didn't he? Tension radiated off him in waves.

I forced my legs to walk across the room and drop me into the chair.

My palms sweated against the cold metal table. I guessed we were going to play this out to the end. "I'm sorry I didn't tell you about your sister earlier." I swallowed hard, my throat working. "Also, Patty Devries didn't kill those three men."

Harry was staring at a spot over my left shoulder, his face as cold and as perfect as polished marble. "I'm aware," he said. His eyes landed on me, terrifying in their clarity. "I also know that all three men were active pedophiles."

I held myself as still as glass. Those of us who'd had our truth stolen spent our whole lives trying to learn how to believe ourselves again. When someone just handed you that treasure, it was terrifying. "I know who killed them. I—"

Harry held up a hand. His expression made clear that he knew, that he'd maybe known for a while. "Don't say it."

I'd walked in the dark for too long. "Harry," I said, "I should turn myself in."

He studied me, his eyes as blue as the sky, as earnest as love. "You might do it again?"

I searched for the truth, but in the end, it found my lips on its own. "Never." I'd decided back in Costa Rica, the first case Harry and I ever worked together, that I would take my own life before I'd take another. It was the truest thing I knew.

He stood, brushing imaginary dust off his arms. "Then you can turn yourself in, or you can help us find your mother and my sister." He straightened his shirt cuffs. "Kyle just texted. He's ready for us."

CHAPTER 75

Van

Harry led me to the conference room where just a couple days ago I'd run our meeting. My bones were cast in lead as I followed. I'd planned to go to prison today. Half of me was still there, shame-walking out of the BCA and into a police car. I needed to pull myself together to help Harry find Caroline, to stop my murdering Mother, to prove Frank had killed the three girls in 1986.

When Harry held the conference room door open for me, I bit the inside of my cheek until I tasted the hot rush of blood. There was only here, only now, only my job.

I stepped inside.

I'd expected to see Kyle and a bunch of empty chairs.

My hand flew to my mouth when I realized what I was looking at instead.

A task force.

Deputy Superintendent Ed Chandler, my boss, sat at the head of the table, his usually stern expression softened with concern. Deepty and Johnna, the forensic scientists whose meticulous work had often been my saving grace, offered small nods of solidarity. Kyle was there, his earnest eyes reflecting determination. But most surprising of all was Comstock, eternal thorn in my side. He'd been an adversary more often than not, but now his weathered face held warmth. He tried to hide it, but I'd already seen it.

For a moment, I was frozen in place, disbelief coursing through me. They were all here. For justice. For Harry. For *me*.

I was no longer fighting the horror of my Family alone, forced to stand by and watch them destroy child after child. I had a team.

"Where do we start?" Comstock asked.

I was so tired that tracers floated in my field of vision. I could weep, or I could get to work.

I walked to the board, quickly sketching all the information I had, starting with Gina's, Robin's, and Lulu's murders. I moved to Caroline Steinbeck's abduction, then covered Frank Roth serving a little more than two years at the Federal Prison Camp in Duluth before showing up married to Marian Vermillion in Florida. I ended with Mother Mary's visit in the early hours, where she'd confessed to Emily's and Alexis's murders.

The room pulsed with life. Papers rustled as Chandler shuffled through a stack of files, his movements purposeful, handing out the appropriate files for each case I covered. Deepty and Johnna took notes, Kyle typed, Comstock and Harry studied me.

"What can you tell us about Judy Morsa's mindset?" Harry asked when I'd finished the recap.

I glanced back at the board. It was more color than white. "She thinks Frank Roth is alive. He may be. But she's the one killing now." I gripped the edge of the table. I hoped I was right. "She mentioned a farm, that it's twice as big as the old one. That they specialize in knitting." My head was splitting trying to pull out the details, still fogged with fear and exhaustion and whatever she'd drugged me with. "Crimson Wool, she said it's called."

"On it," Kyle said, typing away at his laptop. "No Crimson Wool, but there's a Vermillion Enterprises in Cambridge, Minnesota." Some more typing. "They have a storefront there. They sell wool clothing, jellies, canned vegetables."

"That sounds like it," Johnna said, looking to me for approval.

"It does," I agreed.

Comstock was already on his feet, barking into his walkie-talkie. Kyle handed him the address, and Chandler pledged any assistance he needed. We were dealing with an active murderer and at least one abductee who was in danger, if she was still alive.

And they believed me.

Cambridge was an hour north of Minneapolis, but I was willing to bet Comstock's team would reach it in under forty-five. I turned to follow him out, intending to find a place in his caravan. Chandler held me back.

"You're too close to this one, Reed," he said, his bald egg head bobbing. "Plus, you look like freeze-dried shit. Comstock will get it sorted. You and Steinbeck sit this out."

I opened my mouth to argue but felt the world tilt sideways. Harry caught the hand I threw out. Chandler scowled at him. "Keep an eye on her."

And then he followed the rest out, leaving just Harry and me.

"I'm good," I said, feeling awkward.

Harry was studying me. He looked so dreamy, like a cherub. Was he floating? "Are you awake right now?" he asked.

"Of course I am." I tried to push past him to get to my office, but my legs weren't working.

That's when I realized I was falling, for real this time.

CHAPTER 76

Van

Anne Morsa is holding me, rocking back and forth, singing a lullaby. I'm a child, a toddler, a newborn.

"Hush," she says. "Back to sleep."

I try to fight. I need to be somewhere but can't remember where. My head is so heavy I can barely lift it. I'm in her room in the nursing home. She's so old. How can she hold me? Her arms are weak. Besides, she isn't my grandmother, she's my great-grandmother.

"Judy," she scolds. "You know who you are. You're a homing pigeon. The only reason you didn't come back home was because you couldn't."

I'm twisting in her arms when a splash of cold hits my face.

Water. I blinked, looked around. I was lying on the floor of the conference room. Harry stood over me, his face etched in worry. He held a paper cup.

"You passed out," he said. "Or fell asleep standing. I couldn't tell."

You're a homing pigeon.

The only reason you didn't come back home was because you couldn't.

I was scrabbling to stand, moving so quickly that a wash of dizziness almost knocked me back. "She's not in Cambridge," I said. "Mother Mary. She went back to Frank's Farm. The original one, where I grew up. It's something her grandma said, that Judy—if given a chance—always returns to her home. That's gotta be the Farm. She lived there longer than anywhere. It's where she . . . had me."

Harry helped me to my feet and then forcibly sat me in a chair. His strength caught me off guard.

"Frank didn't sell it?" he asked.

I shook my head. Was that a buzzing I was hearing? "I don't know."

Harry suddenly appeared angry. It'd been lying dormant, just below the surface, but he wasn't hiding it anymore. He was furious. With *me*. I couldn't blame him, but I was right about this. I felt it in my bones.

I tried to stand, but he pushed me down again. "You're not investigating anything," he said. "You shouldn't even be *walking*."

"Harry," I pleaded. "Mother Mary is there. I know she is. Just let me go."

"Chandler said I need to keep an eye on you." He considered me for a moment. "Stay here. I'll be right back."

I heard him just outside the door, talking on the phone. I was planning to sneak out of the building without him knowing. Too bad I didn't have whatever paralyzing agent Mother Mary had given me. I could knock Harry out and escape. My best bet was just to lie and tell him I was going home to sleep.

The words were on my lips when he reentered the conference room, his brow furrowed. "Frank Roth's farm was held in a revocable trust in his name when you all lived there. It's never changed hands. The property taxes have been paid every year since."

I leaped to my feet. "I'm driving."

He shook his head. "Not this time."

CHAPTER 77

Van

Harry was rigid, quiet on the drive. I understood why. He might see his sister again today. I was quiet for different reasons. We were driving to my childhood home, my first nest, a place I hadn't seen in well over a decade. I'd experienced severe trauma there, but also good times. Would it seem bigger? Smaller? Would I recognize it at all?

Chandler had given us permission to make the nearly two-hour drive northwest of the Cities—had even coordinated with a pair of agents who were in the area so we weren't on-site alone. He clearly didn't believe we'd find anything but was going to play by the book.

The cold April air tried to pry through the cracks in the car window as Harry navigated the winding roads of rural Minnesota, sending fingers down my spine. The landscape was barren, a patchwork of brown and gray against the dreary sky, a few clots of snow still hanging on.

I was trying to convince myself it was no big deal—just another case—until we hit the gravel road to Frank's Farm, and my heart hammered with old memories. Knuckles stiff from pulling weeds and churning heavy pots of stew for the Family, arms aching from lifting never-ending laundry in and out of icy basins, and the worst of all: the constant fear gnawing at us—no error or hesitation would go unnoticed by Frank.

A cold sweat prickled over my skin. Could I go through with this?

An unmarked car was parked at the end of the drive, where our farm stand used to be. Two agents stepped out when we pulled up alongside them. I didn't recognize either.

"Gate's locked," the older agent said, her posture suggesting she was ready for anything.

"And we're being watched," her partner added, pointing at a camera poised over the gate.

I was having a hard time drawing a breath.

"Is it on?" Harry asked.

Both women shrugged.

Harry sent our location and the situation update to Chandler.

"You want to tell us what we're expecting?" the gray-haired agent asked as Harry typed.

"This was an active commune up until the late aughts," I said. "It might be abandoned, the camera a fake installed to deter trespassers, or there might be a contingent living here—mostly, if not all, women and children—and housing a murderer."

The two agents exchanged a glance. "You're shitting me," the younger one said.

"You can hang back, guard the entrance," I said.

They looked at each other again before the older one hitched up her belt. "We're here. You can give us the rest of the details on the walk in."

We stepped around the locked gate. The crunch of gravel beneath our feet echoed the rhythm of my racing heart. More memories flooded in. The old oak we used to climb, its branches twisted and gnarled. The beginning of the creek whose lacy ice we'd poke at with sticks. The rock pile where we buried our pets. The field where Frank made us keep hoeing the rows even after our blisters popped and made the wood handles slippery.

Then, as we rounded the final bend, it came into view.

The Farm. Dread gripped my throat, every instinct screaming at me to run.

Frank's house stood proudly at the center, flanked by barns and sheds that once teemed with life. Nearby was the industrial kitchen where we processed the food for the Farm plus what Frank sold to the public. The children's dormitories loomed beyond, silent sentinels bearing witness to a past so awful I sometimes wondered if I'd dreamed it. The smell of spring farming hit my nose, fresh hay mingling with the sharp tang of manure, the rustle and moan of animals, and . . .

"Smoke," the agent nearest me said, pointing at a wisp appearing from behind Frank's house.

A cracking noise in the woods drew all our attention, and then another, and then a cry.

It sounded like a group, all of them fleeing.

We'd come to the right place.

CHAPTER 78

Van

I raced toward the smoke, my chest feeling bruised. Time and space flickered, fireworks and snakes. One minute I was charging forward, Harry on my heels, the next I was in the church the day Frank shattered Veronica.

He's just finished his four-hour Sunday sermon. We girls think we're going to the kitchen to prepare the afternoon feast, but Frank has different plans. He asks Veronica to read her school essay to the congregation.

"Sir?" Veronica asks. Her body is in the appropriate submissive posture, her eyes on the ground.

"Your essay." He takes a paper from his lectern, steps off the altar, and walks it over to her. His face is pleasant. Serious, but not angry. "Your teacher called me about it right before I pulled you all out of public school. You don't remember?"

His tone is so inviting, but his eyes don't match. Mother Mary has a wet face, but she averts her gaze, pretends not to see. Does she know what's about to happen? I feel the sudden urge to grab Veronica's hand and run.

Veronica takes the paper Frank is offering her. It flutters like a wounded bird in her hands. "I love living on Frank's Farm," she reads, her voice high and clear. "It is my favorite place. But I do not like the naked punishment—"

"Aha!" Frank booms. We all jump. "You *did* tell them our secrets."

Her eyes widen. I know what she's thinking because it's what all of us who went to school at Frank's behest are thinking: He *told us* to share with the world the wonder of his Farm. I remember because on the day he informed us it was our job to evangelize, I'd thought, *God made me for this. It's in my name.*

Evangeline.

I clear my throat because there must be a mistake, but before I can get out the words, he has her by the neck. Not the neck of her long dress, her *neck*. He drags her toward the door by her tender skin. "Follow, my children!" he bellows. "See the fate that awaits those who speak out against their Father. Bear witness as I share grace with her and wash away her sins."

We freeze for a moment, all of us.

It's going to be a baptism, the very worst of Frank's punishments.

I shove to the front of Frank's Flock, trying to catch Veronica's eye, to somehow signal to her to remember to play dead so Frank lets up sooner, but I'm only eleven and have always been small. I'm behind the others, struggling to push through, but I'm too late because we've reached the trough.

That's what I'm doing now, running toward the trough because that's where the smoke is coming from. Is Harry on my heels? Do my feet even touch the ground?

Frank holds Veronica high. He shakes her, and she whimpers. "Does anyone have anything to say on behalf of this evil child?" he demands.

I want to speak, but I feel tiny, even smaller than I am and more naked than I was that day I stood, unclothed, in front of my Family. But I have to say something. I think the words—*stop, you told us to share our lives, don't hurt her*—but only a grunt escapes. I look to the Mothers, but they're watching their feet.

"Evangeline, stop!"

That was Harry. I can hear his voice, but I'm running between time. I have to save Veronica before it's too late. I can if I hurry.

"You are all party to this grace," Frank says, turning to the trough, clutching Veronica. I expect a speech, but instead, he thrusts her body down with such speed that her head hits the side with a sickening clang. She goes rigid, a raspberry bloom staining her light hair, and then she disappears underwater.

When Frank finally pulls her out minutes later, she no longer looks human. The Mothers hurry her to the infirmary. We're not allowed to ask questions, even after she's carried into the dining hall and strapped to a chair later, mouth open, eyes half-lidded.

I let Frank do that to my Sister.

I am too late. But wait! Veronica's still here, waiting all these years, kneeling by the trough.

I rush to her side, heat stitching my ribs, and drop to my knees.

She lifts her face.

She smiles, her skin stretching like leather.

I scream.

CHAPTER 79

Van

It wasn't Veronica.

It was Judith Mary Morsa, my mother, kneeling in front of the animal trough where Frank Roth cracked Veronica's head. Gore ran down her face, oozing from the sockets where her eyes had once been. A pointed stick glowed orange in the fire alongside her, the muck of her eyes sizzling on the end of it.

"Is it you, Evangeline?" she asked. Her voice was lavender, its dissonance with her face stomach-turning. "Frank said you'd come here today. He saw it in a vision. He's never been wrong. That's why I've given my eyes, do you understand? So your Father can continue to see the future. Don't fear for me. The Lord gives sight to the blind, and he loves the righteous." She reached out blindly, her hands like claws. "Think what power he'll have if you give him *your* vision." Her hand hit my leg, and she clung to me. "Give him your eyes, won't you, Evangeline? Give your Father your eyes. Let him see our future fully so he can lead us all."

I tore her off and scrambled backward, desperate to get away. Harry leaped in front of me even though Mother Mary couldn't hurt anyone, not anymore. One of the agents was calling for reinforcements, and the other had drawn her weapon and was turning in every direction.

"I should have raised you better," Mother Mary called out. "It's our role to take on the sins of the Father. The other children know that, Evangeline. You did too, once."

It was clashing, crashing, the past and the present, my cases, my life.

"Where's Cordelia?" I yelled, lurching to my feet. "Where is she?"

Mother Mary clasped her hands as if in prayer, holding them beneath her chin. She was shivering, whether from shock or religious fervor, I didn't know. "She's gone where no one can find her. Frank told us all about your visions, Evangeline. Tell me about them. Tell me about your gift."

I stepped around Harry to face her, my disgust and fear combining with pity. She'd been an innocent girl once, abducted by Frank Roth. He'd molded her into this, and she'd kept the shape of her cage even after it was removed. Was he alive? I thought no. I also thought it didn't matter as long as the women he'd left behind carried on his sins.

"I will tell you about my visions," I said, "if you tell me where Cordelia is."

Mother Mary's smile grew so wide it cracked. "She's with the Lord."

Harry cried out.

Mother Mary's face twitched. "You are someone who knew her?" she said, raising her voice. "You knew our Cordelia? That one was trouble from the start, you should understand that. But even still, I obeyed the Father, right up until the end." She bowed her head and held out her wrists. "I killed those three girls in 1986. I killed the two women now. I confess."

A surge of anger blazed up my spine. "You didn't. You're covering for him, for a man who abandoned you."

"I am a killer," she said, her empty sockets lifting toward me, seeking me. "It runs in our blood, doesn't it, Evangeline."

The sounds of sirens pierced the air. I turned to Harry. It was all I could do to bear the raw pain in his face. "We're going to find her," I said.

I called to the agent with her weapon out. "We're going to search the outbuildings for survivors. This woman needs first aid." I pulled Harry away. "Let's start in the girls' dorm."

His face was slack, but he followed.

The dormitory door creaked when I opened it, gun drawn. It seemed smaller, cramped even, with a dozen narrow beds pressed against walls. They were all neatly made, the scent of lye soap hanging in the air. The thought of another generation of girls molded by Frank Roth's twisted beliefs nearly drove me mad.

"This was where the girls slept," I said.

His gaze scanned the area for any sign of Caroline. "You think she was here?"

I passed my old bed, remembering the evenings spent lying awake, wondering if tonight was the night Frank was hiding beneath one, waiting to catch us talking about him. "Not unless she was visiting children," I said, the words hurting my throat. "She would have lived in the Mothers' dormitory or Frank Roth's house. We'll check every building, though. If she's here, we'll find her."

I hurried through the long room, touching the cold metal frame of each bed. We searched the closets, the bathroom. I touched a toothbrush. Still wet. There'd definitely been girls here recently, but the place had emptied out. I wouldn't have been surprised if Mother Mary had had an evacuation plan in place.

We moved on to the Mothers' dormitory. It was the same in there. Beds, memories, no people. It was like they'd been zapped away by a spaceship, except for the undercurrent of sorrow, a sense of loss that hung heavy in the air.

The ambulance sounded near when we stepped outside, half a dozen officers swarming the scene. I barked quick orders to the nearest one—rope off the area, be on guard for booby traps, gather any people you find into the central courtyard. I gave a different set of commands to the two agents: Call BCA Deputy Superintendent

Ed Chandler and MPD Detective Dave Comstock and get them out here ASAP.

Then I turned to Harry, my heart lead. "There's only one place left to look."

I led him from the Mothers' dorm and toward Frank's house.

As a Daughter, I'd never been inside.

CHAPTER 80

Van

I shot Harry a glance when we reached Frank's porch. His jaw was set, his eyes narrowed with determination, but he was so pale. Taking a deep breath, I pushed open the door, revealing a surprisingly modern interior. When I was a girl, no technology had been allowed on the commune other than the basics we needed to run water, provide lighting, and cook and process food. The exception had been Frank Roth's house, where radio and sometimes even TV sounds emerged.

There was a lot more than a radio and a TV here now.

The walls were lined with sleek monitors, flashing with data and information. One screen showed several police cars parked at the end of the driveway, another was aimed toward the woods, and still others displayed the officers streaming across the property.

"Keep your guard up," I said, my weapon pointed and my voice low as we stepped farther into the house. "We don't know what we're walking into."

Harry nodded.

Every shadow seemed to hold a threat, every corner a hidden danger. I could feel Harry's desperation mounting with each passing second.

If Caroline was in this house, she wasn't on the main floor.

I considered the evacuation plan Mother Mary would have had. The Mothers and Sisters would most likely be ordered to take off into the woods, carrying any young children with them. Did they have cars stashed nearby, or a bus, waiting for just this emergency? Mary would want them hidden where they couldn't be questioned, couldn't say a word against Frank Roth.

Cordelia she'd send the farthest away. She was the one crime Mother Mary couldn't take responsibility for, not if Cordelia could testify for herself. That's why it made the most sense that she'd been killed. Mother Mary wouldn't risk her being discovered in the forest or being stopped in whatever getaway vehicle they had. No, the smartest plan would have been to eliminate Cordelia and scatter the commune, reassembling them once the heat wore off, exactly as they'd done after Frank's arrest.

Still, I felt she was alive. It wasn't a vision, wasn't even a hunch. It was blind hope.

"Let's check upstairs," Harry said. His voice was thin, his pallor gone from white to gray.

Fear clicked in my ears when we reached the second level. It was too quiet, the air smelling sweet-rotten. Harry sensed it, too. I could tell by the way he held himself tight, every muscle coiled like a spring.

"I'll clear this room," I said, pointing to the nearest door, "and then we'll move to the next."

He nodded.

I opened the door. Looked up. Spotted huge, fluffy clouds drawn on the slanted farmhouse ceiling. Harry stumbled past me, making a strangled noise. They were exactly like the clouds Caroline had painted in her childhood room. I stepped forward, reaching out to touch one. The white paint came off on my finger. *Fresh.*

I glanced out the window, toward the wide part of the river. The realization physically struck me.

I knew where Caroline was.

CHAPTER 81

Van

"Come on!" I yelled, running down the stairs and tearing out of the house. The cold wind hit me like a slap. I raced toward the water, yelling at an officer and an EMT to follow.

My mother's dark words still echoed in my skull. *Give him your eyes, won't you, Evangeline? Give your Father your eyes. Let him see our future fully so he can lead us all.* I'd been too late to help Mother Mary, too late to help Veronica.

I was always too late here.

The woods seemed darker, the cold gripping my bones as I ran toward the river. The same one I used to splash in as a kid, under the careful eyes of the Watchers, those children too heavy to swim. Because that's why they hadn't been allowed in, wasn't it? They'd inherited Frank's dense bones. They wouldn't have been able to survive deep water. But it was Frank's preferred way to kill his Family.

The forest pressed in as I wove through the tangled underbrush. I couldn't seem to move fast enough. Was Harry behind me? I couldn't spare the movement of looking back. There was no time to waste because it had been a vision, hadn't it, my nightmare of my father holding a girl underneath the water.

I'm walking toward the deepwater creek from my childhood, but something is terribly wrong. The once-clear stream is black, its wet oiliness lewd against the blue sky. Its banks are lined by figures I almost recognize, but their faces have twisted into grotesque masks made of bark, their arms twisted branches, their hollow eyes following my every step. The scent of rotting wood is overwhelming.

That's when I spot Frank Roth kneeling at the river's edge, his back turned to me. His shoulders convulse rhythmically, as if he's scrubbing something in the black water.

I'd thought it was me he'd been holding down.

It had been Caroline.

My feet pounded the forest floor, each step echoing my frantic heartbeat. I could hardly breathe, my chest burning. The sound of the creek grew louder, the roar of the spring-swollen water mingling with the rush of blood in my ears.

And then, I saw him.

Frank—my Father—knelt at the water's edge. I'd been unwilling to accept that he was still alive, could hardly believe it even as I stared straight at him. He was facing away, holding someone underwater, her hands clawing at the air, just like in my vision. My entire body felt like it was on fire as panic surged through me.

"You came home," he said loudly, his back to me. His voice sounded raw. "After all these years, you came home." His shoulders flexed, but he still didn't turn. "It was all for you, Evangeline. Everything I did, everything I put you through, it was to make you stronger. To prepare you. You don't understand it now, but you will. You'll see. This place, it's yours now. It always was."

I remembered the way he laughed—sharp and mocking—when one of us was hurt.

The sting of his anger.

The way his voice could drop to a chilling whisper.

How his eyes narrowed as he judged every mistake.

The suffocating air of dread he'd forced us all to live under.

My desperation for his love, despite who he was. I'd loved him nearly as much as I hated him.

My pistol was drawn, but I couldn't shoot. The risk of hitting Caroline/Cordelia—who else could it be?—was too great. Instead I leaped at Frank, howling like an animal, every ounce of fear he'd instilled in me crystallizing into a weapon.

The collision was brutal, a jarring impact that sent us both tumbling into the creek's icy depths. The water was shockingly cold, wrapping around me like a vise. I could feel the weight of Frank's body, his bulk dragging me down as he held me close. I might as well have been wrapped in chains.

Memories flickered in and out like the sun breaking through clouds. Veronica's face as we skipped to the field, the two of us spinning and twirling in carefree abandon. The softness of a kitten in my hands, its tiny purr vibrating against my palm. Harry, his rare laughter sounding like music, lifting me higher than I ever thought possible. The smell of the yeast as Mother Mary taught me to bake bread, the way her hands kneaded the dough.

I fought against the darkness closing in, desperate to hold on to what was slipping away, but my vision was going black from the cold.

Out of nowhere, a quiet calm washed over me.

This was it. The end.

Frank must have felt it, too, because suddenly he released me.

CHAPTER 82

Frank

We all needed love to do better, even when we didn't deserve it.

Hell, that's when we needed it the *most*—when we were at our lowest, when we'd done our darkest. Frank Roth knew that better than most. It was no accident he'd gathered an army of women to give him the unconditional love his mother had been too weak to.

And now the best of his women, Mother Mary, was gone from him forever. No one knew him like Mary, no one understood the agony of his visions, the exultation of his successes.

No one.

He'd borne witness to her gouging out her eyes. That was how his visions worked. He *saw* his women and his girls. Not every second of their day, but enough to bend them to his will. That was how he'd built his Family, convinced them he was a god, because after all, wasn't he? His bones didn't break. He had visions. He was a holy Pied Piper.

Did he wish he hadn't made mistakes in the early days, hadn't allowed his ego to kill those three girls in 1986? Of course. He'd thought they would come to him like Mother Mary had. When they'd refused him, he'd returned later to offer them the poison. It had been easy for him to see if they were alone or with others, at home or in public. Once he chose a girl, he could follow her with his mind's eye.

Two drank the poison willingly, if tearfully. The third he had to force.

It was because of those three girls—plus some other mistakes through the years—that he'd had to eventually stage his death. It was the only way he could guarantee absolute freedom. The plane crash had been the test of his godhood, and he'd passed, hadn't he? He'd walked away. He hadn't expected the way the fire would twist his skin, how he now had to concentrate to walk smoothly, but it was a small price to pay to be free of his past crimes.

Not that he had ever really expected law enforcement to connect the murders and trace them back to him, but one of the things he'd learned in prison was to cover all your tracks. His plan had been flawless, except for one hitch.

His Lucky Bird.

Evangeline.

She'd been the only of his girls he couldn't read. Her revelations interfered with his. She was also the one most like him, and not just in the visions. Charismatic, though she hid it. Driven. Brilliant.

A killer of three.

He loved her.

She was his true daughter, the heir to his kingdom. He hadn't enjoyed punishing her, but it'd been necessary. The red scarves. Drugging her multiple nights. Chewing her fingernails. Sending Mother Mary to poison her associates. Through it all, he'd been hopeful he could bring her back into the fold, though he'd kept that bit from Mary. The poor woman had already sacrificed so much. His kindness nearly cost him Evangeline when Mother Mary went to kill Lucky Bird without consulting him first, believing she was doing what he would want. She shouldn't have taken that on herself.

But then he had the vision, what would be his last.

It was his time to sacrifice for his daughter. He would allow her to push him into the water. She'd understand soon.

Her face was the last he saw before the visions of every evil he'd done dragged across his brain like rusty razors.

For you, Evangeline. It was all for you.

CHAPTER 83

Van

I kicked to the surface and drew a sharp breath that turned to mist in the frigid air. Harry was on the far bank, pulling Caroline out of the water, a medic at his side. But Frank was still below the surface. I could see him down there, a dark shape against the lighter water, his heavy bones anchoring him. For a second, I was paralyzed.

Why'd he let me go?

Then instinct kicked in, and I dived below the surface, my hands outstretched, reaching for him. His mouth opened—was it a silent scream?—but his body was too heavy. The bones that had saved him so many times kept him submerged.

Still, I gripped his wrists and pulled, feeling the cold, slick surface of his skin beneath my fingers. He was a lead weight, unyielding, immovable. My fingers slipped against his wet flesh, the struggle sapping what little strength I had left. My lungs were collapsing under the pressure. I couldn't stay under any longer.

I had to let go of my Father.

I broke the surface, gasping for air, my chest heaving. It was over. It was really over. Frank Roth wasn't going to survive this.

Beneath his god delusions, his deceptions, the facade of power, he was just a man.

I looked down, the cold seeping into my bones. The dark, swirling current had carried me away. I could no longer see his face.

I didn't have the strength to fight either the relief or the soul-cutting grief.

CHAPTER 84

Van

Caroline was alive. Pale, exhausted, nearly drowned by Frank Roth, but alive. She'd been rushed to the nearest hospital. I knew Harry wouldn't leave her side. That was what it looked like to be family. I was so, so happy for them both, even though I'd only ever be on the outside of that sensation. When it came to parents, sisters, I'd been dealt a laughably terrible hand.

But Caroline was alive, and she was reunited with her brother.

I think that's why I was able to sleep for the next twenty-plus hours. I wanted to drive straight to Gina's, Robin's, and Lulu's families, but I was a dead woman walking. After rising from blessedly dreamless slumber, I showered, pulled on the only semiclean clothes I had left, and stumbled out of my apartment, managing to mostly ignore Owl's toys and food and water bowls.

I started in Saint Cloud and worked my way back.

Robert Penchant was wearing the same clothes as the last time I'd seen him. It appeared neither he nor his outfit had been washed. He broke down weeping, falling into my arms when I told him what'd happened to Gina. It was a mixed bag, learning your child had been murdered, but there was a bleak relief in hearing it wasn't suicide.

I asked Robert if he wanted to call his son, but he seemed unable to hear me. I led him to the bathroom, shoved in a pair of clean pants, underwear, and a sweatshirt, and cleaned his kitchen while he showered.

Hand-washing dishes was oddly soothing, wiping dirt from cupboards, throwing out rotten food. I dug out a couple cans of vegetable soup that weren't expired and started their contents simmering. By the time he was clean, at least one room was halfway to habitable.

I was pleased to notice he'd shaved in addition to bathing. "Either you're calling social services or I am," I told him. "You can't live like this."

He ended up making the call. The county told him they'd send someone out this week. He'd either find a reason to claim what remained of this life or he wouldn't. At least he was eating when I left.

Prudence and Lindy would take the news differently, I knew that. The murderer had visited. He'd been close. And if they'd stayed overnight, he likely wouldn't have killed Gina, at least not that evening. I'd need to tread lightly when I told them what'd transpired.

The women met me at Bo Diddley's. They held each other, faces etched in grief, as I told them that Gina hadn't been killed by a demon or taken her own life.

They received the information as well as they could.

They were making plans to call their classmates and possibly set up a memorial when I left. They'd decided it would require them getting together a few more times. I was glad to hear it.

Teresa Seer broke down sobbing when I told her. She said she'd call Chuck.

Martha Geldman just nodded, like she'd expected the news. When I handed her Lulu's diary, she said, "My girl can rest now."

Back at the BCA, I updated my report. It included Judith Mary Morsa's—Mother Mary, to me and Caroline—recent confession, which was corroborated by the claims she made to Comstock when he visited her in the hospital. She was in stable condition, her eyes destroyed but the rest of her in good health. She insisted she'd made the poison that killed all three girls in 1986 and forced them to drink it because she thought they were going to steal Frank Roth from her.

I intended to establish that she couldn't possibly have killed them, but that was all I could do for her. She'd most definitely poisoned two innocent women, Emily Barris and Alexis Zahn. In a sick twist, due to her blindness, it seemed likely she'd be sent to the Carlton County Treatment Center west of Duluth—the nursing home for serial killers central to the previous case Harry and I'd tackled.

Frank Roth was officially, undeniably dead. They found his body wrapped around an underwater log, his bones so heavy that it took a crane to lift him out. His skin and some muscle was horribly melted from the plane crash he'd survived. It must have been incredibly painful, the last couple years of his life. Was that justice? It would have to do.

Mother Mary had claimed that Frank Roth had visions like me. I didn't know if it was true or just more of his Messiah garbage. The fact that he knew I also experienced them suggested the former. What had Mother Mary said? That my visions were a gift. Easy enough to say when you didn't have to endure them.

I needed to personally hand Chandler my report. He'd insisted. I passed Harry's lab on the way. It was empty. He'd taken time off, obviously, his return date open ended.

Caroline Steinbeck was going to make a full recovery. In fact, according to Chandler, she'd already gone home with Harry.

I appreciated the news. I'd been avoiding any mention of Harry, even though I was fiercely happy for him. Privacy was the least I could offer him, after what he'd learned about me.

I was a murderer.

My father had abducted his beloved sister.

Our friendship was over.

CHAPTER 85

Van

I slept deeply the next night, too, a mix of exhaustion and what felt like my soul shattering. I should have done more for Caroline, for the other Mothers, for all my Sisters, sooner. If I'd tracked down Mother Mary, reintegrated her into society, would Emily and Alexis still be alive? That was an unknown I'd have to live with, but I refused to do it standing still.

I was going to locate the rest of my siblings.

Comstock estimated that at least four dozen people had been living at Frank's Farm 2.0. They *did* have an evacuation plan as well as a legal document passing the very legitimate, tax-paying, aboveboard Crimson Wool business off to Hannah and Grace should Mother Mary die, be impaired, or be institutionalized.

Comstock had who he needed—Judith Morsa—and so had no reason to find the others.

I did.

I was going to set them free, if they were still following Frank's twisted doctrine. It was the only way I could imagine quieting the keening that had started in my belly since I'd discovered that both my mother and father were unapologetic killers.

It still didn't feel real, the realizations of the last forty-eight hours twirling and settling, twirling and settling, like a fan made of razor blades working its way through my bloodstream. I kept expecting to wake up, to realize this was just another horrible dream. But no matter how hard I blinked, how much coffee I drank to shake the fog, the truth sat there, staring back at me like a wound that wouldn't close. My parents had destroyed families, ruined lives. I felt dirty. Their blood was in my veins, and I could never be clean again.

But they'd been all I had, as tenuous and awful as our relationship had been. Now, I had nothing. It was a loneliness so deep it untethered my bones.

I bet I wasn't the only one in my Family feeling that way.

Comstock said that even though he wouldn't be actively looking, he'd still let me know if any other members ended up back on his radar. The rat bastard had checked on me twice since Morsa had been brought in. I didn't plan on getting used to him being kind. Kyle had also stopped by, ostensibly to bring me coffee, but I'd seen the worry in the creases of his eyes. And Chandler had all but put a gold-star sticker at the top of my report when I'd handed it to him yesterday.

It was annoying, their attentiveness. I hoped it'd blow over soon.

I was reviewing records for my next cold case when Harry's text came through.

Can you come over tonight? I have something to tell you.

A cold fist squeezed my heart. I had thought it'd take longer, the hard split, but how like Harry to want to "communicate clearly" about the rules moving forward. Well, I'd take my medicine, and then I'd get back to figuring everything out on my own.

It was how I worked best.

CHAPTER 86

Van

Walking up Harry's sidewalk in a numb body was a trip, but no way could I stay physically present for what was about to go down. He was going to tell me that he was grateful to me for bringing him to his sister—he'd be obligated to start there, good manners dictated it—but that it was important we maintain a purely professional relationship moving forward, and that he would appreciate it if I'd request a different forensic scientist on any future cold cases.

Cordelia/Caroline—how could I stand seeing her, knowing what'd been stolen from her, how I'd been party to it?—would either forgive me or scream at me. In either case, the end result would be her calling me out for the monster I was and telling me she would very much like me to leave her brother alone.

I could give them both this. I wouldn't argue. After, I would crawl into the piles in my apartment and make myself as small as possible until it was time to return to the world. Wouldn't be the first time.

I knocked on Harry's door.

Shuffling came from the other side.

I steeled myself.

Harry appeared. I blinked several times. He was blurred, growing older and younger, heavier and lighter, in front of my eyes. I grabbed the doorjamb for support.

"Evangeline?"

I rubbed my face. It was just Harry. Solid. Beautiful. His sculpted face shaded with worry. He was dressed in casual slacks and a long-sleeved lavender shirt that made his eyes look stormy.

"Sorry," I said. I meant *for everything*. I meant *please still love me*. I meant *you can never hate me as much as I hate myself*. But I wouldn't burden him with my pain. He already carried more than his share.

He opened his mouth as if to say more but instead stepped aside. Caroline was sitting in a chair, her legs curled beneath her. The thinnest layer of blond was growing along her scalp, a sharp contrast to her dyed chestnut hair.

"Hi, Van," she said. Her voice was like a melody. I didn't remember that, but she'd so rarely spoken when we were children, hidden away in Frank's house as she was. "That's what you like to be called, isn't it?"

I heard the door close behind me, inhaled Harry's faint, soothing scent. I made my way to the couch. Lowered myself onto it. "I didn't know," I said. "Until recently. Who you were. I am so very sorry."

Her eyes skimmed to Harry, then back to me. "We were all prisoners there."

She said the words as if she were trying them on. It was a good sign that she was willing to consider rejoining this reality. I knew from experience it was going to be excruciating, relinquishing the upside down of Frank's Farm to walk in the world that everyone else lived in. I'd email Harry resources to share with her.

"I remember you lying for me," she said. It was hard to look at her. She was so fragile, an origami bird in a world made of fire. "When I ran away."

I nodded. I didn't trust my mouth.

"And you found me, now." Her smile was tender. "Harry said you're the reason I'm alive."

I shook my head, pain exploding through my veins. *I took too long.*

"Harry," she said, "your allergy pill is going to wear off soon. You should do it now."

Harry strode across the living room and opened a side door.

Owl crouched on the other side, every bit of her trembling with excitement. She couldn't seem to move, could only stare at me with an apology written across her face, like she thought it was her fault we'd been separated.

"My god," I said, my eyes growing hot as I slid off the couch, my body no longer mine. *"My god my god my god."*

I started crawling toward her. She met me halfway, quivering in my arms. I buried my face in her neck.

Harry sat gracefully on the floor next to us. "I reached out to the shelter and confirmed to them that Ms. Barris had been killed. They gave Otto Pusch a chance to claim her, but he didn't want the responsibility now that he was in the clear. So I adopted her."

Owl made a moaning lament and tried to slurp Harry's face without leaving my lap. He jerked back just in time. "For you," he said fussily. "If that wasn't obvious."

My insides felt carved clean. "I don't deserve her," I mumbled.

Owl whipped around and began licking my cheeks wildly.

"Looks like she doesn't know that," Caroline said, chuckling. It was a beautiful sound, water over river stones.

Harry stood, glancing at his watch. "Mom will be here soon," he told Caroline.

I glanced up from embracing Owl—*she was mine!*—in time to see Caroline steel herself. I rose shakily to my feet, already feeling like an intruder here. I'd taken far too much from them. "I'll go so you can be with your family," I said.

Harry shook his head, his expression confused. "But that's why you're here."

I looked from him to Caroline, not understanding what seemed obvious to them both.

"If you'll have us," Caroline said, her smile sad. "We're a bit broken, us Steinbecks."

I glanced down at Owl. She stared up at me like even she understood.

"I don't get it," I said.

Harry took a step toward me, then back. "We know each other's deepest secrets, Evangeline. We take care of each other. You brought my sister back to me." His hands hung at his sides. "I choose you. I choose you as family."

"*We* choose you," Caroline said, leaning forward to grip his hand. "But again, only if you want us."

I could only nod, my face more liquid than solid, my spirit dancing. *I am safe. I am grown. I am free.*

ACKNOWLEDGMENTS

A big charcuterie board of thanks to my editor and friend Jessica Tribble Wells, who midwifed this series by giving a home to the short story "Catch Her in a Lie" and then requested three follow-up books. There is no Van and Harry without Jessica. Jill Marsal, my agent and advocate, thank you for your clear head, tireless dedication, and listening ear. To my editing crew at Thomas & Mercer: Charlotte, Jon, and Kellie, thank you for all you do to cover me up when my intellectual underwear is showing.

Jessica Morrell, you're the first reader on every book I've written since *Knee High by the Fourth of July*, and you never disappoint. Thank you for your guidance, support, and friendship.

Ann Marie Gross, big thanks for lending your beautiful science brain to this series. All errors are mine. Shannon Baker and Erica Ruth Neubauer, sprinters and cheerleaders both, the two of you are the dessert to my writing meal. Carolyn Crane, our regular writing sessions (and our friendship) mean the world to me; thank you for sharing your big, beautiful brain and heart and humor. Sarah Stonich and Kristi Belcamino, there are no two writers I'd rather go to Browntown with. Thank you for your steady support and delightful company.

Thanks to Linda Maul for the idea that sparked one of Frank's secrets. In response to a plea in my reader newsletter (you can sign up for it on my website) asking for help in writing this book, Linda came back with: "What about someone with Van's abilities hunts her as they prey on those like her." JL Corey is another newsletter subscriber who responded, giving me the idea for the red scarves. Much gratitude to both! It takes a village to write a book.

And I can't forget newsletter subscriber Tanya Brooking, who (like me) also worked at a Chi-Chi's in the '80s (hers was in Winnipeg, mine was the City Center location, as described in this book) and reminded me of the cheese dip with chunks that we "hoped were food." I also stole the phrase "flounce blouse" from her. Minnesota salutes you, Canada!

Boundless thanks to all the rescue organizations that not only give shelter to needy animals but also provide temporary pet housing to folks in crisis. I'm proud to foster for the Animal Humane Society as well as Pet Haven here in Minneapolis, though I specialize in kittens and pregnant cats rather than dogs. Owl was inspired by my own boxer, Juni, who passed in 2020 but now gets to live forever in this book. If you have the time and space to foster, I encourage you to check out your local rescue. It's incredibly rewarding.

Finally, I'd like to thank all the readers who've given Van and Harry a chance and who've spread the word about this series. I've grown to love these two BCA agents, and I hope you do, too.

ABOUT THE AUTHOR

Photo © 2023 Kelly Weaver Photography

Jess Lourey is the Amazon Charts bestselling author of *The Quarry Girls*, *Unspeakable Things*, *Litani*, and *Bloodline*, as well as the Reed and Steinbeck thrillers, the Salem's Cipher novels, and the Murder by Month rom-com mysteries. Lourey writes about secrets, fosters kittens, and travels. She's surpassed a million readers; been short-listed for the Goodreads Choice Awards and the Edgar Award twice each; and won the International Thriller, Anthony, and Minnesota Book Awards. She also has an active reader group on Facebook called Lourey's Literati. For more information, including a link to her TEDx Talk, in which she discusses the surprising inspiration behind her writing career, visit www.jesslourey.com.